It is the height of the Roaring Twenties – a fresh enthusiasm for the arts, science, and exploration of the past have opened doors to a wider world, and beyond...

And yet, a dark shadow grows over the town of Arkham. Alien entities known as Ancient Ones lurk in the emptiness beyond space and time, writhing at the thresholds between worlds.

Occult rituals must be stopped and alien creatures destroyed before the Ancient Ones make our world their ruined dominion.

Only a handful of brave souls with inquisitive minds and the will to act stand against the horrors threatening to tear this world apart.

Will they prevail?

## ALSO AVAILABLE IN ARKHAM HORROR

THE ADVENTURES OF ALESSANDRA ZORZI
*Wrath of N'kai* by Josh Reynolds
*Shadows of Pnath* by Josh Reynolds
*Song of Carcosa* by Josh Reynolds

THE FIZTMAURICE LEGACY
*Mask of Silver* by Rosemary Jones
*The Deadly Grimoire* by Rosemary Jones
*The Bootlegger's Dance* by Rosemary Jones

*In the Coils of the Labyrinth* by David Annandale

*Litany of Dreams* by Ari Marmell

*The Ravening Deep* by Tim Pratt

*The Last Ritual* by S A Sidor
*Cult of the Spider Queen* by S A Sidor
*Lair of the Crystal Fang* by S A Sidor

*The Devourer Below* edited by Charlotte Llewelyn-Wells
*Secrets in Scarlet* edited by Charlotte Llewelyn-Wells

*Dark Origins: The Collected Novellas Vol 1*
*Grim Investigations: The Collected Novellas Vol 2*

ARKHAM HORROR INVESTIGATORS GAMEBOOKS
*The Darkness Over Arkham* by Jonathan Green

*Welcome to Arkham: An Illustrated Guide for Visitors*
*Arkham Horror: The Poster Book*

ARKHAM HORROR™

# HERALD
## *of*
# RUIN

TIM PRATT

ACONYTE

First published by Aconyte Books in 2024

ISBN 978 1 83908 297 9

Ebook ISBN 978 1 83908 298 6

Cover art by John Coulthart

Distributed in North America by Simon & Schuster Inc, New York, USA

Printed in the United States of America

9 8 7 6 5 4 3 2 1

**ACONYTE BOOKS**

*An imprint of Asmodee Entertainment Ltd*

Mercury House, Shipstones Business Centre

North Gate, Nottingham NG7 7FN, UK

*aconytebooks.com // twitter.com/aconytebooks*

*This one is for my foes, adversaries, opponents, and rivals, never say I didn't give you anything.*

# CHAPTER ONE
## *The Web*

Carl Sanford's ruin came to Arkham in a dapper Italian suit, with a knowing smile, and no fixed address.

The interloper named Randall Tillinghast had been walking up and down in the city for over a week before Sanford even detected his presence. That was an appalling failure of Sanford's intelligence network, like a spider hearing secondhand about the presence of a new fly in his web. There should have been warnings. There should have been *vibrations*. Instead, the man had nearly ten days to lay his traps and set his snares without interference before word finally reached Sanford about the "humble antiquarian and enthusiast of the esoteric" who'd set up shop somewhere south of the river, peddling his wares, which supposedly included objects of real power.

Either this Tillinghast was a fraud dealing in worthless trinkets, in which case, Sanford would chase him out of the city, or he was a genuine occultist with access to worthwhile relics, whereupon Sanford would acquire everything he possessed of value and then see what further use could be made of him.

Arkham was *Sanford's* city. You couldn't just move in here and join the game without asking permission and paying tribute. Someone had tried to usurp Sanford's place as the preeminent master of the magical arts in Arkham last year, and that person had ended up blasted with a shotgun, blown up with dynamite, buried in rocks, and drowned in the icy Atlantic.

"You're quieter than your brother was, Brother Altman," Sanford said from the back seat of the Bentley, where he gazed out the window at the slow river bleeding silver beneath the bridge.

His driver, bodyguard, and – increasingly – confidant was the slightly younger sibling of one of Sanford's former lieutenants. The first Altman had died in a hotel room, murdered by cultists... and a bit later, the twisted doppelganger those cultists had created to take Altman's place had died in a temple devoted to their dead deity beneath the sea.

The new Altman was broadly similar to his brother in terms of expertise, experience, and discretion, but he lacked the original's sardonic sense of humor. He did still possess both his ears, while his predecessor had lost one in some overseas unpleasantness, which Sanford supposed was a sort of cosmic balance.

"Our mother used to say Reggie wouldn't say boo to a goose," Altman replied, "but that *I* wouldn't say shit if I had a mouthful."

"How charming." Sanford sniffed. The new Altman had come to Arkham last year from a sojourn in Africa, where he'd been doing unspeakable things for some colonial government or another, to attend the funerals of his brother and his niece, who'd also been lost in the unpleasantness last year, when the Lodge was assaulted. Altman the younger had agreed to stay on as Sanford's new personal assistant for a hefty salary and the opportunity to vent some of his rage on the Lodge's enemies. "If you're going to be my batsman and bodyguard and amanuensis, I'll need you to indulge in the occasional conversation. I do some of my best thinking aloud, and without a partner in dialogue, it would just be … ranting."

"Am I all those things, then? All right. I'll try to hold my end up." Altman guided the Bentley slowly into the narrow streets of Rivertown. "No actual address, eh?"

"Frustratingly, no," Sanford said. "Each of my two informants gave me a different location, which means one of them was confused. Both placed this new shop near the graveyard, though. It's called Tillinghast Esoterica and Exotics. How *gauche*. You might see my name on a building at the university someday, but I'd hardly emblazon it above a mercantile concern."

They drove up and down the streets of the Rivertown district but saw no sign of a new shop. "It has a green door, apparently, with a sort of eye painted on the window," Sanford said, though Altman knew that already. "A cheap ploy to appear mystical and draw in the credulous, no doubt." They traversed the densely packed blocks of the Merchant District and passed the former site of Huntress

Fashions, a "For Let" sign in the dusty window, and Sanford felt a twinge in his guts he chose not to investigate. A Lodge member named Diana Stanley had operated that shop for a time, but she'd left town after betraying Sanford's trust... and then saving his life. That last part probably made them even, or maybe put Sanford very slightly in her debt. Better for all involved that she'd left town with her beau. Sanford had resisted the urge to deploy agents to track her down. Let her do as she would, as long as she wasn't doing it in his territory.

Sanford drew much of his strength from the past, of course, but he preferred to look forward to the future whenever possible.

"Dash it, just go to the general store," Sanford commanded, and Altman obeyed without complaint. They parked near the ramshackle structure, a neighborhood institution despite its decrepit aspect, and Sanford said, "You may as well wait here. No reason to scare the plebeians." Altman chuckled, where he normally would have stayed silent. Sanford appreciated the man's efforts.

The magus of Arkham slid out of the car and walked up the warped board steps, nodding to a couple of old-timers who sat in rockers on the drooping front porch. They nodded back, eyeing him with open suspicion. They might recognize him – Sanford was well known in town, of course, and those of his social class weren't very welcome here – or they might simply be reacting to the presence of a man who was wearing a suit instead of stained dungarees or overalls.

He pushed through the door, a bell clanging discordantly

overhead to herald his arrival. The musty general store was crowded with wooden shelves holding everything from tinned foodstuffs to used hand tools, arranged in no discernible order. A sullen, bearded man slouched on a stool behind the wooden counter, seated next to an immense jar of pickled eggs suspended in a suspicious greenish fluid. They reminded Sanford of the peculiar biological specimens preserved in the laboratories deep beneath the Silver Twilight Lodge house.

The shopkeeper – Sanford could never remember the man's name – looked right through Sanford, as if he were a pane of window glass with nothing much of interest on the other side.

Sanford wished he'd brought his walking stick. Smashing that jar of eggs would get a reaction, wouldn't it? Instead, he smiled, strolled to the counter, and rapped his knuckles on the wood briskly. "Hello, my good man. I wonder if you might be able to assist me."

The shopkeeper grunted. "First time for everything."

"I'm looking for a shop that I understand has recently opened in the area."

Now the man barked a laugh, showing off yellowed teeth. "Now why would I send a customer off to one of my competitors?"

Sanford looked around at the dusty bags of flour, the chipped glass jars, and rust-edged shovels, and sniffed. "I don't think your business and his have much overlap in terms of inventory. It's called Tillinghast Esoterica and Exotics–"

When Sanford spoke those words, it was as if the

shopkeeper had downed a revitalizing tonic. He stood straighter, his eyes brightened, and his smile went from sly and knowing to wide and genuine. "Mr Tillinghast! Why, of course. He's a true gentleman! You can look at him and tell he's a man of quality, but he doesn't go around putting on airs like some people do. He even brought me a little gift, did you know that, like he was welcoming me to the neighborhood when it should have been the other way around."

"How very hospitable of him," Sanford said. "Now, where exactly–"

"I'll show you!" The shopkeeper bent down and reached beneath the counter, drawing out…

A snow globe. A perfectly unremarkable example of the form, as far as Sanford could tell. The shopkeeper shook it vigorously, filling the glass sphere atop the rounded stone pedestal with a flurry of white flecks. The artificial snowflakes were usually made of wax, or meerschaum, Sanford understood, but as he leaned obligingly forward and peered at this one, he wondered. This looked very much like *actual* snow. Even after the shopkeeper put the globe down on the counter, the snowstorm inside didn't abate, the fragments not settling as gravity should have dictated, but continuing to fly about in all directions, obscuring the contents. Sanford only caught glimpses of the shape inside, but where he would have expected a snowman or a white deer or a country church, he saw… was it a man, bundled up, bent forward as if walking against the wind?

"The snow just flurries around all by itself in there,

though it goes faster when you give it a shake," the shopkeeper said proudly. "Mr Tillinghast told me it's on account of, what was it… 'a complex chemical interaction among incompatible material elements.'"

*It's a simple magical charm,* Sanford thought. *But such trifles are sufficient to amaze a simpleton.* The flakes had probably been enchanted to abhor the fluid they floated in, and the glass that surrounded them, and one another, and flurried incessantly in a fruitless bid to escape. Still, it seemed a lot of effort to go to, for a child's toy…

He saw a flicker of darkness, a black speck among the flurrying white, and peered closer, almost putting his nose on the glass. Was that glimpse of a humanoid figure… *moving*? Actually trudging through the snow? Why bother with such a detail?

The shopkeeper snatched the globe back, and when Sanford looked up at him, he saw naked hate and avarice in the man's gaze. "This is mine," the shopkeeper said. "You don't need to go touching it."

"I wouldn't dream," Sanford said smoothly. "It's a beautiful piece. I can see why you're so fond of it. Might you direct me to Mr Tillinghast's establishment? Perhaps I could procure a slightly less wondrous item for my own enjoyment."

The shopkeeper squinted, suspicious, then shrugged his bony shoulders. "I'm not sure. I never been there myself. Mr Tillinghast just stopped in to introduce himself a few days ago and had himself a pickled egg – best he'd ever had, he said, I make them myself – and went on his way. I heard he's got a place not far from the graveyard, but beyond that, I couldn't say."

"Capital." Sanford removed a slim white card from his jacket pocket and slid it across the counter. "Perhaps if Mr Tillinghast returns you might give him my card? I'd love to discuss certain business opportunities with him."

The shopkeeper picked up the card – Sanford imagined the edges were instantly discolored, though that might have been mere fancy – and squinted at it with a grunt. "I suppose I could do that. For a loyal customer. A loyal *paying* customer."

Sanford sighed.

Back in the car, he passed Altman a damp, bundled handkerchief. "What's that?" the man asked.

"The best pickled egg Randall Tillinghast ever had," Sanford replied. "Enjoy it with my compliments."

Altman grunted and, to Sanford's surprise, devoured the thing rather than dropping it out the window. The man grunted again and said, "I've had worse."

"Have you *really*? Remind me never to ask you for a restaurant recommendation."

"Where to now?" Altman asked.

Sanford settled into the back seat and glowered at nothing. Why had Tillinghast wasted any magic, even a paltry charm, to ingratiate himself with the proprietor of the general store? What could he possibly offer? Although… the shop *was* frequented by a variegated cross section of Arkham inhabitants and was something of a central point for the dissemination of gossip. Maybe Sanford should have cultivated an informant there. He had numerous connections among the city's elite, and in the Underworld, but dash it, he'd never really had the *common* touch. "We've wasted enough time. I'm supposed to have lunch with Miss Standish soon, so let's hie ourselves back across the river."

"Visiting all the finest people today, aren't we?" Altman chuckled.

"On second thought, I think I liked you better when you were silent," Sanford said. "Forget I said anything."

"Too late now, sir. You've gone and opened up my floodgates."

Ruby had set their meeting place, phoning the Lodge with the location early this morning, as she always did. The young woman had a profoundly suspicious turn of mind, but then, she'd earned it.

Thus, Sanford found himself on the doorstep of the Songbird's Perch, a lively enough place at night, when there was live music playing and, undoubtedly, a general disdain for the constraints of Prohibition. During the day, however, the Perch's carved wooden panels seemed shabby and the red-shaded lamps a bit sad. There were one or two people dining in plush booths, but not much of a lunchtime crowd compared to the more conventional eateries in the area. Sanford made his way to the back, waving off the hostess with a murmured, "I'm meeting someone," and found Ruby in the most distant booth, sucking an olive off a toothpick.

He slid into the seat across from her, nodding toward the martini glass on the table. "A bit early for that, isn't it?"

Ruby smiled at him sunnily. Her hair was dark, lately, and even in her presence, it was hard to pin down her age or extraction – late twenties, early thirties? Some hint of the Spaniard or even Central American in her ancestry, perhaps?

"If I'm awake, it's not too early, Sanford, darling." She wasn't at her *most* glamorous just now – no fascinator in her hair, and no jewels around her neck, dressed neither for speakeasy nor garden party – but her makeup was immaculate, her hair perfectly curled, and her day dress effortlessly *à la mode*, a dark pink with a big black ribbon bow tied at the neck, the trailing ends spilling down her front. Ruby was capable of making herself up to look like the dowdiest hausfrau, or an innocent farmgirl in the city for the first time, or a silver screen vamp to put Theda Bara to shame, depending on which appearance best suited her stratagems. He was tempted to think this version was the "real" Ruby, shorn of all disguises, but Sanford knew better than that. If there even *was* a real Ruby, he didn't think this woman shared her with anyone but herself.

She tapped the rim of her glass with one of the rings on her fingers, making it chime. "Would you like something?"

He settled back into the booth, which was actually quite comfortable, the better to entice visitors to sit and drink awhile. "I'm quite all right. We could simply meet at the Lodge, you know. I don't like talking business in public." Not that anyone was paying them the least bit of attention here.

"They know I like my privacy here. And you know why I don't like to go to the Lodge."

"Tut, tut," Sanford said. "You were hardly locked up in

the basements for any length of time at all. You escaped almost immediately."

"My brief imprisonment aside, I *was* pursued through those basements by a monster. I have unpleasant associations with the place." She made a face, which was, in fact, less revolting than the monster in question.

*You should see the creature now*, Sanford thought. "'Monster' is a bit much," he said. "It was merely a guardian, and you were trespassing. But, yes, I take your point." Sanford's relationship with Ruby was, historically, rather fraught. She was a professional thief who'd robbed his vault below the Lodge of priceless relics some years ago, and he'd even arranged a trap to lure her back to Arkham so he could take his revenge on her. But she'd become entangled in all that business with the Cult of Asterias, and in the process, the two of them had become necessary allies, fighting back-to-back against a common enemy. He'd agreed to forget her transgressions in light of her service, and they now had a reliable (if never totally comfortable) working relationship. She *was* very good at what she did. She must be, if she'd managed to steal something from *him*.

"Why did you want to see me?" she asked.

Right to business. She seldom spent any of her charm on him, which was fine since he was immune to such blandishments. "Oh, I have a job for you. But before we get into all that... have you heard of a man named Randall Tillinghast?" Sanford had myriad connections all over Arkham, since many of the city's most prominent and influential citizens were members of the Order of the Silver

Twilight (known universally, informally, and erroneously as the Silver Twilight Lodge), the social organization and esoteric order that he ruled absolutely. But Ruby had a different set of connections: bartenders, small-time thugs, dock workers, housemaids. The little people who kept the city humming along. Sometimes she knew things he didn't.

He wasn't expecting a reaction like this, though. "*Tillinghast?*" She put her glass down, carefully, but her hand was shaking, and gin sloshed over the rim. "You don't mean... Tall, thin, white hair, in his sixties? Likes to wear expensive Italian suits?"

Sanford cocked his head. "I haven't met the man myself, but that fits the descriptions I've received. You mean to say you know the man? Personally?"

Ruby stared at the tabletop. "I can't... he was... I did some work for him. A while back. I shouldn't talk about it. I have to be discreet, in my business, you know." A tremble crept into her voice.

"You needn't give me details about your business relationship," Sanford said. "I mainly want to know: is he the genuine article, in terms of his association with the occult? There are a lot of charlatans in his business–"

She laughed, the sound as short and harsh as a crow's caw. "Tillinghast is the real thing. The... item... I procured for him... It belonged to very serious people, and they wanted it back. Badly. There was this policeman, too, who came after the relic afterward, and it was a lot of work to shake him. To be honest, I still look over my shoulder sometimes." Ruby narrowed her eyes. "Is Tillinghast *here*? In Arkham?"

"That is the rumor, yes. You hadn't heard anything about a newcomer?"

"No! And you'd think I would have…" She chewed her lip, clearly vexed. "Do you know what he's doing here?"

"Business," Sanford said. "He's opened a curio shop, though I've had trouble finding out exactly where it's located. He should fire whoever does his advertisements. Miss Standish… Ruby… does this man frighten you?" He'd seldom seen her react so strongly, even in the face of imminent peril.

"Frighten?" She seemed to take the question seriously, rolling the glass between her hands as she pondered. "No, that's not quite right. He unsettles me. Tillinghast can be very friendly, solicitous even, and he paid me fairly, plus extra to make up for the trouble I encountered down in the swamps. But… I can't explain it. Have you ever stood on a bridge at night, looking down at the water all dark beneath you, and for a moment it feels like you're just suspended in the void? Like you're surrounded by nothing? A kind of… *active* nothing?"

Sanford nodded. He'd glimpsed the emptiness at the heart of reality on more than one occasion.

She nodded back. "That's how I felt, sometimes, when he'd look into my eyes. Like I was staring into the abyss… and the abyss was staring back at me."

"The thief who quoted Nietzsche!" Sanford scoffed.

Ruby managed half a smile. "I'm an educated woman, Sanford. It just wasn't a typical education." She turned serious, her eyes fixed on his. "What do you want with Tillinghast?"

"I want to meet him, first of all," Sanford said. "I want to peruse his wares and see if there's anything worth acquiring, especially now that you've told me he might have objects of real value. I wish to take the measure of the man and see if he could be useful to me." *Or dangerous to me*, but he'd hardly admit that concern out loud. Sanford leaned forward. "Can you give me any other impressions of him, apart from his voidlike gaze?"

"Not really," Ruby said. "He hired me, I did the job, he paid me, we parted ways. I only met him face-to-face a few times. He definitely has the manners of a gentleman, and he probably has the soul of a shark."

It was Sanford's turn to grin. "I've been told I can be a trifle sharklike myself. I'm sure in my presence this Tillinghast will become like unto a minnow. Would you please make some inquiries for me, and see if you can find the location of his shop? A surprise visit could be in order."

She shrugged. "I'll see what I can do."

"Excellent. Once you've found him, perhaps you could offer to... renew your association? I'm sure he could use someone with your skills, whatever his precise intentions are. And in the process, if you pick up any useful tidbits of information about his plans here in Arkham, you can pass them on to me."

"You want me to be your spy, Sanford?" Ruby shook her head. "That's going to cost you."

"I would expect nothing less. You know the depths of my purse. I'm sure we can reach a satisfactory arrangement."

"I'll see what I can do," she repeated. "No promises,

but if the opportunity to renew my acquaintance with Tillinghast comes up, I won't let it pass me by."

Sanford nodded. "Fair enough. On to our main business, then. There's a certain shipment arriving from South America this week, bound for the university, and I'd appreciate it if you could intercept something for me."

# CHAPTER TWO
## Dark Deeds on the Docks

The Arkham River Docks were never a particularly cheerful place to visit, even in the bright morning with the birds singing and the sun shining, and so much less so deep into the evening with the mists rising and the only songs the swearing of the toiling stevedores.

Skulking around this area in skirts at night wasn't a safe proposition, so Ruby was in one of her more seldom-used disguises, wearing patched trousers and battered boots, with a baggy old shirt to hide her figure, and her hair bundled up under a newsboy cap. A few smudges on her face in lieu of makeup made her resemble a boy prowling the docks in search of work or amusement or both. She was hardly immune to trouble in this guise, but it was a less troublesome sort of trouble than she could expect if she prowled around wearing a dress and kitten heels.

The docks rambled along a lengthy stretch of the river near the Merchant District, home to crumbling piers, rambling warehouses, unsteady stacks of cargo, cheap accommodations, booze that would blind you in time, and people desperate enough to drink it anyway. She saw Abner Weems, a local drunk who was occasionally lucid enough to pass messages or provide a useful tip, but not tonight; he was sprawled on his back beside a bottle at the mouth of a narrow alley, even his coat and shoes too worn for anyone to bother stealing.

A little farther along, Joey the Rat skulked past her, shoulders in a perpetual hunch, eyes darting everywhere; he was a small-time crook with an encyclopedic knowledge of the comings and goings of every ship, and she'd paid him for information before (and dislocated a couple of his fingers when he patted her bottom once). His peripatetic gaze didn't even pause when it reached her, which meant her disguise was solid.

Still, she kept to the shadows, staying close to the warehouses and heaps of crates, trying not to catch the eye of any of the big-shouldered men shifting cargo. Walking near the water was, theoretically, more pleasant, since you could look at the river, but while the Miskatonic had a certain beauty in the daytime, at night, the river just made her uneasy: those murky depths could hide anything, and nowadays she knew too much about the foul things that sometimes lurked beneath the surface. Of the water, and of everything else.

The river docks never entirely shut down, though they were a lot busier in the afternoon than they were in the dark of night. There were certain visitors who preferred to arrive in the wee hours, and certain cargo better unloaded in the dark – whisky sent down from Canada, for example. The most corrupt cops patrolled the docks overnight, and the skeleton crew of officials weren't averse to bribes, either.

Ruby had dealt with the harbormaster, "Tick" Scanlon, before, and figured he was her best bet. She was a cat burglar by training and preference, but she couldn't move a crate that took two men to carry all by herself, and while it was possible to just filch the contents, it was hard to be quiet with a crowbar. Nails tended to squeal when you wrenched them out.

Tick was sitting in his office, a shack of wood and corrugated metal positioned to give him a good view of the busiest berths on the dock. The upper half of the river-facing wall of his shack was hinged, and when that panel was open and propped up, he had a giant window and an awning to keep the rain off, unless the wind was blowing from the north, of course. On those days, he shut the window, and to hell with keeping a close eye on things.

Tonight was mild, though, and the wall was open. Tick lounged in a swivel chair with his feet up on the counter, with one of his ever-present pulp magazines propped open on his belly. He usually tended toward two-fisted detectives and bold explorers, but tonight he was reading that new scientifiction magazine, *Amazing Stories*. She'd read the same issue when it came out. Maybe Tick liked it because it had sailing ships on the cover, though they were run aground, and there was a big ringed planet looming over them in the background sky. No wonder he spent as much time as possible in imaginary worlds when the docks were his main habitation in the real one.

She sidled up to the counter and muttered a gruff, "How are ya?"

Tick's eyes flicked up briefly, then went back down to the magazine. He was reading slowly – she hadn't seen him flip a page during her whole approach, and usually he went through two or three of those magazines in a night. "No work for you tonight, kid. Run on home before a crate falls on you or something."

Ruby leaned over the counter and tipped her cap back. "Come on, Tick, be a pal. There's always work for me. I make work wherever I go."

He looked again, squinted, and grunted. He usually smoked a nasty cigar to cover the smells of tar and river stench, but not tonight. "It's you. Nice get-up. You trying out for the Vienna Boys' Choir?" His eyes drifted back down to the page. Must be riveting stuff, though as Ruby recalled, that issue was all reprints of old stories by Wells and Poe and Verne, which you'd think a bloated bookworm like Tick would have read a hundred times already.

"You know me and fashion. What do you think of the magazine?" Ruby leaned over the counter to get a look at which story he was reading and blinked. Were the images on the page *moving*? Almost like a movie projected on a screen... but no, it must be a trick of shadows from the lantern hanging behind him–

Tick slammed the magazine closed and lowered his feet, slipping the pulp – reverently, Ruby thought – under the counter. He glared at her. "Whaddya want? I'm busy."

Ruby didn't mind getting straight to business, though Tick was usually chattier, since shooting the breeze broke up the boredom. "A ship came in about an hour ago, bringing in a load of finds from an archaeological expedition down south, headed for the university. I'd like a chance to nip on board, take a look around, maybe carry off anything that appeals to me. What do you say?"

Tick sighed. "And how am I supposed to explain the missing whatever it is?"

"Come on, Tick. You know all the tricks. Mix-ups on the manifest, cargo lost overboard, breakage during travel. This stuff came all the way up from the Amazon or someplace – the eggheads at the university can't expect it *all* to arrive intact."

"Yeah, yeah." He sounded sour about the whole idea, but that was just his way. He liked making deals like this. They made him think he was a criminal mastermind in a story, probably. "Usual rates?"

"Why not? I'm feeling generous tonight." She slid an envelope across the counter, and he made it disappear. Normally Ruby didn't pay up front, but Tick had proven himself reliable and unambitious often enough.

"Gimme a second." He glanced down, reached under the counter, and gazed at something Ruby couldn't see. Did he have a flashlight under there? For a second, she could have sworn there was light flickering across his face, from underneath…

The light vanished, and he rose, holding a battered leather folder. "All right, let's go inspect the cargo." He emerged from the side door of the shack and set off swaggering, walking with the rolling gait of a lifelong sailor, though as far as Ruby knew, the closest he got to sea was visiting the cargo holds of the boats at his dock.

Ruby walked beside him. "Good magazine?" she asked.

He glanced at her with surprise. "Yeah, the greatest." He sounded strangely sincere. She would have bet that Tick and sincerity hadn't been acquainted since childhood.

Take interesting conversation wherever you could find it – that was her philosophy. "It's got 'The New Accelerator' in it, right? That old HG Wells story? I always liked that one. I wish I could take a potion to make myself flit around like a hummingbird, the people around me standing still as statues – that would come in handy, in my line of work." He didn't say anything, which wasn't like him. "But I guess you'd rather use the other potion, the one that slows you down, and makes the people around you seem to zip around at super-speed, so an hour passes in a second. You could get through those long boring nights in a blink that way, right?"

"Huh?" Tick seemed distracted, glancing over his shoulder at the shack, like he'd left something important behind. "Right, yeah, Wells. That's a good one." He led her around a heap of moldering crates that had been piled there for so long they seemed like part of the infrastructure, over to a beat-up little river barge. "Here you go."

"This thing didn't come up from the Amazon," Ruby said.

"Nah, they shifted the cargo a few times along the way."

Ruby grinned. "Easy to see how something might get lost in transit then, huh?"

He grunted again and stepped onto the ship. "We're not unloading this one until morning. The university is sending somebody to pick things up before lunch. Come on." He led her to the back of the ship, then folded back a tarp, revealing a dozen crates, varying in size from steamer trunk to casket. "Do you know what you're looking for? I'd rather not have to open all of these."

"What do you take me for, an amateur? Give me that flashlight, would you?"

Tick handed it over, and she scanned the crates in the weak yellow beam. Most of the crates were made of the same dark wood, stained and splintered, held together with nails gone rusty from long exposure to the elements. She checked the letters and numbers painted on the sides until she found the one Sanford had told her to look out for, A-24. That designation marked an unassuming crate that looked just big enough to hold a case of wine. That should be the one, but better to be safe. "Ticky, what's the manifest say about this box here?"

He flipped open his folder, and she shone the light on the pages for him. "Crate A-24, contents: one cup, stone."

"That's the one. Do you want to do the honors?"

"I don't open crates, Rube. I'm a harbormaster." He picked up a short-handled crowbar leaning against the wall and handed it over. "Help yourself, and hurry up about it, I want to get back to my magazine."

"It's not like a movie, Tick. You aren't going to miss the action if you spend too long in the bathroom during intermission." She took the crowbar and jammed the edge under the lip of the crate while Tick pointed the light in vaguely the right direction. Ruby levered up a corner of the crate, then moved down, popping the other corner, and worked her way around until the whole top panel was loose. She picked up the lid and set it upside down on the crate beside her, shiny steel nails gleaming in the flashlight beam, then turned her attention to the contents.

The crate was packed with straw, and it was always a little harrowing to stick your hands in that stuff – she imagined bear traps, set to snap on the hands of innocent hardworking thieves like her – but plunge she did. She made contact and lifted out the object nestled inside.

"I was expecting like a wine glass, but that's more of a loving cup," Tick said. "What's it supposed to be, the holy grail?"

"Unholy grail, knowing my luck." The goblet was nearly a foot high from rim to base, and when she held it up to the light, it glittered. The cup was made of shiny black stone, something like onyx but not, and it was elaborately faceted, twinkling in the flashlight beam. It looked like the thing Sanford had described, anyway. Something niggled at her, made her uneasy and uncertain, but she couldn't trace the sensation to its source. Probably she was just suspicious because this had gone so smoothly, but sometimes jobs were easy, right?

"I'm satisfied, Tick. Nice doing business with you." She wrapped the cup in a burlap sack and stuffed it into the leather bag dangling over her shoulder.

"I'll break up the crate and toss it in the river, make like this box never made it from the last stop," Tick said.

"I have total faith in your methods. See you next time, Ticky. Enjoy your magazine."

"Oh, I will."

Ruby kept to the shadows on her way out and managed

to avoid getting cracked on the back of the head and having her bag stolen. She got into her car and drove through the deserted streets toward French Hill, parking right outside the tall wrought-iron gates that surrounded the fading grandeur of the Silver Twilight Lodge.

It was hard to believe that she'd broken into this place to pillage its vaults, not once, but twice, most recently in the company of her friends Abel and Diana. Both of *them* had demonstrated their good sense by leaving Arkham, heading west to live someplace that didn't touch the sea, but Ruby had stuck around, tempted by the opportunities provided by working with Carl Sanford, instead of against him. She still didn't like going into the Lodge, but Sanford had insisted she bring the treasure straight to him, and it wasn't like she had to go into the strangely vast basements. Those, she'd avoid forever if she could.

She wanted to stay on Sanford's good side, and not just because of the money. Now that she had a true understanding of the terrible things that lurked beneath the surface of the world, sticking close to someone powerful enough to stop those monsters seemed like a good idea. Sanford had his issues, but he was formidable, and he took care of his allies… as long as they stayed useful to him, anyway.

Ruby got out of the car and went to the iron gates. They opened when she shoved, hinges squealing, and she stepped onto the path of paving stones crowded by the long grasses growing wild on either side. The Lodge looked like a great house that was beginning to crumble, its grounds extensive but unkempt. Sanford called it "protective coloration."

There was no reason to let outsiders know the Lodge was one of the most luxurious and well-appointed houses on the hill, after all.

Ruby carefully stayed on the center of the path. There were dogs hidden in those grasses – or, anyway, things that looked like dogs. Ruby had never satisfied herself fully regarding the true nature of the hounds, but had decided that, on balance, she preferred ignorance anyway.

The Lodge Warden, Sarah Van Shaw, was sitting in a straight-backed wooden chair on the porch by the front door. She wasn't knitting, or reading by lamplight, or sipping a cup of tea; she was just sitting, hands folded on her lap, eyes fixed ahead and unmoving, like a life-sized doll of herself.

"Good evening, Ms Van Shaw," Ruby said.

"Cheeky," Van Shaw murmured, looking Ruby up and down. The warden had long red hair and green eyes, and wore a well-made but old and unfashionable dress. "I suppose you're here to see the master."

"He's expecting me. But I'm in no hurry. We could pass a pleasant half hour in conversation, maybe play a few hands of cards, swap stories. Did you do something to your hair? Say, are you seeing anyone? Got a new beau I don't know about?"

Van Shaw didn't smile, exactly, but she showed her teeth. "You are welcome here, Ruby Standish, though you are not a member of the Order. It would be in your best interests if you made some efforts to remain welcome."

Ruby should have left it at that, but this woman was an enigma, and Ruby couldn't resist trying to unravel those. It was a character trait that had gotten her into trouble more than once. But what was life if not a series of troubles, and the effort to get out of them?

"Why did you join the Lodge, Sarah?" She leaned against a pillar on the porch. "I know you're sort of the guardian of this place, and that you run that pack of dogs, but what do you get out of the deal?"

Van Shaw didn't speak for a long moment, and then said, "I made my bargains, Ruby Standish. I made them with clear eyes and complete understanding… or as complete as I was capable of, at the time. I keep the Lodge safe. The Lodge keeps me safe in return. There are worse arrangements." She waved a dismissive hand. "Go on in. The master awaits."

"I just love our girl talks." Ruby opened the imposing front door of the Lodge and stepped into the anteroom, where the splendor of the house began to reveal itself. A fire burned eternally in the great hearth, across from a wall of shelves that held priceless volumes, including a Gutenberg Bible and a few Shakespeare folios, though the truly valuable books were kept elsewhere, locked away from the eyes of non-members. There was a Chesterfield sofa beside a lamp, perfect for curling up and reading, though Ruby had never seen anyone actually doing that. There were little niches in the walls holding ancient statuary, valuable not because of their beauty but because of their age – mostly they were hideous things to look at, all bulges and spines. She wondered if the cup she'd stolen would be displayed in the Lodge, but she thought not. Sanford wouldn't have sent her after the cup if it hadn't been unusual in some way, and he kept his magical relics in more secure quarters. Still in the vault in the basement, she assumed, probably with increased security these days, but who could say for sure? Sanford had never been trusting, but since the Cult of Cain had pillaged his Lodge, he'd become even more paranoid and secretive.

She pushed on deeper into the house, traversing its well-appointed corridors. Despite the late hours, there were a few Initiates within, one reading in a corner by himself, and others murmuring together over brandies. The Initiates varied in age from wet-eared youths to grizzled great-grandfathers, but that didn't matter here; only their rank did. They were the rank-and-file, members who'd never seen the basements. Not yet inducted into the Lodge's vile mysteries, they were welcome to enjoy the dining rooms and social gatherings and believe themselves part of something exclusive, when they had no *idea* what was hidden beneath their feet. Most of them never would. Sanford inducted citizens he considered useful to his cause, but only a few knew the Silver Twilight Lodge was anything other than a run-of-the-mill secret society like the Masons.

The Initiates glanced at Ruby when she passed by, and as quickly glanced away. No one knew quite what to make of her – she wasn't a member of the Order (she'd steadfastly refused induction), but she was known to have the master's ear, so most of the Initiates thought it best to pretend they didn't see her at all. Though the fact that she was dressed like a ragamuffin probably helped with avoiding conversation, too.

Sanford was waiting for her in his office. This was the

room where he met with the Initiates and other honored guests, and it was the picture of a great man's study, all dark wood and leather, but the *real* work took place in other rooms, deep below.

Ruby stepped into the office, shut the door behind her, and smiled at the man behind the huge carved desk. He was tidy and well put-together as usual, hair and beard neatly trimmed and touched with gray, dark gray suit immaculate, hands laced together on top of the desk. Ruby had seen him fight monsters in a cavern beneath the sea, and even then, he'd scarcely had a hair out of place. "Please, have a seat." He gestured magnanimously, king of all he surveyed or might wish to.

Ruby dropped into one of the leather chairs positioned across from the desk and looked around at the tasteful paintings, shelves full of gilt-lettered books and assorted civic trophies and awards. There was even a framed honorary doctorate from Miskatonic University on the wall. "I always feel like I've been called into the headmistress's office when I sit in here. Like I was caught smoking in the restroom or something."

"I do nothing to discourage such associations with authority," Sanford said. "Do you require a drink? Something to eat? A cigar?"

"Look at you, being the perfect host. You must *really* want what I've got in my bag here." She patted the leather satchel.

He chuckled. "I am... more than mildly interested. I read about this cup many years ago, and when I heard this expedition had actually found it, and several thousand miles from its last rumored location, on an entirely different continent… My curiosity was thoroughly piqued."

"What's the goblet good for?"

"Accounts vary," Sanford said. "But I'm looking forward to settling the question definitively." He reached out with both hands and made a "give it to me" gesture. "Enough suspense. Let's move on to the gratification portion of the evening."

Ruby opened the straps on the satchel, lifted out the cup, and set it on the desk in front of Sanford.

He leaned forward, gazing at the cup, then reached out and rotated it slowly through a full revolution, considering every side. Then he picked it up, peered at the underside of the base, made a small *hmm* sound, and set it carefully back down. "This, Ruby, is not the goblet I sent you to steal. It is, in fact, a very good replica."

Something clicked in her mind. Ruby closed her eyes and swore. "I should have realized. The *nails*, Sanford! The nails in that crate – they were all shiny and new, but the nails in the other crates were rusty. I can't believe I missed that. Someone must have gotten to the crate first, pried it open, made off with the real goblet, and swapped in this fake. The original nails probably got bent or broken in the process and they had to use new ones to seal it up." She groaned. "I'm sorry, Sanford. Really."

He nodded thoughtfully. "I suppose Doyle's Sherlock Holmes or Poe's C August Dupin might have noticed a detail like those nails, but no one else could have been expected to, especially in the dark. Did you meet with your contact at the docks during this acquisition?"

Ruby nodded. Sanford had plenty of connections all over town – all over the Eastern Seaboard, and beyond, probably – but his contacts tended to stay above the poverty line; he counted on associates like Ruby and his driver-slash-bodyguard, Altman, to handle things on the seedier end of the social scale. "Tick, the night harbormaster. He must have known somebody else got to that crate first! Nothing happens down there that he doesn't get a taste of. The cheating bastard. I'll go shake the truth out of him."

Sanford shook his head. "No, no. I have great faith in your abilities, but I believe a different set of skills will prove more useful in the current situation."

She whistled. "You're sending Altman after Tick?" She shook her head. "Then I take back 'cheating bastard.' Make it that *poor* bastard, instead."

# CHAPTER THREE
## *An Avid Reader*

The next morning Altman walked through the narrow lanes of the River District until he reached the house he was looking for. He didn't find the damp walls and uneven stones and trash-strewn alleyways especially off-putting – he was no stranger to slums and shantytowns, and even the poorest denizen of Arkham had it better than people in some parts of the world he'd visited. These people didn't know how lucky they were.

Or, in one case, how unlucky they were about to be.

Tick Scanlon lived in one of the nicer dwellings, as befit his station – a little bungalow set apart from its neighbors on a fenced square of weedy lawn. The front door hung straight, and the roof still had most of its shingles: the height of luxury by local standards.

Altman opened the waist-high front gate and stepped inside, glancing around automatically to see if there were witnesses, though it hardly mattered here. The people who lived in this damp and squalid sector of Arkham had never willingly spoken to a copper in their lives, and even if the law did make trouble, Altman had a powerful patron these days. Still, there was no reason to let his professional skills get rusty. He moved swiftly along the path, ignored the front door, and went around the side of the house instead. Back doors were left unlocked more often, and if he had to break in, a splintered doorframe or broken window was a lot less noticeable in the rear.

The backyard held a wooden Adirondack chair painted in flaking gray, with a more-or-less flat stump for a table beside it. The latter held a lumpy clay ashtray overflowing with butts. The chair had a view of nothing but the tall boards of the back fence with moss growing up them. Did Scanlon sit back here and watch the grass grow? No, wait, he was a reader, Ruby said. Probably posted himself back here and smoked and perused. Altman himself hadn't voluntarily read anything since he left school at age twelve. Life was his library.

The windows at the back of the house were shaded, but the back door was indeed unlocked. Altman eased it open and peeked into a dirty bachelor's kitchen. No sign of Scanlon, but he was probably sleeping, since he worked the night shift. Altman closed the door quietly behind him and stole into the dim house. It wasn't a big place, and he sussed out the layout immediately – kitchen in the back, then a small corridor with a bathroom on one side and a bedroom on the other, and the living room up front. The door to the bedroom was ajar, and light flickered inside, casting colored blobs on the hallway's walls. Altman frowned. That wasn't candlelight or lamplight. Did Scanlon have a toy magic lantern in there or something?

Altman crept silently down the hall, one hand drawing a sap from his coat pocket. Just a pouch full of lead birdshot, with a leather handle attached, good for putting out lights or breaking the odd wrist. He ducked low and peeked through the crack in the door, into the bedroom inside.

Scanlon was sitting on his bed – a mattress on the floor, really – with his back against the wall, gazing at something glowing in his lap, colorful lights flickering across his slack face. The bedroom floor was filled with haphazard stacks of pulp magazines, some nearly waist high, and more magazines covered the top of a dresser, and stuffed a makeshift shelf constructed from bricks and boards. Scanlon seemed to be holding a magazine open on his lap, but magazines didn't glow.

Altman stood up. The man looked practically hypnotized, mouth gaping open, and even if he'd been watchful and alert, he wasn't much of a threat – out of shape, in an undershirt and gray boxer shorts, big toe poking out of a hole in one of his socks. Altman gave the door a kick and strode inside, slapping the blackjack against his open palm… but Scanlon didn't even look up.

"Scanlon. Tick. *Hey.*" Altman kicked the end of the mattress, and Scanlon finally lifted his eyes from the thing in his lap. Altman tried not to look at the glowing object too closely himself. For all he knew, it might turn him into a drooling fool like Scanlon. He'd seen stranger things.

Tick slapped the thing shut and shoved it under a pillow. It *was* a magazine, or at least, it looked like one. "Who are you? What are you doing in my house?" The questions were spoken mildly, without heat, and Scanlon still seemed vague around the eyes, though it was harder to see his expression in the dim light creeping in from around the window shade.

"You made a deal with my associate last night," Altman said. "You helped her acquire a certain cup. Except you didn't, did you? The cup was a fake. Somebody stole the real one before she even got there." Which was pretty impressive, Altman thought. Sanford usually had the best information, and Ruby was no laggard herself, as far as he could tell. There was a new player in town. Was it this guy Tillinghast they'd been casting around for? Seemed likely.

Scanlon gazed up at Altman, making no effort to rise from his vulnerable position. "Oh. Yes. Ruby. Right. Sorry."

"*Sorry?* You cheated us, Tick."

He shook his head. "She paid me to… let her open a crate… and take what she found. That's what I did. No cheating."

"People in my line of work don't care too much for, what do you call it, semantics. You knew someone else stole the real cup first, didn't you?"

Scanlon became slightly more animated, shaking off some of his strange torpor. "Look, buyer beware, and all that. I don't have some exclusive arrangement with Ruby. Somebody else made me an offer, and… and I took it…" He looked away from Altman, incredibly, and at the pillow where he'd stashed his magazine.

"You're going to make this right, Tick. Why do they call

you that, anyway? Is it because you're all bloated up and full of blood? Maybe we'll see how *much* blood, eh?"

Scanlon wrenched his gaze away from the pillow. "What? No. Just go away. I was reading."

Enough. Altman reached down, grabbed Scanlon under his armpits, and hauled him out of bed, throwing him onto the floor and knocking over a pile of *Black Mask* and *Adventure*. Scanlon tried to get up, and Altman booted him in the ribs. "Who took the cup? Who paid you off?"

The harbormaster cowered, holding up his hands to shield his head. "I never saw her before! She had long black hair in braids, and she was wearing a black dress, she had silver bracelets, I remember her fingernails were painted purple, but I don't *know* her, I never saw her before!"

That didn't sound like Tillinghast. Huh. "Not good enough, Tick. You did business with a stranger you'd never met before, with nobody to vouch for her? You're smarter than that, or at least, that's what people say."

"She..." He licked his lips and looked toward his bed. "She gave me the magazine. It's the most wonderful... the stories... I'd do anything..."

Altman spat on the floor, disgusted, then stepped onto the mattress and kicked the pillow aside. The magazine looked ordinary enough when it was shut, some junk called *Amazing Stories*, but he was glad he was wearing gloves when he picked it up. You could never be too careful with these occult things. Sanford knew about enchantments. Maybe he could figure out where the magazine came from, or what had been done to it. Ha, maybe this *Amazing Stories* was what the detective magazines probably called a *clue*–

Altman was entirely unprepared for the ferocity of Scanlon's attack. "No! *No*! It's mine!" He slammed into Altman's legs and knocked him to the floor, then began to climb up Altman's body, reaching with desperate hands for the magazine Altman still clutched in his own.

Fighting was Altman's area of expertise, though. He rolled onto his side, tossing Scanlon off him, and a moment later, he was on top of the harbormaster, his knees pressed into the man's meaty chest. He tapped Scanlon on the side of the head with the sap, which was usually enough to get the job done, but the man's eyes were wild, and his teeth still gnashed, so Altman gave him a harder wallop.

Scanlon went still, but Altman waited a moment to make sure he wasn't shamming. When a small trickle of blood oozed from the man's ear, Altman thought, *There's no faking that.*

He rose and looked around the room, wondering if it was worth his time to search in case Scanlon had the cup somewhere in here himself. Altman doubted it – he was practically certain, in fact – but Carl Sanford wasn't a big fan of assumptions. He set down the strange magazine and went through the dresser drawers, and the closet, and checked the bathroom and kitchen cabinets, and even underneath the shabby furniture in the living room. No cup.

He returned to the bedroom, checked to see if Scanlon was still breathing – disposing of bodies was such a chore – and found him still alive. He looked at the magazine, which still appeared entirely harmless with its cover closed, but he was reluctant to touch it again, even with gloves on. He tore off a stained pillowcase and scooped the magazine into his makeshift sack.

Then Altman slipped out of the house to give his boss the bad news.

Sanford sat at his desk, peering at the open magazine through something like a jeweler's loupe, though the lens was topaz. "Most curious," Sanford murmured. "You say it was glowing?"

"Glowing, flickering, like a movie was playing on the pages."

"Curious indeed. Ruby said she gathered the same impression, of light and motion, when she saw Scanlon poring over the magazine at the docks. I detect nothing out of the ordinary, however. Of course, there are many forms of otherworldly adulteration, and even I am not conversant in all of them. Perhaps the effect is limited to one particular page." He began to leaf through the magazine, slowly, one page, at a time, and then stopped suddenly. Sanford plucked a small rectangular card that had been stuck between the pages. He held it up to Altman. "What do you make of this?" His voice was strained.

The cardboard rectangle was printed with the words:

*Tillinghast Esoterica and Exotics*
*Rare Books and Curios*
*By Appointment*

It bore no phone number or address. He grunted. "Our mysterious new shopkeeper again, eh? Maybe he sent this long-haired lady with the purple fingernails to deal with Tick. Tillinghast is in the book business, right?"

"It's hardly what anyone would call a rare tome. They print thousands of the things, and this issue is quite new."

"Most of those thousands of issues don't glow, though," Altman pointed out.

"No, they don't," Sanford said. "I suppose these things would be even more popular if they projected a moving picture you could hold in your hands. No need to go to the theater and bear the noises and odors of the hoi polloi if you could enjoy such things in your own home, hmm?" Sanford set the card aside, then riffled quickly through the remainder of the magazine. "Whatever ensorcellment this once possessed is gone, or else its magics are dependent on the presence of the intended recipient."

"Want me to bring Scanlon in? Take him down to one of the basements, see what more we can get out of him?"

Sanford picked up the business card and tapped it on the desk. "No. No, I think we should pursue other avenues instead. Ones more likely to provide satisfaction."

Altman had never been to the courthouse in Arkham before, but he'd certainly seen its type plenty of times: the entryway featured marble floors, vaulted ceilings, noble pillars, and there were friezes and frescoes of stern-faced New Englanders doing allegorical things with scrolls and swords and scales and sheaves of wheat on the walls all around. It was a place designed to impress upon the public the might and majesty of law and order and civil society.

Altman was not impressed.

Sanford nodded to a dozen people as they walked across the shining floor, murmuring asides to Altman as they went – this or that judge was a member of the Lodge or wasn't, this lawyer was just crooked enough, this other lawyer was annoyingly un-bribe-able and impoverished as a result. "I have close associations with the county sheriff and his deputies, but I have friends among the city police forces, too, of course," Sanford confided.

Altman soaked in the information. He never knew when Sanford might dispatch him to have a face-to-face discussion with someone, and the more he knew about the complex associations of power and privilege in Arkham, the better. He'd always had a gift for names and faces, but handling the complex web of entanglements that surrounded Sanford was testing the limits of his faculties.

They eschewed the corridors that led to the courtrooms and instead went up a grand staircase. On the upper floors, the polish started to fade a bit. Here the floors were scuffed, the wooden doors a bit dingy, and the lights less warm. This was the part of the courthouse where people actually got work done.

Sanford walked the halls with total confidence, entering a warren of offices and leading Altman across threadbare carpeting until he finally reached an unassuming door painted flaking white, and pushed it open.

Altman followed him into a little break room, set up with a scarred kitchen table, mismatched chairs, a small stove, a kettle, and some sad plants drooping in brown pots. A little rectangular window high on one wall let in a slice of distant sunshine. There was only one person in the room, a compact pretty brunette in a neat skirt suit, shaking salt over a peeled hardboiled egg. She widened her eyes and stood up, then looked hurriedly around, as if to make sure she wasn't being observed, before dropping a curtsy. Altman had never seen anyone curtsy while holding an egg before. At least it wasn't pickled.

"Master!" she said. "What are you doing here?"

Sanford swept toward her, took the hand that wasn't holding an egg, and kissed it. "My dear Sister Madeline," he said. "I recalled that you customarily took your lunch around this time. Please, sit."

She did, although a bit stiff and flustered, while Sanford arranged himself comfortably in a chair across from her. Altman slid back and stood against the wall, arms crossed. Madeline clearly didn't know what to do with the egg, so she just kept holding it. Altman couldn't tell whether she was terrified of Sanford or merely in awe of him, and decided it was too close to make any distinction.

"Madeline, this is my associate, Mr Altman." Sanford gestured vaguely backward.

The woman frowned, and Altman thought that little worry-furrow in the center of her forehead was pretty close to becoming permanent. She was a little older than he'd thought at first, perhaps even thirty – those wide eyes just made her seem younger. "But I heard that Mr Altman..."

"I'm his brother." Altman spoke up. "Just joined the family business, as it were. It's a pleasure to meet you, miss...?"

"Mrs. Mrs Ostler. Madeline."

"Sister Madeline is an Initiate of the Order, Altman, and

a very valued member indeed." Sanford could sound so warm when he wanted to. "She works at the courthouse as a stenographer, and I couldn't ask for a better set of eyes and ears on the legal system."

She blushed, rather prettily, if you liked that sort of thing; Altman could take it or leave it. "It's nothing, really," she said.

Sanford leaned forward and briefly patted her knee in a paternal fashion. "But Madeline has other skills, and those are what have brought me here today."

She didn't blush this time. She went pale instead. "Oh, sir, must I?"

"You know I wouldn't ask if it weren't essential," Sanford said. "The magazine, Altman?"

He opened the briefcase and extracted the magazine, stuffed into an oversized envelope – he was still reluctant to touch the thing with his bare hands, even if it did seem inert. Sanford showed no such squeamishness when Altman handed it over, extracting the magazine from the envelope and showing it to Madeline. "A woman handled this, not long ago. I need to find her."

"What is she, a bloodhound?" Altman asked.

"A tracker, of sorts, indeed," Sanford said. "Madeline is an accomplished psychometrist."

Altman grunted. He'd attended his share of séances (most were shams, and the ones that weren't were… alarming), and he'd heard of psychometry before. "So she can handle a dead man's handkerchief and tell his wife he still loves her from beyond the grave, things like that?"

Madeline shook her head. She made no attempt to take

the magazine from Sanford's hands. "Not really, no. I pick up… impressions… of the people who've handled things. It's stronger if the handling was more recent, and stronger still if they touched the object often. Sometimes I can see a sort of… silver thread… connecting the person to whatever they touched."

Sanford nodded. "Madeline has been a great help to the police over the years, though most in the department don't realize it. Her late fiancé was a detective, and took frequent advantage of her skills, sneaking her into the evidence room and letting her handle knives and guns and clubs, and more often than not, she could point him straight to the hand that most recently wielded them. Of course, her evidence is hardly admissible in court, but a motivated detective can manufacture whatever proof is required."

"He passed on, then?" Altman said. "I'm sorry for your loss, ma'am."

"Two years ago," she murmured, her eyes far away. "Shot by smugglers. I… I helped find his shallow grave… I can still feel him, in the cemetery now, even though it's consecrated ground, it doesn't help… you see, he touched me so often… our connection…" She wrung her hands, and Sanford put a hand on her knee again.

"I hate to ask it of you," Sanford said softly, and Altman could almost believe it. "But it's a matter of grave importance. Do you think you could try?"

She nodded, tears standing in the corners of her eyes, and took the magazine. She bowed her head, eyes closed. Altman was expecting the sort of dramatics he'd seen among the spiritualists – table rapping, gouts of ectoplasm, or at least her head flung back and her eyes rolling to show the whites. But instead, she simply seemed to concentrate very hard, and spoke softly. "You touched this, and Mr Altman, and before them, a man... he's in a house near the river now. I think he's sobbing? His connection is *very* strong. He didn't hold the object long, but he held it often..."

"A woman," Sanford prompted.

"I... yes. Yes, I see, she didn't hold it long, but it was recent, so I can follow the thread. She had long dark hair. I see her in candlelight. Northside... A lonely house, across from a field, with horses... yellow paint... I think there's a sign... Kersh Lane? That's all. I'm sorry." Her voice croaked, like she'd gone days without water.

"That's very helpful, my dear. Can you see... any farther? Who gave her the magazine?"

*Trying to get a fix on Tillinghast*, Altman thought.

"The thread stops at her," she said. "I don't understand... normally, something like this, I could reach back and find the hand of the newsagent that sold it, the man who packed it for delivery, the printer who took it from the press... but after this woman, it just stops." She opened her eyes, blinking furiously, mouth downturned. "I'm so sorry, master, I've failed you–"

"Tut, tut," Sanford soothed. "Nonsense. You did very well." He took the magazine from her, put it back in the envelope, and handed it to Altman. Then he reached into his jacket and removed a small tin, closing it in Madeline's hand. "Here. These will help with your headaches. And any... dreams."

"Thank you," she whispered. "For everything... everything you did... I owe you... anything you need... I can never repay..."

Sanford rose and said his farewells, and they swiftly departed the courthouse. Once they were back in his Bentley, Altman said, "What did you do for her, to make her so grateful and eager? You could tell doing her trick cost her something."

"Hmm?" The magus was in the backseat, and distracted, gazing out the window, looking northward. "Oh. I tracked down the men who killed her fiancé, and took them to a remote location, and drove Madeline there. Then I gave her a knife and let her take her revenge. I'd intended to keep proof of her crime and use it for blackmail, you see, to force her to use her powers whenever I needed them – I kept the knife, covered in blood, with her fingerprints, and even told her I'd dispose of her bloodstained clothing, and kept those, too. But do you know, I never even needed to threaten her? She doesn't even know I intended to. It just goes to show, sometimes the soft touch is the better way. She was so grateful for the opportunity to take revenge, she's been utterly devoted ever since, and even joined the Order. I've considered promoting her to Seeker, though I worry about letting her handle some of the more potent objects in the basements. She's very sensitive. Even that little display today will have her down with a splitting headache for days."

Altman grunted. "She cut the killers up herself, did she? I'd say she doesn't look like a killer, but, well. I know better."

"Killers can look like anyone at all," Sanford agreed. "How do you fancy a drive to the north side of town?"

# CHAPTER FOUR
*Gloria in Excelsis*

As Altman drove through the winding streets of Arkham toward Northside, Sanford tried to decide whether Tillinghast was going to be a problem, or merely an annoyance. He certainly didn't seem to be an opportunity any longer.

It was interesting that Madeline had been unable to feel Tillinghast's connection to the magazine. If anything, the woman had understated her own powers when describing them to Altman – she should have been able to reach all the way back to sense the printer who set the type for the magazine, the papermaker who'd pressed the pulp, the logger who felled the tree to provide it, the hand of a hiker who'd touched the tree. Instead, she'd hit some sort of psychic dead end, something she'd never done before in Sanford's experience.

That suggested Tillinghast had enough power to hide himself from psychic discovery – or that he possessed a relic that provided such camouflage. Sanford had encountered such items, once or twice, though he didn't currently have any in his own possession. He'd certainly *like* to. If Tillinghast had such relics, and he'd brought them to Arkham, then, ultimately, he'd delivered them to Sanford. This was *his* city, after all, and anything he desired in its limits would be his eventually. Sanford might have been willing to make room for Tillinghast, if the man proved useful, but now he'd stolen the so-called Grail of Dreams out from under Sanford's very nose and *that* insult could not be borne.

"Coming up on Kersh Lane now," Altman said, stirring Sanford from his reverie. They'd left Eastside and traversed downtown and made their way to Northside without the magus even realizing.

This Tillinghast was taking up far too much of Sanford's time and attention. He wanted to track the newcomer down, retrieve the grail, drive the interloper out of town, and move on with more important business. "I don't recall a yellow house around here," Altman said, "but I haven't committed every little shack to memory."

"I'm impressed you know as much as you do about our environs, given your relative newness to the city."

"Oh, I visited my brother from time to time, and he liked to ramble around and point out places of interest. I'm naturally an attentive person."

"Surely it's training as much as inclination," Sanford said. "Noting potential escape routes that should be eliminated, composing a mental map to use in the case of house-to-house fighting, and the like." Sanford didn't know exhaustive details about Altman's life, but he knew the man had been a mercenary like his brother before him, and he'd observed this Altman long enough to draw certain conclusions.

"Let's just say I've learned it pays to keep my eyes open and my wits about me." Altman cruised slowly along Kersh Lane, peering left and right methodically at the houses they passed. The dwellings were spaced out a bit more widely here, on the edges of things, with backyards merging seamlessly with fields or stretches of woodland.

"Do you know, I worried about employing you at first," Sanford said. "I was afraid you'd blame me for your brother's death. I feared you might seek revenge."

Altman barked a laugh. "I would have sought revenge against the cultists who killed Reggie, not the man who employed him. You got all the revenge for me before I reached town, anyway. Left the whole cult in a watery grave, and in pieces at that."

"True. But I was surprised you took my word for that."

"Oh, no, I got Ruby drunk. Or tried to. She's got a high tolerance, for a flap. She told me what she knew about my brother's fate, and her story accorded with yours well enough, but not so perfectly I thought you'd rehearsed it together."

Sanford chuckled. "It gratifies me to know you did your due diligence before accepting my offer of employment. An excess of trust can be a danger in our line of work."

"What line of work is that, exactly? I know we're looking for artifacts and relics and items of unnatural provenance, but you've been a little short on details when it comes to the ultimate purpose of all this acquiring."

Sanford clucked his tongue. "Don't be foolish, man. Power is its own purpose. Sufficient power permits one to do whatever one wishes."

"So… it's freedom you're after, then."

"Succinctly put," Sanford agreed. "And freedom means making sure no one else has the power to limit me." Something outside the passenger window caught his eye. "There, Mr Altman. I see a flash of yellow through the trees. Looks like fresh paint."

"That explains why I didn't recall it from my last meander around these parts." Altman didn't slow from his already stately pace but swiveled his head to look at the house. It was a single-story structure, neat and trim, set well back from the road behind a split-rail fence, with open fields lying fallow on either side. A curl of smoke rose from the chimney. It looked like a picture postcard for cozy country living.

Altman drove on until he reached a side road and followed that on a meandering course toward the back of the house. He pulled off to the side, behind a copse of trees, glimpses of the yellow backside of the house visible here and there between the branches. "How do you want to play this?" Altman asked, pulling on his gloves. "Shall I slip in and… prepare the ground? Get her in a receptive mood for your questions?"

"I think–" Sanford said, and then flinched when someone rapped on the window beside his head. He turned and looked into the startling green eyes of a woman crouching beside the car. Black braids framed her face, and she smiled an open and guileless smile.

"How did she creep up on us like that?" Altman twisted in the seat to look back at her.

She made a twirling motion with her hand (her finger-nails were, indeed, painted a deep purple), and Sanford rolled down his window. "Carl Sanford, I presume?" she asked, her voice like bells and flutes.

"You have the advantage of me, madam," Sanford said.

"I'm Gloria Dyer. My employer said you might drop by. Would you like to come in and have a cup of coffee and talk things over?"

"I suppose we should." He glanced at Altman and gave a minute nod. His driver nodded in return and slid out of the car – he towered over the Dyer woman, who was far more diminutive than her confidence implied – and gestured for her to step back. She moved gracefully away, and Sanford took in the whole of her for the first time. She wore black trousers, a black silk shirt with pearl buttons, pearl earrings, and a leather cord around her throat that disappeared into her neckline. Her boots were knee-high and extravagantly heeled, which made him revise his estimate of her size yet again. She might be four foot eleven in her bare feet, he supposed, but not much more than that.

Altman opened the door for Sanford, and he emerged, bringing his walking stick, with the sword blade hidden inside. He didn't need the stick to walk, or the sword to fight, but it never hurt to be underestimated and overprepared. He leaned on the stick and gave her a nod. "Lead on, madam."

She smiled sunnily. "It's miss. Never been married.

Never found the right man. Not many people can put up with someone who travels so much, and I can't put up with anyone who stays in one place. It's an appalling character flaw, I know, but I can't help how I was made, can I?" She positively twinkled. "Come along, we'll go through the trees, it's nicer."

Dyer set off confidently through the weeds toward the trees, and Sanford followed, Altman just a step behind him. Sanford knew the man carried a knife – his late brother's kukri, in fact – and had a pistol and a blackjack as well. All that seemed far in excess of requirements to deal with a tiny thing like Dyer, but Altman had doubtless learned not to underestimate people, too.

They emerged from the trees and stepped into her backyard, a neatly mown lawn with a single crab apple tree standing sentinel in the middle of the space, and she gestured at the house as she approached. "Isn't it lovely? I had it painted before I moved in. I just adore yellow. It's such a sunny color, don't you think?"

Sanford's associations with the color yellow were rather less pleasant – yellow was the color of certain sigils he'd seen scrawled on crumbling walls in Europe, where cult-maddened crowds had run riot during the Great War. Worst of all, the shade reminded him of a figure once glimpsed down an alleyway, wearing a mask of tattered yellow cloth; a figure that he was sure saw him, too, though the mask lacked eyeholes. But Sanford merely said, "Yes, it's very… bright."

She opened the back door and gestured for them to precede her inside. Altman went first, scanning for signs of ambush, and checking all the rooms while Sanford smiled benevolently at Dyer, and she beamed happily back at him. After a few moments, Altman returned and beckoned Sanford to enter. He went up the steps slowly, leaning on his stick, just as he'd slowly traversed the woods, playing up his age. Dyer skipped in after them and shut the door.

"I have fresh coffee, unless you prefer tea?" She bustled around with cups and carafes, and a silver creamer and sugar bowl, and tongs and a tray of small ginger snaps, arranging everything on the kitchen table, which was also painted yellow. Dyer sat down at the table and looked at Sanford expectantly.

"We're fine, thank you." Sanford perched on the edge of a chair across from her. Altman took up his usual position, back to the wall by the door, eyes watchful. "But your hospitality is appreciated."

"As you like it." She poured herself a cup from the carafe, dropped in more lumps of sugar than seemed prudent, and stirred in a splash of cream, tiny silver spoon *tink*ing against the china cup. She took a sip, then held the mug, steam blurring her face when she met Sanford's eyes. "I understand you have some questions for me?"

Sanford didn't expect honest answers, and didn't like the fact that he'd been expected, but even lies could provide useful information. "You work for Randall Tillinghast."

She cocked her head. "*Was* that a question? But yes, I do. I'm his – well, it's funny, he called me his herald, isn't that a strange way to put it? Like he's a king and I'm in front blowing the trumpet to announce him. I'm just his personal assistant, though, really. I came to town before him, secured lodgings, looked at potential locations for his shop, took care of the business licensing and registering with the tax authorities, set up phone lines, purchased some of his fixtures, made preliminary introductions..." She waved a hand. "All the little details a businessman doesn't always have time to handle himself. I'm still helping him settle in, running errands for him, and so forth."

"How long have you been in Tillinghast's employ?"

"Oh, just a few months. I was working as an executive assistant at Bethlehem Steel, in Pennsylvania, at the time. Before that I worked as the personal assistant for–" She paused. "Well. I think I'm still contractually forbidden to divulge who I was working for, but suffice to say, a very wealthy titan of industry, who traveled extensively, and I traveled with him, making all his arrangements along the way. He passed away, sadly, when we were in Morocco, and I was at a loose end for a bit, then took the job in Bethlehem, for something to do more than anything else... sorry, I'm twittering on a bit, aren't I?" She laughed in a way that suggested she was delighted by her own minor foibles. "Mr Tillinghast approached me on my lunch break one afternoon and offered me a job, short-term, on a contract basis, for a frankly irresistible sum. After this I'll be able to travel without having to worry about paying my way. I think that answers your question, though I'm sorry I also answered all those questions you *didn't* ask. I can get a bit chatty when I meet new people. Nerves, I expect."

Sanford thought she seemed no more nervous than a heavyweight boxer facing the prospect of a bar fight with a drunken laborer. He waited a moment to make sure she was done, then said, "Have you any interest in or knowledge of the occult, Miss Dyer?"

She put a single fingertip to her lips. "The occult? Oh, of course, I know Mr Tillinghast deals in all sorts of rare books in that line. Grimoires, I think they're called? And relics of old religions." She shrugged. "None of that is really within my purview, though. You don't need a working knowledge of Egyptian hieroglyphics to get a phone line installed, fortunately!" She laughed that self-delighted tinkle of a laugh again.

"You said you came to town, and arranged introductions," Sanford said. "Introductions to whom?"

She took a bite of a cookie and chewed thoughtfully. "Oh, gosh, who can remember? Some experts in antiquities at the university... there were some other book dealers, the proprietors of a curiosity shop and a so-called magic shop in town..."

That was irritating. The owners of the Curiositie Shoppe and Ye Olde Magick Shoppe should have notified Sanford of any unusual contacts. Unless they'd been bribed with enchanted objects to refrain...

Gloria continued, "There were a few business people Mr Tillinghast thought might be interested in investments... I didn't do that much, honestly. I just passed along my employer's card, and sometimes delivered gifts–"

"Gifts?" Sanford interrupted.

"Oh, yes. I think Mr Tillinghast spent some time in the East. He told me he'd picked up a delightful custom of offering small gifts to those he hoped to do business with.

Just baubles, usually, nothing of great value, but I've found people are most appreciative of the gesture."

Sanford couldn't tell if this woman was truly guileless, or so full of guile she could pretend to be so at an expert level. "Why, may I ask, didn't you contact *me* when you were making these introductions?"

She looked puzzled. "Introduce you in what capacity, sir? I know who you are, of course, and I understand you used to be involved in imports and exports, but that you are largely retired these days. You are known as a patron of the arts and a philanthropist, and a pillar of Arkham society, but not someone with whom Mr Tillinghast would expect to do business. He is essentially a humble shopkeeper, as he will be the first to attest."

"Mmm. I see." The problem with ruling a secret society was that sometimes it was *too* secret. Sanford was provisionally prepared to believe Miss Dyer didn't know what he *really* was, but he was quite certain that Tillinghast did. "You mentioned little gifts. You gave such a gift to the night harbormaster at the river docks recently, did you not?"

"Oh, yes, that nice Mr Scanlon." She brightened even further. "It was nothing much, just a magazine Mr Tillinghast thought he'd like. I imagine the shop will be receiving all manner of shipments, and he wanted to smooth the way with the officials on the waterfront – it never hurts to ingratiate oneself a bit with the people in charge, does it? You get much friendlier service that way."

"Yes, yes. Did you give Mr Scanlon anything *else*?" *Like a great stone cup, for instance?*

"No – well, there was a note, tucked into the magazine, from Mr Tillinghast."

"What did it say?" Sanford demanded.

For the first time, she frowned, though only slightly. "I'm afraid I don't know. It was sealed. Mr Tillinghast is so delightfully old-fashioned; he uses a blot of wax and a little stamp, in the shape of an eye. Anyway, I didn't read it. Mr Tillinghast told me to honestly answer any of your questions when you came by, but I can't tell you things I don't know."

If she was telling the truth, she didn't know anything about the Grail of Dreams. Tillinghast must have arranged for the theft and the swap in the note he'd given Scanlon – and the man had been so entranced by his "bauble" that he'd doubtless been eager to obey any instructions, no matter how strange. "Perhaps you can tell me how you knew I was coming at all?" Sanford asked, doing his best to sound mildly curious instead of furiously outraged.

She shrugged. "Mr Tillinghast simply said I should be expecting you, probably no later than mid-afternoon, and to cooperate with you fully."

"And didn't that strike you as odd?" Sanford demanded, losing his composure slightly.

Another tinkling laugh. "Mr Sanford. For what I'm getting paid, I can stomach a great deal more than *odd*. Have I answered all your questions?"

"No. Where is Tillinghast's shop? I haven't been able to locate it."

"You know, he hasn't quite settled on a final location yet," she said. "I've shown him a dozen places, and none of them strike him as quite right. It's something of a moveable feast, you might say! He's been taking meetings with people here and there, auditioning different places, but so far, all his custom has been arranged by appointment. Would *you* like an appointment?"

Sanford seethed. People made appointments to see him, not the other way around; Sanford just turned up, and the people he wanted to see dropped everything to accommodate him. It had been that way in Arkham for years. "Yes. Please make the arrangements as soon as possible. Mr Tillinghast and I have much to discuss." He handed over one of his cards, and she scanned it briefly, committing the details to memory as a dedicated and eager assistant should.

"I'll be in touch the *moment* I've made the arrangements," she assured him.

"You said Tillinghast hired you for a short-term contract?" Sanford said.

She nodded. "Yes. Once all the arrangements are made and Mr Tillinghast is settled in Arkham, he says he won't have need of my services anymore. I'll only be here for another month or two at most, probably."

"Only a month or two," Sanford said. "And yet, you had the house painted?"

She blushed. "An indulgence, I know, but what's the point of all this money if I can't live as I please?"

"Freedom," Altman murmured, the first time he'd spoken since they entered the house.

Dyer grinned at him. "Exactly."

Sanford rose. "I thank you for your time and hospitality.

We will speak soon. If I am unavailable to take your call, please leave the salient details with my secretary." He couldn't remember which Initiate he had answering phones just now – at a certain point, they all became a bit interchangeable.

Gloria rose, too, and said, "Before you go, Mr Tillinghast left a gift for *you*." She reached under the table to pick up something resting in the empty chair beside hers and straightened with a small box in her hands.

Sanford took a step back, and Altman took a step forward, and they stood shoulder-to-shoulder. Dyer looked back and forth at each of them, puzzled, and laughed. "You act as if I was about to hand you a poisonous snake, or a lit stick of dynamite!" The box she proffered was gaily wrapped in red paper with a green ribbon, and was big enough to hold a book, perhaps, but nothing larger.

"What is it?" Sanford said.

"I'm sure I don't know. I was given the box already wrapped. But Mr Tillinghast has a wonderful ability to choose the right gift. People are always delighted to receive his presents."

She kept holding out the box, and so Sanford nodded to Altman, who took it, as if afraid it might explode. "I appreciate the kindness," Mr Sanford said. "I look forward to reciprocating it in good time."

They bade their farewells and headed back across the lawn and through the trees. Altman held the box out before him at arm's length. "What do you want me to do with this thing?" he asked.

"Put it in the trunk, for now," Sanford said. "And as soon

as you can, put it in a sack, weigh it down with rocks, and drop it in the river. Don't tell me where."

"You really think it's that dangerous?" Altman said.

"So far, I've seen two gifts Tillinghast has given, a snow globe and a magazine, and both seemed to utterly entrance the men who possessed them. I like to think I'm made of sterner stuff, that my will is like unto adamant, but..." He shook his head. "Why risk it?"

"Who *is* this Tillinghast, do you reckon?" Altman asked.

"A fellow connoisseur of power, I suspect," Sanford said.

He glanced behind him, through the trees, and saw Dyer standing at the window in her kitchen, smiling and waving, waving and smiling.

# CHAPTER FIVE
*A Humble Shopkeeper*

Ruby sat in her favorite booth at the Perch, picking at a plate of veal and damp boiled vegetables, thinking about terrible encounters she'd had in a certain Louisiana swamp years earlier. The Perch never drew much of a dinner crowd, and it was a bit early for the rowdy late-nighters who'd come later for drinks and song, which meant it was quiet enough for her own thoughts to dominate her attention. Unfortunately.

Blessed distraction arrived in the form of a stranger sliding into the booth across from her. Usually, the people who did that were men, slightly or very drunk, ties loosened, eyes shining, full of misplaced confidence regarding their own charms, asking Ruby what a pretty girl like her was doing here all alone. The smart ones took a verbal brushoff. The less smart ones tended to scurry when she jabbed one of her heels into their shins. For the terminally clue-deprived, she'd signal the bartender, and the staff would help her out – they loved her here.

Ruby made friends easily, but only the friends she wanted.

This intrusion came from a woman, though, and she seemed sober, which was two deviations away from the norm. She had bright green eyes and black hair in the sort of elaborate braids that made Ruby tired just to think about. The stranger was wearing billowy purple palazzo pants and a blood-red top that left her arms bare, showing off silver bracelets. Her fingernails were painted a shade of purple Ruby had never seen in a paint pot before, and her smile was like a sunrise after the longest night of the year. "Are you Ruby Standish?" She slid into the booth as casually as if they were old friends reuniting.

"Who's asking?" Hardly snappy repartee, but then, Ruby wasn't trying to impress anyone just now.

"My name's Gloria Dyer. I hope you don't mind me interrupting your dinner. I ordered us a couple of gin fizzes. I hear they don't even make their gin in a bathtub here." As if on cue, a waitress plopped two glasses down on the table. "I love how Prohibition stops at the front door in this place," Gloria said. "The owner is the mayor's second cousin or something, isn't that right?"

"I never inquired about his family tree," Ruby said, though of course she knew how everyone around her was connected to everyone else.

"Well, anyway, it's a safe harbor. I've spent most of the past decade overseas, and it was pretty strange to come back and find my own country had become as sober as some of the Emirates I visited." Gloria shook her head. "But even in those places, you can get a drink if you know where to look." She held up her glass, and Ruby lifted her own in return. She was naturally suspicious, but Gloria hadn't touched Ruby's glass, and the staff here wouldn't slip Ruby anything, so she sipped. Bad choice of a cocktail, though; Ruby had first tasted a gin fizz down in New Orleans, and drinking this one brought those lurking memories even closer to the top, like a gator surfacing in the bayou to feed.

"Since you bought me a drink, I might as well tell you, yes, I'm Ruby. What brings you to my table?"

Gloria laughed. "I like how you didn't say 'What can I do for you?' It seems like I always say that, even when I don't mean to, and especially when I don't want to do anything at all for whoever's pestering me." She turned her glass around and around with her fingers. "We have an acquaintance in common. My current employer, and your former one."

The gin tasted even worse all of a sudden, and Ruby pushed the glass away. "Tillinghast." She looked around, half expecting to see the slender, elegant fellow leaning against the bar, watching her with those deep, perceptive eyes, but there was no sign of him. Ruby wondered if Sanford knew about Gloria yet. It made sense that Tillinghast would have an associate running errands for him. He'd always struck her as more of a "work from the shadows" type.

"That's the one." Gloria cocked her head. "You say his name like it's a swallow of sour milk. Is there anything I should know? He's been a perfect gentleman so far, but I know some men come across that way so you'll let your guard down, and then make a move you didn't see coming."

Ruby shook her head. "No, he never… it's nothing like that. He was fine. A little strange, like he was in on a joke nobody else could understand, but he's rich, and rich men are all peculiar in their own ways. It was just… the job I did for him got a little hairy. He paid me for it, paid me a bonus even, for the trouble I saw, but…"

"But money doesn't erase your memory," Gloria said. "I get that. He's had me do some odd things since he hired me, but nothing I'd call hairy."

"He sent you to talk to me?" Ruby said. She nodded. "How did he even know I was here?"

Gloria shrugged. "I don't know. Sometimes I ask questions, but he doesn't usually answer them, and if I had more sense, I'd probably give up on trying to understand him entirely."

Tillinghast had possessed inexplicable inside information about the job Ruby did for him, too. He'd sent her down south to acquire some disgusting little relic called the "Horror In Clay." The people who'd owned the lumpy statuette had been *very* attached to it, and exceedingly cross with her for liberating the object of their affections. Ruby still had dreams, sometimes, of torches flickering all around her in a dark swamp as she fled, wondering if the alligators or the cultists would get her first.

She leaned back in the booth and took a closer look at Gloria. She was well put-together, relaxed, and friendly; dressed fashionably but not aggressively so; and she projected a sort of "we're all in this together" bonhomie. Ruby never trusted first impressions. Too often, people were just putting on the costume they wanted you to see, knowing once you'd made up your mind about the kind of person they were, that impression would be established, and subsequently hard to shake. Ruby used that trick too often herself to let it work on her.

But, damn it, Gloria was likeable, and there was no harm in listening. Sanford *had* tasked Ruby to track down Tillinghast and wriggle into his good graces, and here was an opportunity, served up on a platter. Sure, it seemed too easy, just like the job at the docks, but didn't Ruby deserve an actual lucky break every once in a while? "What's mister long, tall, and mysterious want you to tell me?"

"He wonders if you'd meet with him to discuss a potential business arrangement."

Ruby hadn't really enjoyed the last job she did for the man, though it had turned out all right in the end. Except for the nightmares. "Did he tell you what kind of business arrangement?"

Gloria smiled, her dimples deepening. "He did! He said to tell you 'the lucrative kind.'"

She snorted a laugh despite herself. "The old man does know the way to my heart, I guess. Do you know what I used to do for him, Gloria?"

"He told me you were one of the finest acquisition agents he'd ever employed." She paused. "I assume that means you're good at negotiating purchases."

"That's an assumption, all right. Where and when does Tillinghast want to meet?"

"At his shop," Gloria said. "And now, if it's convenient?"

Ruby had a set of brass knuckledusters and a Derringer pistol in her purse, so she was as ready for a meeting as she'd ever be. Those were just the usual precautions, though. Ruby didn't think she was in any danger – she didn't have anything Tillinghast was likely to want, and even if she did, without knowing it, he knew she was easier to buy off than to threaten. Ruby considered ducking out to give Sanford a call, and let him know things were in motion, but the old man was such a meddler – he'd probably dispatch Altman or someone else to follow her around and muck up everything in the process. She decided to call Altman after, when she had something solid to report.

"Let me settle up here, and then we can go," Ruby said.

"I'm *delighted*," Gloria replied, and seemed to mean it.

Dyer's car was parked just around the corner, and it was a real looker: a long, sleek, canary-yellow convertible roadster with shining running boards and leather interior, and a hood ornament like a winged Viking helmet. Ruby whistled. "Is that the new Imperial 80?"

"Fresh off the assembly line," Gloria said. "It's barely got a hundred miles on it. Shipped down from Detroit on a train, apparently. I found it in the driveway of the house I'm renting the day I arrived here, with a note from Mr Tillinghast that said, 'To aid you in your errands on my behalf. You may keep it when our business is concluded.'" She laughed, a silver-bell tinkle. "Talk about a starting bonus, huh?"

Ruby shook her head, impressed. Tillinghast was generous enough, in her experience, but then, if your personality doesn't inspire loyalty, money can be a great help. She went around to the passenger side, climbing in while Gloria settled behind the wheel. The engine started up with a rumble, then roared like a barely tamed beast. "I found a nice straight empty back road that first day and pushed her up past eighty miles per hour." Gloria patted the wheel affectionately. "She didn't break a sweat or even start to shimmy. I call her Helios. My chariot of the sun."

"You're a pretty bright and perky person yourself, aren't you, Gloria?"

Dyer put the car into gear and pulled around the corner, angling her way westward. "I've had my share of shadows in my life, so when I have a chance to stand in the light, I make sure to appreciate it. But maybe my fortunes are finally turning. Mr Tillinghast is being so generous, I might be able to pursue some of my own dreams for once, instead of just making other people's come true."

Ruby leaned back, closing her eyes and enjoying the feel of the wind in her hair. For once, the breeze was blowing the right way, and didn't even smell like tar and fish. "What dreams are those?"

"Oh, now, a girl has to keep some secrets, doesn't she?"

"Amen to that, sister," Ruby agreed. "Well, I hope you get everything you want and nothing you don't."

"That's very kind of you," Gloria replied.

Ruby opened her eyes and watched the buildings slide past, Gloria deftly weaving around the inevitable double-parked delivery trucks and plodding, inattentive pedestrians. "We're headed to Northside? Funny place to put a shop, isn't it? It's mostly offices and factories over there. Not likely to attract much passing trade."

"Mr Tillinghast is mostly open by appointment anyway," Gloria said. "Though it's unclear if he'll actually settle in Northside. He's had me show him so many different spaces. He'll decide on one, only to change his mind and pack up the whole inventory and move to a better prospect. The local real estate agents are quite put out with me, I'm afraid."

"Tillinghast moves around all the time, huh?" Ruby mused. "Like some sort of fugitive, almost. Or a crime boss staying one step ahead of the G-Men."

"Oh, I don't get that impression," Gloria said. "More that he's… very particular. He's looking for perfection, and nothing less will do." She glanced sidelong at Ruby. "Do you think he is involved in legally dubious activities? I'd hate to find myself embroiled in something unsavory. But I'm not stupid. Given how free Tillinghast is with his money, I've certainly wondered."

Ruby waved a hand. "Everyone who deals in ancient relics and artifacts operates in legally gray areas, Gloria. They pay off dockmasters, they bribe customs agents, they spirit away objects that probably ought to be in museums… even your ordinary book dealers cheat and connive and scheme and backstab, and when the texts in question get really rare, it all turns even nastier. But it's not like Tillinghast is running the Capone mob or something. Even my boss–" She paused. It was entirely too easy to talk to this woman. Gloria had that trick of making you feel like the most interesting person in the world, gazing at you, all wide-eyed fascination. Ruby had used that technique herself often enough to make others tell her things they shouldn't have, and it galled her a little to find herself falling for the same technique. Gloria seemed so genuine, but Ruby would proceed with caution anyway. "Let's just say, even some of the most prominent and upstanding people in Arkham have hands that aren't totally pristine.

You don't get money and power without getting a little dirt under your nails in the process."

"Surely you have to draw the line somewhere, though," Gloria said.

Ruby shrugged. "Sure. I don't like violence. For one thing, working with violent people means you might find yourself the subject of that violence sometime, and that's not for me."

"As good a limit as any, I suppose," Gloria said. "We're here." She pulled into a narrow street, almost an alleyway, between a defunct cannery and a squat brick building that seemed to be held together more by inertia than mortar.

"When I worked for Tillinghast, he had an office at the top of a private library," Ruby said. "He's gone down in the world."

"It's nicer inside," Gloria said. "You see the wooden door there, with the square window? It should be open, so just let yourself in."

"You aren't coming with me?"

"More errands to run," Gloria said. "A helpmeet's job is never done. Mr Tillinghast will get you a cab wherever you want to go, if I'm not back by the time you're finished." She offered her hand and shook Ruby's briskly. "I hope we have the chance to chat again, or maybe even work together. I enjoyed meeting you."

"Same here," Ruby said. "Us career gals have to watch out for each other, right?"

Gloria gave her a wink, and Ruby slipped out of the car and watched her drive the purring convertible around a corner and out of sight. She looked around the alley, strewn with dried leaves and newspaper pages, and muttered, "I get to visit such nice places."

Ruby approached the ornate and polished dark wooden door, which seemed out of place set into the crumbling bricks. The square window was stained glass, mostly white except for a green triangle with a stylized eye in the center. She'd seen sigils like that before in various mystic texts – eyes and pyramids were common motifs among secret societies – but never one exactly like this; there was something sort of reptilian about this eye, though she couldn't put her finger on what. She knocked once, said, "Hello?" and then put her hand on the copper doorknob when there was no answer. *Gloria said to just go in…*

Ruby twisted the knob and pushed. There was a popping sound, like a seal being broken, and the door swung inward.

The interior of the shop *was* much nicer than the outside, a cozy space with dark wooden floors scattered with colorful rugs in peculiar geometric patterns, lit by the soft glow of brass lamps. There were shelves everywhere, crammed with books bound in leather and cloth and less obvious materials, and other shelves that held curios and statuary and peculiar objects, and occasional freestanding pedestals with objects of presumably greater value displayed under glass.

She stepped in, shutting the door behind her, and called, "Mr Tillinghast?" There was no answer, so she looked around, peering at some of the most eye-catching objects on the shelves: a figurine of a broad-hipped woman carved from white crystal; a sparkling cracked-open geode, the crystals inside the color of rich burgundy wine; a copper sphere surrounded by silver rings; an astrolabe and matching sextant that appeared to be made of solid gold; a squat statuette of a man with the head of a beetle; a book with a black binding that sported a snarling wolf's face on the cover, complete with real teeth–

"Ah, Miss Standish." The voice purred from behind her, and Ruby made herself turn slowly, with a smile, instead of startling.

Tillinghast was there, standing behind a long glass counter that she hadn't noticed before, with a tarnished brass cash register at his elbow. He was the same as she remembered, down to the smallest detail: a tall, thin white man, probably in his sixties, with gray hair cut short and a gray Italian suit of an immaculate cut. He didn't look at all like a humble shopkeeper; he looked like the patriarch of an aristocratic family, full of centuries of dignity. Except for that dark little twinkle in his eye, like there was a joke only he knew, but if you could understand it, you'd be just as amused as he was. The twinkle was only there when the man smiled, though. She remembered well that when his face went slack and impassive, the eyes became like black wells. "You're looking well."

Ruby dredged up a smile. "Last time you saw me, I still had muck in my hair from running through a swamp. I should hope I've cleaned up since then."

"Your innate glory always shines through, my dear." Tillinghast picked up a stool and carried it from behind the counter, setting it carefully on the floor. "Have a seat, would you?"

Ruby sat on the stool, tucking her skirts around her. "Gloria said you had a job offer for me?"

"Straight to the particulars, then? You don't want a glass of brandy or a cup of tea first?" He was still half-smiling at that secret joke of his. Ruby just hoped the joke wasn't on her.

She didn't want to be around Tillinghast any longer than necessary. He still made her skin crawl. She was only here because Carl Sanford had asked her to renew the connection, and he was the one providing her with martini money lately. "Maybe we can have a drink to seal the deal, if we make one," she said. "What's your offer, Mr Tillinghast? I trust you won't waste my time."

"Nothing too strenuous, really," Tillinghast replied, leaning against the counter. "I just want you to betray your current employer, Carl Sanford, and come work for me instead."

# CHAPTER SIX
## *The Hourglass*

Altman was supposed to be off Tillinghast duty for the day. Sanford had spent the past two months tracing rumors and rumblings about a visiting professor of philosophy at the university, Reginald Detwiller, who was dabbling in matters best left undabbled in. The professor was supposedly messing with time, somehow, or trying to, and Sanford didn't like people conducting occult experiments in his city unless he got to supervise and take a cut of any useful proceeds.

So Altman was sitting in the professor's apartment, in the dark, in an armchair, with a pistol in his lap, waiting for the fellow to get home. Sure, the whole setup was a little theatrical, and something of a cliché, but it really was pretty effective. Just *being there* in someone's supposed place of safety tended to shake them up thoroughly, and shaken people were easy to push around. The only problem was, the technique required a lot of waiting, and a lot of patience, and that left Altman alone with his thoughts.

Too often, lately, after a lifetime of placid calm, those thoughts had been troubled. Ever since the death of his brother Reggie, really. The elder Altman had always been a titan to his younger sibling, an unstoppable force, effortlessly deadly, a killer with panache, brute force with a bright mind... but he'd been bested and killed by cultists, and the surviving Altman hadn't even been able to get revenge on them personally.

Sanford had gotten that revenge instead, and Altman respected the man for it, and was even grateful, but Sanford had also been the one who led the older Altman into the cult's clutches to begin with. Altman didn't blame his employer for that – this was a dangerous business, messing with the occult – but it did make him a little nervous. Altman had no doubt that Sanford would sacrifice him, too, if it furthered his interests, or even enabled the magus himself to survive five minutes longer than he would otherwise. That was fine, too, honestly; you didn't become the head of an organization like the Silver Twilight Lodge without a streak of ruthlessness as wide as the Yangtze River, and Altman knew what he was signing up for when he took the old man's coin.

But more and more he found himself wondering: *How do I stop working for people like Sanford, and become a person like Sanford instead?* It would be nice, for once, to wield the power, instead of just being an element of the power that someone else wielded.

Shortly after nightfall, Altman's brooding was interrupted by the creak of the front door's unoiled hinges. The university put up their temporary professors in fairly small and dingy apartments that clung to the outskirts of campus, but that's what the life of the mind got you.

Detwiller bustled in, a small man in a worn plaid suit, with a parcel tucked under one arm. He was bursting with energy, like a small and nervous dog, and his hair was combed meticulously over a bald spot the size of the Aral Sea. Altman had spied on him once or twice and developed the impression of a man who was deeply concerned about his appearance but didn't have much to work with in the area. He didn't notice Altman at all, just carried his paper-wrapped package to the table in the eat-in kitchen, and picked up a knife to slice apart the strings binding it.

Altman eased up out of the chair and padded silently to stand behind Detwiller. He watched as the man unwrapped the package and tore open the box, then removed an ornate foot-tall hourglass, delicate blown-glass chambers filled with sand the color of ash – maybe it *was* ash – in a black wooden frame carved with small, intricate spirals. "Finally," Detwiller breathed, and that's when Altman put his hands on the man's shoulders and boomed, "What's this, then?"

Detwiller shrieked and tried to spin, but Altman pushed down, holding him in place. "Put down the hourglass and take a seat, professor. We'll have a little chat, shall we?"

"What are you – who – what do you want?" He clutched the hourglass to his chest. "This is mine! You can't have it!"

"I think you'll find the only thing that's truly yours is the breath and blood in your body," Altman said. "And you've only got those for as long as I allow it." He squeezed, fancying he could feel the man's collarbones compressing, and Detwiller whimpered. "Do as I said. I don't like asking for things twice."

Detwiller put the hourglass down on the table, reverently, and Altman eased up on his grip to let the man drop into a chair at the table. Altman then sat across from him, holding the gun so it was visible, but not pointing at the man. Yet. It was always important to leave room for escalation in negotiations like these.

Altman prodded the hourglass with the butt of the gun and watched Detwiller wince and start to reach for it. He scowled, and the professor clasped his hands before him on the table instead, fingers writhing like a nest of snakes. "Who are you?" he croaked.

"I'm a representative of an interested party. What's the hourglass for, professor?"

"It's just – an old family heirloom, it has purely sentimental value–"

"I'll put a bullet through the glass if you don't tell me the truth," Altman said mildly. "And since you're sitting on the other side of the glass, it's possible the bullet will carry on through your body as well. You're only useful to me if you tell me something I want to know. I don't keep useless things around. Better to be useful, yes?" He decided to show a little mercy. "We know you're trying to send yourself back in time, anyway, like the fellow in that old HG Wells story."

Detwiller shook his head violently. "No, that's not – I don't believe it's possible to travel bodily in time."

"You want to project your mind back in time, then," Altman said. The magus had talked about that sort of thing – apparently there was a dame locked up in one of the

Lodge basements who'd come to Earth from some future time, taking over the body of a local woman in the process. Not a very good arrangement for the local woman, Altman supposed, but people with power made their own morality.

"I… yes." Detwiller bowed his head. "It doesn't – I won't hurt anyone. I'm going to send my mind back, you see, into the body of my own grandfather. It's easier if it's someone in your bloodline, at least, that's what Mr Tillinghast said–"

"Tillinghast?" Altman said sharply. "The shopkeeper?"

"The… yes." Detwiller smiled, as if he'd forgotten all about the stranger with a gun. "He's been such a great help. I was working so hard, with nothing to show for it… I came to Miskatonic University to gain access to certain texts about a prehuman, or maybe posthuman, species that had unlocked the secrets of time. I wasn't making much progress, and then Mr Tillinghast introduced himself. He said he'd read one of my papers on the circularity of causality in a finite universe, and that he could help my research. He didn't ask for much in return, not *so* much, just a few texts from the special collection here. They were the same texts I'd come to study, so I had access. I had to smuggle the pages out, and I suppose I'll lose my privileges if the librarians realize they're gone, but it doesn't matter, you see? I would have paid any cost for what he gave me."

"Tillinghast sold you the hourglass," Altman said. "In exchange for some books. What kind of books?"

"Not even books. Just fragments of the *Pnakotic Manuscripts*. I couldn't make much sense of them anyway, so it was no great loss for me. Perhaps Mr Tillinghast can make more sense of them. He's very wise."

Altman made a mental note of the name of the texts and waved his hand. "All right. Where did you meet with Tillinghast?"

Detwiller blinked. "Nowhere, really, he just came to me when I was sitting on a bench on campus, and we met there again, this afternoon, to make the exchange."

That didn't help with tracking the shopkeeper down. "All right. What's the hourglass supposed to do, anyway?"

"Once I complete the proper preparations, it will make me immortal," Detwiller said. "I will project my mind back into that of my own grandfather, and then I will sire my own father, and of course in time my father will sire *me*, and then I will grow up to obtain the hourglass, and then I will send my mind back in time again to inhabit my grandfather, and – don't you see?" His eyes shone behind his round spectacles, feverish and bright. "I'll live forever, in a closed loop, eternal, my consciousness repeating, never dying, never – never having to face judgment for..." He closed his eyes and mouthed something Altman couldn't decipher. "It's my way out. It's my secret passage, my trapdoor, it's perfect, and I never would have found my way if not for Mr Tillinghast–"

"I'll be taking this," Altman said, reaching for the hourglass.

Detwiller leapt across the table, snarling like an animal. He knocked the hourglass onto the floor in the process, where it rolled but didn't break. He crashed into Altman, right out of his chair, the two of them tumbling to the floor, where he clawed wildly at Altman's face, howling, "No, no, no, no!"

The experience was a bit like being attacked by a very small but rabid dog. Altman managed to roll over, pin the man down, and got his hands around the professor's throat. Sanford hadn't sent him to kill Detwiller, to discover what he was up to, but the magus hadn't insisted he be left alive, either: "Use your best judgment, Altman, as you always do."

Judgment. "Looks like you'll have to face that judgment after all," Altman said. "I'm sure you've never done anything worse than I have, and I'm at peace with the whole thing." He bore down, and after a time, Detwiller stopped struggling, but Altman held on for longer. In films and such, people died after mere seconds of choking, but in reality, humans were resilient, and it took time to squeeze the life out of them irrevocably.

The time came. Altman rose, picked up the hourglass in his gloved hands, and put it back in the box it came in. He considered staging the scene, making it look like a robbery, or even concocting a suicide note, then decided not to bother. Detwiller was new in town, with no particular connections or friends, and Sanford had plenty of pull with the university and the police. Even if someone had noticed Altman creeping in, no serious repercussions were likely to come his way.

Still, he checked carefully to make sure he was unobserved before leaving the apartment and returning to his car. Just because you had a powerful patron didn't give you license to abandon *all* your tradecraft, after all.

"Fascinating," Sanford said. "I've never seen markings

like these before." The two of them were in his study at the Silver Twilight Lodge, a space paneled in dark wood and furnished with leather chairs and a desk that seemed the size of a banquet table. Sanford had the hourglass on the blotter and was examining it through a jeweler's loupe with a topaz lens. Magic of some kind. Altman didn't know much about magic, but more and more, he was interested in it. Magic had gotten his brother killed. Maybe it could help keep the surviving sibling alive.

"I think we should go speak with the Scholar." Sanford put the loupe into a desk drawer and picked up the hourglass, handling it nonchalantly. He'd touched more relics than Altman had ever seen. "I haven't introduced the two of you yet. I think you'll find her interesting."

"This is the woman you mentioned, who sent her mind through time?"

"She's not really a woman," Sanford said. "She's just in the body of a woman. But yes, that's the one."

"I don't suppose she can tell us who's going to win the next World Series?" Altman said. "Or offer up some stock market tips? You could make a tidy sum if you had the right news from the future." An idea occurred to him. "Wait, *is* that how you've made your riches? Inside information from your Scholar?"

Sanford chuckled. "I'm afraid her knowledge isn't usually that practical. She's not from the future of this world, but from a distant place and time, among the stars. I'm not sure she even knows what baseball is, or the stock market, for that matter. She comes from a species obsessed with knowledge, who project their minds elsewhere in order to study other peoples and other worlds. They call themselves the Yith, or, sometimes, the Great Race."

"Modest, then, are they?"

"The farthest thing from it," Sanford said. "Indeed, based on my limited interactions with their kind, the Yith make me seem humble."

"Hard to believe, sir," Altman said, and was rewarded with a smirk. Sanford seemed to enjoy a certain degree of informality from his closest lieutenants in the Order. Altman supposed that sort of thing made the magus feel more like a human and less like the embodiment of an institution.

Sanford led Altman through the corridors of the Lodge, to an undistinguished closet in the old servants' quarters, and through a hidden panel, down a set of secret stairs, and into the first of the Lodge's basements.

Altman had accompanied the magus into the depths a few times, but he still didn't have a proper understanding of the size and scope of the place. There were long corridors with wooden floors and whitewashed walls, and occasional iron doors bound in chains, and strange sigils painted on the floors and ceilings. There were tiny reading rooms where the books were chained to the shelves, and a ballroom with a floor of mirrored glass, and guest quarters for visiting members of the Order, and a horrible room full of bubbling aquaria, the immense tanks filled with murky water and the faint movement of unseen creatures. There were spiral staircases and seemingly bottomless pits and round bank vault doors. Strangest of all were stone-lined archways that opened onto courtyards or gardens or snow-covered vistas that appeared, impossibly, to stand beneath dark skies, some full of red and festering stars. Altman had only entered one of those rooms once, the night he swore his oaths, and his memories were fragmentary. Those strange skies must be illusions, Altman supposed, though perhaps some of the doors really were portals to other places. Sanford was cagey about the particulars: "I'm the head of a secret society, Altman. I have to maintain some secrets, even from you."

They didn't pass through any of those latter doors, fortunately. Instead, Sanford knocked an elaborate sequence on a wall at the end of a corridor, and a hidden panel swung open. They ducked through and into a narrow brick passageway like a bootlegger's tunnel, except the bricks were painted black and marked with twisting sigils in red paint... *probably* paint, Altman mentally amended.

The corridor doglegged several times, taking sharp curves for no apparent reason, until they finally reached a steel door with a barred window. Sanford knocked on the door and called, "Are you amenable to visitors?"

A woman's voice within said, "Enter."

The magus took a large key from his pocket and unlocked the door. Altman couldn't help but wonder – why had Sanford given an apparent prisoner the courtesy of a knock and polite inquiry? The magus seemed to understand his expression, for he smiled and said, "The Scholar and I have come to an understanding. She used to be held here under duress, in unpleasant circumstances, but now... while she'd prefer to leave, she cooperates enough to earn certain privileges, and in return, I treat her with a fraction of the respect she feels she deserves." He pushed open the door, and Altman followed him in.

Because of the door, Altman had expected a filthy dungeon, but the interior was a nicely appointed studio, with comfortable furniture, ample electric lighting, shelves spilling over with books, a small kitchen with a hotplate and sink, and a curtain that presumably led to a bathroom. There was artwork on the walls, even. Abstract and monochromatic, yes, but still, purely decorative, as far as Altman could tell.

The Scholar was a pale middle-aged woman of no great height, with locks of gray hair framing her face. She wore a robe of gray silk and comfortable house slippers and sat in an armchair with a thick book open on her lap. She didn't look up when they entered, and Sanford closed the door behind him. "There is tea," she said, turning a page. "Please help yourselves."

*Civilized, for an alien body-snatcher,* Altman thought.

# CHAPTER SEVEN
*Incursions*

Sanford handed Altman the hourglass, then went to the little kitchen and busied himself with a kettle. "Scholar, this is my associate, Mr Altman."

She did look up, then, scanning Altman from top to bottom and seeming to inventory him with a glance. "The sibling of the doppelganger. Interesting. What is that you hold in your hands, Mr Altman?"

Altman glanced at Sanford, who gave an indulgent nod. The lieutenant cleared his throat. "It's an hourglass. Purported to be capable of sending someone's mind back in time, to inhabit the body of another."

"What a peculiar way to go about it," the Scholar said. "For my people, such projection is purely a matter of mental preparation and willpower." She glanced over at Sanford, who was pouring hot water into a delicate china cup. The Scholar's preferred tea was foul stuff, but the rituals of hospitality seemed to please her, and Sanford saw no reason to create unnecessary friction. "Though our techniques can be inhibited by certain rituals, which your employer has seen fit to perform."

"You're really from another world, then?" Altman asked.

"I have seen thousands of worlds," she replied. "This is not the worst, but it is likewise far from the most pleasant."

"It gets more pleasant here all the time, though, doesn't it?" Sanford carried his teacup to one of the other chairs, sat down, and crossed his legs, balancing the cup on his knee. "Altman, give her the hourglass."

He raised an eyebrow. "It won't, ah, allow her to slip away?"

"I am quite contained," the Scholar said. "Indeed, I am contained many times over, so even if I were to circumvent multiple measures your employer has taken, others would still stand in my way." She held out her hands, and Altman gave her the hourglass.

The Scholar turned the relic over in her hands. "Interesting. Useless to you, however, Sanford." She gave the device a shake and held it up to the light. "The contents include ash from human remains, among other substances. I deduce that the ashes belong to an ancestor of the intended recipient of this device and serve to create a crude connection to the past through the bloodline, allowing the user to enter the body of their own forebear. Rather limited in application, I should say. These designs *are* from one of the alphabets used by my people, though from a long-ago iteration of our civilization, as perceived from my home point of temporal and spatial origin, anyway. The origin of these symbols come from the deep past, as reckoned by our current space-time position, however, which suggests it was created by someone with a high degree of occult knowledge." She shook the hourglass, just once, then put it down on the table beside her. "Unless this object is returned to its intended recipient, it has no particular use now. In any of your hands, it is simply an ornate funerary urn."

Sanford was unsurprised, but a bit disappointed. "You have no idea where the hourglass came from?" Sanford said.

"I have never seen a device of this precise nature," she said. "Its uses and methods are simply obvious to me, just as you would immediately apprehend the purpose of... oh, a doorknob, even if it took a somewhat unusual shape. If you filled the vessel with the ashes of another person, and made the appropriate alterations to the sigils inscribed on the frame and etched in the glass – you didn't notice those, did you? They're quite subtle – then it could serve to send another's mind back into an ancestor. I will happily supply the appropriate sigils for you, if only you–"

"Grant your freedom, yes, I know. I have no particular desire to stand in a dead Sanford's shoes." His ancestors were of no particular distinction. He was the first of his line to truly become someone of consequence. "If the hourglass could be used to send me to the future, however..." He quirked an eyebrow. To possess that power would be valuable indeed.

"To project your mind *down* your bloodline?" the Scholar said. "No. This vessel is far too crude for that. It only sends you into the body of the person whose remains... remain, in the glass. I could make certain alterations to the design, but it would be dangerous. Unless you know for sure that you will have descendants in the chosen era, you might find your mind projected into nothingness, and be lost forever, leaving your body an empty husk."

"Let's put that bit of research and development aside for the moment, then," Sanford said. "Can you estimate the age of this relic? Perhaps if I know what era it came from, I can narrow down the civilization that produced it–"

The Scholar blinked at him. "No, Sanford. This is no object of antiquity. In fact, I would say this object was constructed within the past week. Certainly, no earlier than the past month."

Sanford was usually the picture of sangfroid even in moments of great trial, but he couldn't stop his eyes from widening. "Then… Tillinghast is constructing magical objects?" Such artificers were rare in these fallen times, and most of those only combined and modified objects created by wiser figures from the past.

"I do not know anyone named Tillinghast," the Scholar said. "Do you have any further questions, or may I return to my work?"

Sanford schooled his face to blankness once more. "The man who made this hourglass traded it to someone for fragments of the *Pnakotic Manuscripts*. Those writings concern your people, don't they?"

"My people are the authors of those texts," she said, with not a little pride. "They were housed at our library in Pnakotus for a time, hence their vulgar local appellation. The manuscripts include some of our research on various civilizations, though the original texts were corrupted by later additions from ill-informed fools. It is possible to extract a certain amount of useful information about my people from them, however." She smiled. "Is someone trying to study my kind, Carl? For what purpose, do you suppose?"

"I do not yet know," he admitted. "But I intend to remedy that deficiency soon." He rose, putting down the unsipped teacup on a side table. "Until next time, Scholar."

"I need more books," she said. "And those star charts and oceanographic surveys I told you about. And where are those photographic plates of the sky, taken from the coordinates I supplied?"

She was terribly demanding, for a prisoner. "I have agents en route to the godforsaken islands you indicated, Scholar, but it will take some time for them to arrive. It's not as if their destinations are located on regular trade routes. I wish you'd tell me *why* you want all this information."

"There are indications of movements in the sea, and I wish to see if they are mirrored in the sky," she said, rather cryptically, Sanford thought. "The stars are not yet right, but I feel there is a… culmination, growing nearer. When you bring me more information, I might be able to provide more coherent answers."

"This has been a pleasure, as always," Sanford said. "Come, Altman. We have work to do." He left the room, followed by his bodyguard, and the door's many locks, seen and unseen, engaged themselves.

A *maker* of relics! Could this Tillinghast be more formidable than Sanford had supposed? He needed to get in touch with Ruby and find out what, if anything, she'd discovered about the man's business in Arkham. Perhaps he should reach out to that Dyer woman, too, and light a fire under her about arranging that appointment.

When they returned to his study, Sanford stopped dead, staring. There was a damp box in the center of his desk, wrapped in waterlogged paper and bedraggled ribbon, standing in a puddle that smelled strongly of the river. "Altman. Is that the gift from Tillinghast I told you to dispose of?"

"I tossed it into the river myself!" Altman said. "In a sack with rocks, like you said. How the devil did it get back here?"

"It seems we have a serpent in our garden," Sanford murmured. He'd once believed his Silver Twilight Lodge to be unassailable, home only to those who gave him their unwavering loyalty... or at least loyalty to his ability to help them achieve their petty dreams of power and success. In order to reach anything beyond the rank of Initiate, there were certain tests of devotion, after all. But a member named Diana Stanley, who'd attained the rank of Seeker, had disabused him of such rosy notions last year, when she turned against the Order and began working against his ends from within. Since discovering her treachery, he'd become vigilant toward signs of rot and ruin at home, but apparently not vigilant enough.

Someone with access to the Lodge, and his office, was in league with Randall Tillinghast.

"Take this box down to the basements," Sanford said. "There's an empty workroom just beyond the Threshold of Light, on the left." Until last week, one of Sanford's pet archaeologists had been teasing apart a mummy there, supposedly the remains of a high priest of the notorious pharaoh Nephren-Ka, in search of genuine magical tokens secreted in the wrappings, but he'd found only the usual gimcrackery: mundane amulets carved in the shape of scarabs and scepters and beetles and the like. But there were still magical protections active in that laboratory, and Sanford could use them. "I'll be down shortly."

"Where are you going in the meantime?" Altman asked.

A hot, short spurt of fury ripped through Sanford, but he didn't allow it to show. Now, moments after discovering someone in the Lodge was working against him, Altman chose to ask questions? When immediate obedience was clearly the better choice? That was the problem with having close lieutenants; they began to think of themselves as *more*, even when Sanford didn't want them to. "I will begin investigating this breach in security."

Altman nodded, thoughtful, and picked up the soggy box without apparent fear. Well, why not? Tillinghast had proven that he could attune his gifts to their recipients, enthralling the minds of only those he chose, not anyone who looked upon the things. Sanford had seen an enchanted snow globe and pulp magazine, and neither had ensnared his mind, but whatever was in that box… it well might. Altman was almost certainly safe from it, though, and he departed for the basements with the poisoned gift in hand while Sanford went storming through the Lodge.

Initiates scattered at the very sight of him, finding

other things to occupy themselves and other places to be occupied in. Sanford was not what anyone would call convivial with his underlings, maintaining an air of aloof gentility so they would never doubt that he was the master, but he seldom displayed anger. The rare occasions when he *did* let his temper slip had become the stuff of legends, and no one wished to be nearby should his fury make itself known. The fact that he stared balefully at everyone he saw, wondering *Was it you?* didn't help to calm the nerves of his fearful adherents.

Sanford found his target outside, on the grounds, beneath a twisted old hawthorn tree with burn marks on its trunk. The grounds of the Lodge were deliberately left untended to cultivate an air of neglect, in order to deceive onlookers about the power of those who dwelled within, and to discourage unwanted visitors.

The day was drawing down to dusk, but the shadows were always thick, back here among the trees. Though the rear wall of the Lodge building was only a few score yards behind him, this part of the grounds felt like the forest primeval, a suitable habitat for wolves and bears and witches' sabbats. Sanford wondered sometimes if there were fragments of wild magic back here, left over from long ago, connecting this forest to darker places, but he'd never had time to undertake the proper experiments.

Sarah Van Shaw knelt in the leaf litter, seemingly unconcerned at soiling her long blue dress. She gazed into a hole at the base of the tree, her head cocked to one side, and hummed quietly to herself. There was no sign of the variable number of immense, slavering black mastiffs that usually accompanied her, but Sanford had no doubt they were nearby. No matter. The dogs couldn't hurt him, because *Van Shaw* couldn't hurt him, and the hounds were extensions of her will.

"Warden," he barked. "We need to talk."

"Just a moment, please, master." She opened a dirt-colored sack beside her and began rummaging around inside.

More impertinence! What was wrong with everyone today? Had he let standards slip so far? "You do not bid me to *wait*, warden. You serve me, do you not?"

"I am the servant of the Silver Twilight Lodge, and you are its master, and so also mine." She kept rummaging.

Sanford found her reply pointlessly circuitous when a simple "Yes, master" would have done. "Then stand and face me!"

She put down the bag and rose, standing before him with her hands crossed primly at her waist. Somehow her dress was unmarred by the damp soil. Van Shaw was a striking woman, tall and strong-featured, somewhere between not-quite-young and middle-aged, with long red hair she wore loose most of the time. Her current expression was a sort of ferocious blank, but that was usual for her. "How may I help you, master?"

"As warden, it is your duty to prevent unauthorized entry to the Lodge, is it not?" Before she could answer, he went on, "Someone brought a package into the Lodge today, a package sent to me by an *enemy*, and placed it on the desk in my office."

Van Shaw nodded. "I see. You wish to know who brought

this package in. I will investigate, but if the perpetrators wish to hide their involvement, it may be difficult to track them down. This has been a busy day at the Lodge, with preparations for the annual orphans and widows charity rummage sale underway – we've had twenty-two Initiates enter the gates today, plus six Seekers, a Brother of the Dark, two Knights of the Stars, and even the current Keeper of the Red Stone, back from Morocco for the day. We can question them all–"

"And so we shall, but I want to know how someone brought a dangerous artifact into the Lodge at all without you knowing!" Sanford let himself shout. It felt good. Being in control was important, of course, but a show of pique might motivate her. A distant keening sound reached Sanford's ears, and annoyed him, like the buzz of a fly, or the whine of a lumber saw.

Van Shaw shook her head. The dark trees loomed around her, and she seemed perfectly at ease in this pocket wilderness. His shouting made no more impression on her than a raindrop upon a rock. "No one brought anything dangerous into the Lodge, master. Nothing occult, anyway. Such a breach is simply not possible. After the unpleasantness last year, with the Cult of Asterias, I made alterations to my security methods. My hounds have been granted certain… improvements. They now sniff everyone that passes through our gates, indeed, anything that draws near our gates, and if they detect any whiff of the arcane, they bar the affected individual from entering, and summon me. In turn, I would summon you. No one has brought anything but mundane objects through those gates today."

"We are dealing with a very powerful adversary, warden." Sanford paced back and forth in front of her, kicking the moldering leaves aside with each step. That buzzing had gotten louder and had been joined by a chittering counterpoint. Why did the world conspire to vex him? "A man named Randall Tillinghast, new to town, and possessed of numerous relics of power. He has used his baubles to ensnare the minds of some of my allies and may very well be capable of shielding his poisonous gifts from your perception."

The warden frowned, which wasn't much of a change from her default expression. "I see. I did not realize we had a new and active foe." Her voice held not even a whisper of reproach, which made the implied criticism sting Sanford even more. He should have told his warden that he was tangling with Tillinghast; he'd just been so damned busy lately, chasing ghosts. "I can institute more thorough security checks of incoming members–"

"Shutting the barn door after the horse has already fled!" Sanford said. "Or more like locking up the chicken coop after the fox has already eaten his fill."

"I only await your instructions, master. Bid me to serve, and I shall obey." She'd gone completely stony and blank, so much so that her previous expressions seemed animated in comparison.

He took a deep breath. Antagonizing Van Shaw was pointless. And the fault was, he had to admit, not entirely hers. "Warden, I apologize for speaking intemperately. I know we share a desire to protect the Lodge from – blast it, what is that noise?"

"The things in the tunnels beneath the hill have discovered the bait I set below the tree." Van Shaw gestured at the twisted trunk behind her. "We've had a few incursions of late, and I finally traced them to this place – an old animal den beneath the tree collapsed into the tunnels below, allowing the dwellers in the hill entry to the upper world. I thought it best to kill the beasts before I sealed up the opening, lest they seek another avenue and return. They will likely emerge from the ground in search of more meat shortly. They become frenzied when they feed." She glanced over her shoulder. "I was just about to pour the poison into the breach when you arrived and commanded my attention." Still not even a whiff of reproach in her voice.

Sanford winced. "Go ahead, woman, get about your business!"

She shook her head. "I fear it's too late for the poison, master, but my dogs will deal with whatever emerges. A messier outcome, to be sure, but no less definitive." Half a dozen huge black dogs – or things that looked like dogs – came out of the trees, slinking low to the ground, their hackles raised. They arrayed themselves around the warden, three on each side, and stared at Sanford with their red-rimmed eyes.

Sanford didn't let his instinct to take a step back spur him to action. He couldn't control the dogs directly, but he could control the warden, and that was enough. She was an arcane thing in her own right, with a deep connection to the Lodge that brought along with it certain powers... and certain restrictions. The most potent of those was her inability to leave the grounds of the Lodge house for more than a few hours at a time without growing sick; too long away, and she would die. Van Shaw almost never left the grounds at all, unless he called upon her to do so, and if her leash chafed at her, she never let it show. As long as Sanford was the head of the Lodge, the warden's loyalty to him was absolute. As a result, he did call on her to assist him off the grounds, sometimes, for short periods. It was so rare to find someone you could completely trust, after all.

Sanford nodded and attempted a conciliatory tone. "I killed some of the dwellers under the hill last year and have no desire to splash their ichor on my clothes this evening. I'll leave you to your work. Do let me know when you find out who brought that package into the Lodge. I'll want to question them." He turned away, though a deep, atavistic part of him protested mightily at presenting his back to the predators arrayed behind him. Sanford was the master of himself as well as the Lodge, however, and he departed with a straight back and a steady tread.

The chittering and keening got louder, and ferocious growls and snapping sounds and squeals erupted behind him, but Sanford did not look back to see the carnage. *Such petty problems are beneath my station*, he thought. Others could deal with the rot beneath this house, the pests beneath this earth. His real problem, Sanford increasingly believed, was Randall Tillinghast.

It was time to see what kind of gift the stranger had sent him.

# CHAPTER EIGHT
## *The Honest Thief*

"The problem with betraying your employer is, once word gets around, it's hard to find future employment." Ruby abandoned her stool and leaned against a sturdy table of heavy dark wood, the legs carved with things that looked like gryphons, but with the heads of snakes instead of eagles. She wanted a little more distance from the shopkeeper.

Tillinghast nodded, green eyes twinkling. "And so we arrive at the paradox of the honest thief, yes? The criminal with a code? You will do whatever you promise to do, so long as you're paid appropriately?"

Ruby shrugged. She picked up a dark purple crystal from the array on the table and pretended to look at it. Tillinghast's gaze was even more disconcerting than she remembered – his gaze said he knew something about you that even you didn't, and that whatever it was profoundly amused him. "Playing fair with the people who pay me leads to a less paranoid existence. Someone lured me to Arkham under false pretenses last year, and I was lucky to survive the whole business. Deception is exhausting, so I prefer to be honest in my dealings, insofar as honesty is possible in this business."

"Most commendable!" Tillinghast said. "I would certainly prefer that you never betrayed *me*, after all." Tillinghast moved the stool she'd departed a little closer to her and sat down. He was still a few feet away, but the proximity was entirely too intimate for her taste. "But imagine, Ruby, being so rich that you didn't ever have to work for anyone else again. Wouldn't that be worth a little bit of treachery? It would also solve the whole 'future employment' problem."

Were Tillinghast's pockets that deep? She supposed they might be. "I would entertain that sort of offer." Sanford had asked her to work for Tillinghast again, in order to get information, after all. In this case, contemplating betrayal was no betrayal at all. She just had to keep her loyalties straight in her head. Not that she was *loyal* to Sanford, exactly, but he was the one paying her first, which bought him some kind of consideration, didn't it?

"I am likely to need your services in several capacities, in the months to come." Tillinghast twisted a ring on his finger, idly, the great green stone winking. "I am working toward certain long-term goals, and someone with your knowledge, skill, and experience could be invaluable to me. I wish, therefore, to put you on retainer, as it were. If I call upon you for a service, you will fulfill that service immediately, placing my needs before all other considerations. In exchange, you will be compensated handsomely."

"What kind of services?" Ruby said. "I like to know what I'm getting into, and there are some jobs I just won't do."

Tillinghast waved a hand airily. "Oh, fear not, I will only call upon you for purposes of acquisition – that is, to acquire certain items for me, or else to acquire useful information."

"So, thieving and spying." She sighed. "Those are both things I have been known to do for money."

"And you do them so well. Money, I have in abundance." He rose from the stool and came a step closer toward her. "For you, money means freedom, doesn't it? To be your own woman? To pursue your own interests? With a proper foundation of funds, you could stop working for other people, and work only for yourself, isn't that right?"

"That's the dream." Ruby had spent too much of her career stealing things for other people, working as a mercenary of the illicit, and even when she'd researched and organized her own scores, there'd always been some local crime lord who needed tribute, or some specialist who'd taken an outsized cut because Ruby needed their assistance with an element of her plan. If she had enough money, she could hire her own specialists instead of cutting people in on the profits, and maybe even get people paying tribute to her eventually. She was still pretty young. She had a plan, and she was making progress. But a nice fat payoff from Tillinghast could accelerate her timeline significantly. Especially if she could wrangle a bonus from Sanford at the same time...

"Would the promise of such a sum serve to overcome

your hesitations?" Tillinghast said. "Or are you loyal to Carl Sanford for more than merely philosophical reasons? A personal relationship is always more durable than a professional one, I know."

Ruby snorted. "Sanford tried to have me kidnapped last year. I ripped him off a while back, and he held that against me. Before he could lock me up and torture me, we ended up on the same side of some unrelated trouble, and joined forces against a common enemy. I kept him from dying, and Sanford agreed to wipe the slate clean afterward, as payment for services rendered. We've done some business together since then, but I'm not loyal to him. I don't even like him." All that was true. Whenever possible, Ruby tried to tell the truth; that way, you didn't risk any little tells, the kind of tics and gestures and fleeting expressions a shark like Tillinghast might look for. She just omitted certain things, selectively, to convey the impression she wished to create.

Tillinghast smiled, his teeth so white and even. Sharks didn't always look like sharks. "Then you're amenable to the arrangement I propose?"

"You mean the one where I steal some stuff and sniff out some dirt for you, and you give me the riches of Croesus in return? Sure, I'm agreeable. In theory. On a case-by-case basis. If you ask me to do something I won't do, I won't do it."

"Unless I increase your compensation accordingly, anyway," Tillinghast said.

Ruby spread out her hands before her. "I am a businesswoman, Mr Tillinghast."

"Please, call me Randall."

"I don't see that happening," Ruby said. "A guy like you will always get his mister."

"Then I will continue to call you Miss Standish, for the sake of balance." He stroked his goateed chin. "Perhaps that's better. To remind us both that this is a business relationship, first and foremost."

Ruby nodded. "All right, then. I'm on retainer. Just like I went to law school or something, how about that?"

He went stern. "No. More like a samurai in service to his feudal lord. A member of my personal household, as it were. That's how close this relationship will be, Miss Standish." She suppressed a shiver while he went on in his brisk, matter-of-fact tone. "You will serve my interests, and in return, I will protect and enrich you. We will not need to meet in person like this often. I will convey my instructions through Miss Dyer, for the most part. I wish to keep a low profile in Arkham, as they say, lest I attract unwanted attention."

Ha. "Attention, you've got. You've been handing out gifts to all sorts of people, and you've certainly annoyed Sanford. I'd hate to see how you'd act if you wanted to make a splash."

Tillinghast bowed his head modestly. "Yes, but the recipients of my largesse were all people I *desired* to meet. As for Mr Sanford, well. I gather that our interests have already clashed. Regrettable, but, I suppose, inevitable, for men such as ourselves."

Ruby decided to push a little. "What is it you're trying to do here in Arkham, anyway?" she asked. "What do you have against Sanford?"

"I am pursuing my interests. That is all you need to know. And Sanford?" Tillinghast flicked imaginary lint off his lapel, then locked eyes with Ruby. "He stands in my way. He has things I need in his possession, and worse, he will attempt to stop me from acquiring *other* things I need, and will generally make a nuisance of himself, if permitted to buzz around uncontained. He has sufficient resources to cause me real problems, or at least, to disrupt my plans while they remain at a delicate stage. I need him neutralized."

Ruby whistled. "You're already causing him trouble, so he's going to try to neutralize you, too. He knows you did something to the dockmaster. Enthralled him, or something."

Tillinghast clucked his tongue in disappointment. "Enthralled? Please. I gave the dockmaster something he desired, in exchange for his help acquiring something I desired. That is the essence of commerce. There was no coercion involved."

Ruby wasn't in the mood for evasions. "Mr Tillinghast. I saw the way Tick looked at that magazine. He was practically hypnotized. Why didn't you use the Svengali routine on me?"

The old gentleman nodded, his eyes half-lidded, which made him look sleepy, but Ruby knew that was deceptive. "Fair enough. For very simple tools, such crude methods can be useful. I need the harbormaster for one purpose only – to let me take whatever I want from any vessel that passes through his purview. A single function, you see? And thus a simple machine. But you." He smiled. "I will need you for many things, Miss Standish. You require flexibility, and so I need your thoughts unclouded, nimble, and capable of rapid improvisation. Dazzling you with a trinket would serve to improve your obedience but at the cost of befuddling your mind. The promise of wealth is the only enchantment I need for you, anyway." He frowned, just slightly. "But if I may ask... if you thought I might enchant you... why did you agree to accompany Miss Dyer to meet me? Surely you value your autonomy more than that?"

"I know men like you, Mr Tillinghast." She put the crystal back down, carefully, in the spot she'd taken it from.

"Oh, I doubt that," he murmured, but she ignored him and kept talking.

"You sending Gloria to pick me up was the soft touch. If I'd refused to come with her, the next people you sent for me would have been a lot bigger and a lot less polite, and I would have made the journey trussed up in the back of some jalopy instead of sitting pretty in the passenger seat of a convertible. I knew I was going to end up meeting with you either way, so I figured I'd do it the easy way."

"I suppose I might have been somewhat insistent on our reconnection, now that you mention it," Tillinghast said. "Though I am glad the heavier touch was unnecessary. This way, I feel we've started our renewed relationship on a positive footing."

"Am I done here, then?" Ruby glanced longingly at the door. "I should just wait for Gloria to track me down when you need me?"

"Gloria will be our liaison going forward," Tillinghast said. "But since we're together now, I may as well give you your first assignment. Upon completion of this task, I'll give you your first payment, as well."

"Those vast riches you mentioned? Good."

Tillinghast shook his head minutely. "Not so vast, initially. If I provide you with too much lucre at the outset of our relationship, you might be tempted to book passage on the next ship headed to the continent. No, I'll give you a taste first – an amuse-bouche, to tempt you – but you'll have to wait until my current business is concluded to collect the entirety of your bounty. That work shouldn't take more than a few months… a year at most."

She sighed. "Why am I not surprised?"

"Fear not. Things will proceed quite quickly once Sanford is neutralized."

"You've used that word a couple of times now," Ruby said. "Neutralized. What does it mean? Do you want him dead? Because I'm not–"

"Acquisitions only, Miss Standish, never executions or assassinations." Tillinghast drew a finger across his throat, then shook his head, smiling all the while. "I will not try to use you for any purpose to which you are unsuited. Simply killing Sanford would have negative repercussions, I fear. I have no doubt he has certain safeguards in place, contingencies that will spring into action in the event of his death. I simply wish to remove his ability to pose a threat to my interests. There are ways to do that besides murder." A smile ghosted his lips. "Crueler ways, for a man like him."

"You don't want to give me more details?" Ruby said.

"I'll give you one," Tillinghast said. "I want you to steal

a certain jewel called the Ruby of R'lyeh from Sanford's vaults."

Ruby blinked. "I stole that *for* Sanford, months ago, from a bastard in Boston!"

"Then you already have familiarity with the item. That should make things easier, surely?" He cocked his head and gazed at her, unblinking, which put her in mind of creatures seen at the reptile house in the zoo.

"I've never been sent to steal the same thing twice before." It struck her as an unlucky proposition. "Why do you want it? You're already rich beyond measure, or you'd better be, with the payday you promised me. What do you need with a big red jewel in an ugly metal setting?"

Tillinghast sighed, and the sigh was theatrical, like almost everything about him. She'd never met anyone who did so much *seeming* and so little *being*. "You don't need to know my reasons, Miss Standish, but in the interests of continuing our relationship on the right foot, I'll tell you. The gem is a relic. It has certain properties that will aid me in my endeavors. Specifically, the jewel grants whoever wears it a certain... freedom of movement... in a place where movement is otherwise quite difficult."

"Very enlightening." Ruby had always suspected the jewel had arcane properties – why else would she have been sent to steal it in the first place? – but she'd hoped to find out some details. Sanford had certainly never provided any.

"I will provide more clarity when necessary," Tillinghast said. "Suffice it to say there may come a time when you will be *very* glad we have the jewel in our possession. Will you have trouble acquiring it?"

Ruby huffed out a breath. "I'll have a *lot* of trouble acquiring it. Sanford was never cavalier about his possessions, and he's gotten even more careful in the past year. But… I'll see what I can do. It'll take some time, but I'm on it."

"Wonderful. Call Gloria when you have the jewel in your possession." He took a step closer, close enough to touch, and extended his hand.

She shook it, trying not to show her revulsion at making contact with his dry, lizardlike skin. "I'm sure this partnership will be very fruitful." He headed back behind the counter and disappeared into a back room.

Ruby looked around the shop. He'd left a known thief unattended in a room full of treasures. Why would he do that? Because he was just that confident that he owned her, she realized. She considered pocketing some trinket – an ugly little statue, that hunk of crystal – just to show him, but decided the risks outweighed the benefits… since the only benefit would be feeling like she was still her own woman, and not Tillinghast's creature.

*I'm not*, she thought fiercely. *I'm not really working for him, I'm working for–*

For Sanford. So she wasn't really her own woman then, either, was she? She was a pawn two sorcerers were using against each other. That did not sit well with her.

*I need to figure out a way to work for myself*, she decided. *And not because Tillinghast bestowed that freedom upon me like a gift.*

"He could have at least called me a taxi," she muttered, heading for the exit. "I'll never get one in this neighborhood."

She stepped out into the alleyway and shut the door behind her – and was surprised to find Gloria sitting in her yellow convertible, smiling and waving.

"I finished up my business, and I thought you might want a ride," she said as Ruby approached. "And maybe you could show me where to get a drink in this town? Unless you don't like socializing with coworkers. We are coworkers now, aren't we? Mr Tillinghast told me he planned to make you a job offer."

Ruby liked Gloria… but Gloria was Tillinghast's creature, and that meant Ruby needed to be careful. "We're all in business together," Ruby said. "And I could definitely use a drink. But the old man has given me a task, and I should get started, so we'll have to paint the town another time. I'll take that ride, though, if you're willing to get me back downtown?"

"Tillinghast can be a real taskmaster," Gloria said, patting the seat beside her. "Let me help speed you on your way."

Ruby got out at Independence Square and waved goodbye to Gloria as she zipped away, a bright streak of yellow in a gray town. Once the woman was out of sight, Ruby caught a taxi and said, "Take me to the top of French Hill, please."

She spent the ride across the river thinking things through, and decided she'd tell Sanford everything, holding nothing back. There was no percentage in playing things any closer, at least not yet, and there might be significant downsides to double-dealing. With the right set of moves, she could win Tillinghast's trust *and* deepen

Sanford's faith in her... and maybe even fleece both of them in the process. Or at least get paid twice.

The taxi dropped her off a street over from her destination; such basic track-covering was so automatic for Ruby that she didn't even think about it. She walked up a narrow, crumbling set of steps to an alleyway between two grand old houses that had seen better days. The streetlights were few and far between around here, but the moon was high and bright, and she knew the route, so she made her way swiftly enough. Soon, the Silver Twilight Lodge appeared before her, a weathered mansion behind imposing iron fencing. A few lights burned in the lower windows of the house, some of the Initiates and Seekers taking advantage of the excellent dining room for their evening meal, no doubt.

Ruby went up to the gate and pushed it open, stepping onto the cobbled path between the long grasses – and froze when two black dogs appeared from the long grasses to block her way, heads low, teeth bared, wiry muscles quivering. She lifted her hands placatingly. "Easy, there, I'm a friend, you *know* me."

The animals approached her, moving in tandem, as if they were one animal and not two. She could smell them, wet fur and something rotten, like they'd been rolling in dead things. Ruby tensed, ready to leap backward and slam the gate shut between her and the animals. She didn't rate her chances of finishing the maneuver very highly, but it was always better to try than to stand there and take it.

"Do not run." That was the voice of the Lodge's warden, Sarah Van Shaw, who now stood behind the hounds. Where had *she* come from? The dogs could hide in the grass, but it wasn't tall enough to hide her. "They will give chase if you flee, and nothing will stop them until they bring you down."

"What's happening here, warden?" At least the dogs had stopped advancing, though their hackles were still raised, and drool spilled from their mouths. They wanted to *eat* her. Ruby had never thought of herself as a potential meal before, and she didn't much like it.

Van Shaw stepped between the animals to face Ruby. "The Lodge has been closed to all non-members, as we investigate a security incident. You are not a member of the Order, Ruby Standish."

"No, but I work with Sanford. He gave me a task, and I need to give him an update." She kept one eye on the dogs, though really, the warden was probably the scarier one. One reason Ruby tried to banter with Van Shaw sometimes was because the woman unsettled her so much, and Ruby was always one to whistle past the graveyard.

"I know of your association with the master," Van Shaw said. "That is why the dogs merely stood in your way, instead of taking more serious action, as they would have against genuine trespassers. They will need to smell you before you can proceed, though."

"Smell me? For what?"

"For your own safety." Van Shaw gave a thin smile. "If you're carrying something into the Lodge you shouldn't be, that would be very unsafe for you. I know the master sometimes sends you on shopping trips. If you possess any relics or objects of power, you should declare them now."

She shook her head. "Not this time. I'm just here with information."

The dogs circled Ruby as she stood, stock-still, afraid even to tremble. "How long will this take?" she asked through gritted teeth, as the noses of the monsters nudged at her calves.

"They are finished." The dogs coursed away, their paths revealed initially by the motion of the grasses as they moved, but soon even that subsided, as if the dogs had tunneled underground like moles. "You are clean."

"Clean, upright, and sober, that's me. What's all this about, warden? Did something happen?"

Van Shaw lowered her head, one of the most human gestures Ruby had ever seen her make. "Come along. I'll walk you to the door. If the master wants you to know about our current situation, I'm sure he'll tell you."

She walked alongside Ruby, up the steps and onto the porch, then opened the front door, though not as deferentially as the doormen at the Independence Hotel. "We'll need to check you again before you leave, to make sure you aren't carrying out any contraband."

Ruby huffed in irritation. "Oh, come on, warden, I know you hold my past exploits against me because I evaded your security once or twice, but we're all on the same side now–"

"Do not take this so personally," Van Shaw said. "It's true that I don't trust you, but as of this afternoon, we don't trust anyone."

What in the world, or out of it, had happened here since Ruby saw Sanford last?

"The master is currently occupied," Van Shaw said. "Why

don't you get something to eat for now? I'll send word that you've arrived."

Ruby wasn't all that hungry – her early dinner at the Perch wasn't so far in the past – but who was she to turn down a free meal? The Lodge kept an excellent wine cellar, too. "Thank you, warden. I'll see you when I leave, I guess."

"That you will," the warden promised.

# CHAPTER NINE
## *A Gift for the Magus*

Altman sat in the work room downstairs, gazing at the sodden box from the river, which rested in the center of a metal autopsy table. He wondered, what kind of work *normally* went on in this laboratory? The package seemed out of place where a fresh corpse should be. Altman tried to find the package menacing, as Sanford did, but it just looked sad, like a party gift caught in a downpour.

Sanford entered, carrying a hand mirror – an ornate thing, backed with engraved silver decorated with a confused profusion of wings and eyes. Hideous. Must be European.

"Has the package done anything?" Sanford asked.

Like what? Performed a monologue? Danced a bit of *Swan Lake*? It was a ridiculous damp box. "Not a thing," Altman said.

Sanford grunted and circled around the table, examining the package from all angles. "I think it's safe to say, if there's a trap inside, it is a trap meant for me. Therefore, you will be the one to open the package, and give me a preliminary report on its contents."

"I didn't realize I'd signed on to be your royal poison taster, Sanford."

"Your duties are manifold and changeable, Mr Altman. Do you object?"

Altman shrugged. "The pulp magazine didn't hurt me any, so I follow your logic. Since you pay me to run straight into danger with a knife between my teeth, I suppose I can open a box for you." He approached the table. "In a room like this, I feel like I should be wearing rubber gloves and a leather apron and holding a bone saw."

"Have you donned such garb often?" Sanford asked lightly.

He shrugged. "Chopped up a body or two. It's messy work if you aren't prepared. But you know the broad outlines of my employment history. Are you surprised?"

"I wouldn't have made you a Knight of the Stars if you weren't possessed of a plethora of useful talents."

Altman chuckled. He'd inherited not only his brother's job but also his rank in the Order, one of the highest titles available, which was good for impressing the Initiates and getting access to the good Scotch. The bottles were locked up below the bar after all. Altman hadn't even needed to undergo all the tedious intermediary steps, from Initiate to Seeker and on up.

He'd merely been given a few tests meant to prove his effectiveness and been forced to demonstrate his resilience in the face of supernatural horrors. Down in these very basements, Altman had been confronted with sights that, in Sanford's words, "have caused lesser men to howl into the void while voiding their bowels." Altman could take it though, as well as anyone alive could, anyway. He'd seen things in the caves of Afghanistan in 1919 – ancient creatures awakened by the British conflict there – that had forever inoculated him against shock or surprise when it came to such matters. He knew there were terrible things beneath the world.

He'd killed some of them with a stolen British cavalry sword, and tasted what they had instead of blood, and even seen visions.

The final ritual had involved swearing loyalty to the Silver Twilight Lodge, his body supine on a stone, in one of those strange rooms that seemed to have its own sky... but the details of that night skittered away from his memory when he looked too closely.

All of which meant he was more than man enough to open a soggy box. He unpicked the ribbon and put it aside, then peeled back the damp paper, revealing a slightly malformed cardboard box. Once unbound from its wrappings, the closed flaps on the lid were not further secured. Altman lifted them open, gingerly, one after another, and then shut one eye before peering inside – if there was something mind-searing in there, perhaps its impact would be lessened if it were only *half* viewed.

Altman grunted. "Looks like wet paper."

"Please be more specific."

"There's a gilt-edged card with something written on it, but the ink has run, and underneath it, a lot more paper, in a stack, but it's all damp… I can't tell you much more without taking things out and looking more closely."

"Not yet," Sanford said. "Now that the box is open and you've made your preliminary examination, we'll find out if what you're seeing is what's really there."

Altman lifted his head. He was, frankly, a bit let down. Maybe the contents wouldn't sparkle and glimmer for him, but he'd expected something at least as interesting as a pulp magazine. What the box held was more like if a mundane comic book had been disassembled, its pages stacked in no particular order, and then the whole lot doused with the contents of a teakettle, with a Victorian era calling card dropped on top. "I assume the shiny mirror in your hand has something to do with that step? One of the relics from your vault?"

"What do you know about my vault?" Sanford could pivot from bonhomie to suspicion in an instant; it was one of the man's more irritating qualities, though Altman understood where the habit came from. The master of the Silver Twilight Lodge had been subjected to numerous betrayals… and doubtless committed many more himself. A life like that would give anyone a paranoid streak.

Altman shrugged. "I've seen the odd shiny metal door down here. And the rumor is you have a secret vault down here somewhere, full of priceless relics, guarded by an abomination you conjured from an icy hellscape."

Sanford relaxed a fraction. "Oh, that. The more ignorant people are regarding a given subject, the more likely they are to chatter about it, haven't you found?"

"It is a truth the world over." No answer to his question,

then, but that was typical. Altman inclined his head toward the object Sanford was gently turning in his hands. "So. The mirror?"

Sanford held the mirror before his face and gazed into the glass for a long moment before answering. "This once belonged to the occultist John Dee, who served as court astronomer to Elizabeth the First, among other endeavors. Dee claimed the mirror was created by Hermes Trismegistus himself."

Occultish stuff, then. "Hermes? Any relation to the fellow with the wings on his helmet and the snakes around his staff? Saw a statue of him once in London."

Sanford shook his head, but smiled a little as he did so. "Hermes Trismegistus is a legendary figure, a sorcerer and scholar, and the founder of Hermetic mysticism. He is associated with both the god Hermes, your winged-helmet fellow, and the Egyptian god Thoth, who invented writing and was renowned for his wisdom and magic. It's doubtful that Trismegistus actually existed, and if he did, it's doubly doubtful that he ever worked as a silversmith... but regardless of its true provenance, this mirror is an object of considerable power."

"Ugly as sin, though," Altman asked. "Why's it covered in eyes?"

Sanford turned the mirror over and considered the ornate back. "Angels, as depicted in artwork – as winged human figures, most often – do not match the descriptions given in the ancient texts of the Abrahamic faiths. Angels are often described by those who witnessed them as monstrous, often with numerous eyes, and bodies composed of revolving wheels, or rings of fire. Sometimes they have wings, yes, but not the sort you likely imagine. The seraphim, highest order of angels, are said to have six wings each, which they fold up to hide behind, and are reputed to be 'full of eyes within.' Some of them have the faces of animals. Some of them have ten *thousand* faces, each with ten thousand mouths, and each mouth with ten thousand tongues."

"I can see why they don't paint them that way," Altman said. "It would take forever to get all the tongues right."

His wit was wasted on Sanford. "There may indeed be creatures that match such descriptions, but whether they are the servants of a benevolent god... I have my doubts."

Altman grunted. "You have a lot of doubts, it sounds like."

Now Sanford looked at him, and even offered a smile. "It is important for those who traffic in the occult, as we do, to remain skeptical. We mustn't become overly credulous. Just because we have seen impossible things, it does not follow that *all* impossible things are real." He tilted the mirror this way and that. "I believe this decoration depicts one of those creatures some call angels. The numerous eyes also serve to indicate something of the relic's nature: this mirror is a glass of true seeing." He met Altman's eyes. "Whatever glamour a person or object hides behind, this mirror can reveal the truth beyond the illusion. There is no guile in the glass. Magic is revealed in the reflection, too – as a shimmering cloud of silver if the magic means the bearer of the mirror no harm, and as a seething cloud of darkness if the magic has malice in it."

"I can see how that could be useful." Altman took a step back from the table and made an "after you" gesture.

Sanford approached the table and extended his hand, tilting the mirror so that the glass reflected the contents of the box. He looked at the image, and he frowned.

"What do you see?" Altman asked.

"Nothing," Sanford said. "Nothing unusual at all! If the mirror is to be believed, it's just… paper in there."

He looked around, then spotted a row of medical instruments on a table nearby. Sanford picked up a long metal surgical probe and reached into the box with it, presumably moving the contents around a bit, then put the probe aside and looked inside with the mirror again. He slowly lowered the mirror and set it on the metal table, glass side down. Altman tried to remember when he'd seen the magus look so troubled, and couldn't. "I thought perhaps Tillinghast had hidden something under the papers," Sanford murmured. "But… no." He straightened his shoulders, arranged his features into a scowl, and reached decisively into the box, removing the gilt-edged card.

After a long moment, he let out a chuckle, but Altman thought he detected a note of despair or dismay in it. "Take a look at this, Altman." Sanford handed the card over.

Altman took the heavy thing, paper stiff as a board, edges heavy with gold, and read. The words were written in flowing purple ink, and said, "Greetings, Mr Sanford. Randall Tillinghast requests the honor of your presence at his shop. Please accept this humble gift by way of introduction. If it suits your schedule, please meet him…" The words beneath were so thoroughly blotted by water

*Arkham Horror*

that they were just a smear, the date and time eradicated by river water.

Sanford, meanwhile, was lifting the sopping stack of papers from the box, and he suddenly uttered a strangled cry anguished enough that Altman reached into his coat for a knife, ready to kill whatever serpent had slithered out.

But the magus just gazed wide-eyed at the wet manuscript in his hands, damaged pieces of it peeling away and drifting to the floor. "This is… this *was*… a portion of the *Pnakotic Manuscripts.*" Sanford closed his eyes and murmured what looked very much like a prayer.

"That rare book that Detwiller was talking about?" Altman said. "The one he nicked for Tillinghast?"

"Acquired, apparently, as a gift for me. And now, ruined, or at least seriously damaged." He put the waterlogged sheaf of parchment aside and met Altman's eyes. "I need a brandy. How about you?"

"May as well," Altman said. "It's medicinal, they say." Seeing the magus like this, outfoxed and nonplussed, was distressing, but also – Altman could admit in the sanctum of his own mind – a little gratifying. The old man was always so smug, so master-of-his-domain, that getting a glimpse of the actual human underneath was a bit of a thrill.

They didn't return upstairs, but descended instead to a region of the basements that Altman had never seen before. It seemed to him the warren of hallways and rooms down here must fill the entirety of French Hill… but it was more likely that some portion of the Lodge wasn't exactly located in the real world. Geometry and topology could be made malleable in the right hands, after all. In nightmares, when you ran down a hallway, fleeing from monsters, the corridors could extend forward infinitely, telescoping away from you, and Altman had learned that nightmares really could come true. He wondered if they were going to drink brandy beneath red skies in a haunted wasteland. He hoped not.

Sanford led the way to a thoroughly mundane room, though, one that could have been the private office of a university president: dark wood shelves crowded with clothbound volumes, an impressive desk, leather club chairs, thick Turkish rugs on the floor, and a wet bar that held bottles of the promised brandy.

"This office is an exact replica," Sanford said, busying himself at the bar. "Most of the furniture is from the original. The room looks just as it did years ago, when I first came to Arkham and met a fellow named Alexander Peterman. This was *his* office."

Sanford seldom reminisced about his past, preferring to present himself as eternal and unchanging, and Altman listened with interest.

"Peterman was an occultist, and led a small group of like-minded individuals. They liked to think of themselves as a powerful secret order, and they did some interesting, if unambitious work, though in the process they pledged allegiance to monstrous forces. They called themselves the Order of the Silver Twilight, though *their* organization bears as much resemblance to the one of today as a lightning bug does to lightning." Sanford held up a bottle. "Does Armagnac suit you?"

Considering some of the swill Altman had sipped over the years, Armagnac was more than all right. "Oh, indeed." He settled into one of the club chairs. Sanford didn't really seem troubled anymore. He just seemed... thoughtful.

The magus poured a tiny measure of Armagnac into a snifter and handed it to Altman. He made himself a glass, too, but didn't sit down. Instead, he remained standing, gazing around at the room. "I took over Peterman's organization, which has existed in some form or another practically since Arkham's founding. First, I joined his group, and played the role of the eager neophyte, and learned all I could about their finances, their connections, and their... troublesome associations. Once I'd gathered sufficient information, and leverage on the other members, I simply... Hollowed. Peterman. Out." He sighed. "The old man tried to take revenge, of course, after I left him penniless and powerless, and took up residence in this very office. He attempted to summon up those same dark forces he'd trafficked in. To call in what he thought were favors they owed to him. That didn't end well for him." Sanford swirled the brandy and took a sip, closing his eyes and savoring the liquid. Altman did the same. The Armagnac was sweet and warm, and a portion turned to aromatic vapor as he held it in his mouth.

Sanford went on. "The creatures, if you can even call them that, which dwell beyond this world, or behind it... they aren't particularly interested in transactions. Sometimes you can get them to react to stimuli, in somewhat predictable ways, but there's always a chance they'll turn on you. Fundamentally, those entities don't care about people at all – and that's to our benefit, Altman! Indifference is the best we can hope for. Because when those entities do take an interest in us, it's often the same interest a sadistic child takes in pulling the legs off a spider." Sanford finally moved to sit in a chair. He gestured with his glass, indicating the office as a whole. "Peterman removed himself from our conflict, rather messily, and I soon transformed his organization into something grand, but I kept his office. When I expanded the basements in the Lodge, I brought the contents here, and arranged them just so. This room is a reminder, Altman. Do you know what it's a reminder of?"

"That kings can fall, I imagine." Altman cleared his throat. "'Two vast and trunkless legs of stone stand in the desert. Near them, on the sand, half sunk a shattered visage lies... Look on my Works, ye Mighty, and despair!'"

"Ozymandias!" Sanford cried in delight. "You amaze me. Your brother never quoted poetry, Altman."

"Even so, Reggie was more the reader in the family," Altman admitted. "But I've got a mind that holds on to things, and that bit stuck from some English class or another in my youth."

"At any rate, yes, you're quite right. I toppled Peterman, left him shattered in the desert, and took everything that belonged to him. He believed he was founding an empire that would shake the world and persist through the ages, but it all turned to dust. I kept this office to remind me – to make sure that *I* never became too complacent, too sure of myself, so comfortable on my perch that I take my eyes off the people who want to knock me off it. This morning has been an even sharper reminder."

"You'd think after that business with the cult last year, you wouldn't need reminding." Was that too close to a rebuke? Altman waited to see if the magus would snap at him.

Instead, Sanford shook his head. "Cain was a zealot, maddened by his association with the monster he worshipped. He had raw power, which took some effort to defeat, of course, but he possessed no finesse. No subtlety. Tillinghast *does*. I also knew what Cain wanted – to raise a ravening god to devour the world. I have no idea what Tillinghast wants… so I have to assume he wants what I wanted from Peterman."

"Which is?"

"Everything." Sanford chuckled. "I look quite the fool, now, don't I? I had you drop that gift into the river, even though it was harmless! I threw away an invitation to a meeting I've been trying to arrange. Hardly my finest hour, eh?"

"It could be seen in that light," Altman allowed.

"I don't believe it for a *moment*," Sanford snarled, his voice suddenly sharp as a lash. "The gift the Dyer woman gave me is not the same gift that showed up dripping wet on my desk. *That* gift, I have no doubt, was some bauble meant to ensnare my mind – a stratagem that Tillinghast did not expect to succeed, but that he had to try, nevertheless, just as any decent lawyer files a motion to dismiss first thing, even knowing the judge will reject it. When you threw that cursed box in the river, Tillinghast dispatched someone to leave that wet ruin on my desk instead. But it's a trick, Altman. Designed to make me doubt my own judgment, and to question myself, and to make me feel foolish and chagrined."

"That could be," Altman admitted. "It would have taken some effort to go into the river to get the original box back. I put it in a sack weighed down with rocks, but even so, the package was in pretty good shape, better than I would have expected, unless someone was watching me, and pulled it out as soon as I left–"

"I am certain of my interpretation," Sanford interrupted. "Do you know why? Because it's something that I would do. Tillinghast is good, but he's not better than me. No one is better than me."

"Of course, sir," Altman said. But privately, he thought the magus was misunderstanding the lesson of Percy Shelley's poem about the king who'd once ruled the known world, only to have his name forgotten by history. The point of that poem wasn't to be on guard against would-be usurpers; the point of that poem was that every great endeavor turned to dust, eventually, no matter what you did to stop it.

"I want you to find the Dyer woman, right away." Sanford rose from the chair. "I'll make her take me to Tillinghast, without delay. The spider wants to scheme and move in shadows, creating a network in my city while he hides at the center of his web? No. I won't have it."

Altman liked having a straightforward assignment. "Right you are, sir. Seems the right way to go."

They returned to the upper levels of the Lodge, the

magus striding forward, clearly invigorated and ready for
the next stage in the conflict. Some people are the most
alive when they're in the midst of a battle. Altman had
known plenty of fellows like that, and he understood them.
He liked this pugnacious version of Sanford better than the
one he'd glimpsed briefly in the autopsy room – the one
with the lost and baffled gaze.

A pretty, young Initiate was waiting outside Sanford's
office, standing at attention with her hands clasped before
her, eyes wide at proximity to the leader of the Order.
"There you are, sir! The warden sent me to find you. She
says you have a visitor."

# CHAPTER TEN
## *The Twins*

"Yoo-hoo!" a cheerful voice called from the other side of the fence at the back of the Lodge grounds.

Sarah Van Shaw was roaming the dark estate, looking for further signs of infestation, and she flinched at the unexpected voice. Her dogs twitched in sympathy. She felt them, almost like extensions of herself, like extra hands… and jaws.

Van Shaw swept across the leafy ground toward the black iron barrier that separated her domain from the world. Why was someone back here? There was nothing to the rear of the Lodge, no streets or dwellings, just the stony, weedy slope of the hill dropping off to the east. But there was someone standing there anyway. Van Shaw's eyes were better suited to seeing in the dark than most – she was the guardian of this place, and needed to see everything at all times – and she was thoroughly surprised at the sight of a stylish young woman with black braids framing her pretty face.

"Are you Miss Van Shaw?" the woman asked, as if they were standing at a party, and not on either side of a twelve-foot-high metal fence with bars so close together you could barely fit a hand through them.

"I am," the warden said. "And who are you?"

"Oh, my name is Gloria, but that's not important. My employer sent me here to talk to you. I would have come to the front gate, but I was passing by and spotted you walking, and thought I'd call you from here instead."

Patently false. No one had a reason to just pass by this part of the fence. "Who is your employer, and what do they want with me?" Three of her dogs bounded out of the night and took up positions around her.

The woman let out a high-pitched squeal, and bent forward, hands on her knees. "Oh, what beautiful pups!" Gloria cried in evident delight. "Are they mastiffs? My father raised dogs, you know, I just love them, did you know he had one that weighed over two hundred pounds? And these are even bigger! How wonderful!"

The sole purpose of the beasts that served Van Shaw was to protect the Lodge, and they were scarcely even creatures of their own anymore, but closer to extensions of the warden's will… but even so, she felt an unfamiliar flutter of pleasure deep in her chest. The dogs were often feared, but she couldn't remember when they'd last been admired. They were beautiful, in the way anything perfectly suited to its purpose is beautiful. "Thank you. I ask again: what do you want?"

Gloria twinkled, giving the dogs a little wave, and they didn't even growl at her. She straightened up and turned her smile on the warden, which had about as much effect as snow falling into the mouth of an active volcano. Smiles tended to shrivel, when confronted with Sarah Van Shaw's implacable visage, but Gloria's was undiminished. "My employer heard about your plight, and he thinks it's terribly unfair. He asked me to give you something to help with your troubles." She extended a tiny hand through the bars, then twisted it, dropping a pendant to dangle at the end of a chain from her fingers.

The dogs snarled, sensing the arcane. Van Shaw flinched away – the master had said they had an enemy, striking at the Lodge – but nothing happened. The warden steadfastly refused to look at the pendant. "You work for that Tillinghast. He's sent you with one of his baubles, to mesmerize me."

Dyer laughed like bells. "That's not what he does. He just gives people what they want, or, in rare and special cases, what they need. Everyone is mesmerized by their heart's desire. It's only natural."

Van Shaw sniffed. "I have everything I desire here."

Dyer shook her head. "No, you don't. It's just that what you desire is incompatible with your sense of duty, and your sense of duty is *so* very strong. But what if you could have both, Sarah?" She moved her hand, and the pendant at the end of the chain swung. "What if you could fulfill your duties as Warden of the Lodge, while also having the opportunity to actually live your *life*? Go to a restaurant, walk in a park, maybe even kiss someone under the stars?" That smile again, and that twinkle. "You can have that. We can *give* you that."

"I don't see how," the warden said, then cursed herself silently for even granting the girl's premise. "And even if I could, what would your master want in return?"

"He would ask far less from you than *your* master does," Gloria said. "And he'd be a lot more grateful. Come, now. You aren't loyal to Sanford, anyway, not really. You're the guardian of the Order. The organization itself, not just its current leadership. And, let me assure you, my employer has no desire to harm the Silver Twilight Lodge. Quite the opposite. Mr Tillinghast wishes to see your Order flourish and achieve great things. Sanford uses the Lodge as his personal piggy bank and wrecking ball – he enriches himself, and destroys his enemies, all for the pettiest of reasons. Don't you want to be part of an Order that does great things instead? Don't you want to be part of an Order that matters?"

"That's Tillinghast's plan, then? To usurp Carl Sanford?" The warden shook her head. "Many have tried. None have triumphed."

"Everyone always loses until they win, warden," Gloria said. "But aren't *you* tired of losing? Just look. Look at the pendant. I swear to you, it won't do anything to your mind... except, I hope, change it."

Curiosity got the best of Van Shaw. If something did happen to her mind, the dogs would bite the woman's hand off, pendant and all, which should go a long way toward breaking any spell.

The pendant was silver, and looked a bit like the roman numeral II, but with unusual curves. "Is that the symbol for Gemini?" Van Shaw said, peering closely. "That's my sign of the zodiac." Some of Van Shaw's only contact with the outside world came in the form of the daily newspapers like the *Arkham Advertiser*, and one of her few guilty pleasures was reading her horoscope there, even though the promises and predictions never came true really, because her life was very much the same, and essentially unchanging, day after day.

"The Twins," Gloria confirmed. "Mr Tillinghast acquired this pendant from the collection of a sorcerer who had a fondness for the zodiac, as part of an incomplete set. There's also a Taurus pendant that gives the wearer tremendous strength, and a Sagittarius that grants perfect accuracy with bows or guns or slingshots, and a Leo that I really wouldn't recommend anyone put on – it removes fear entirely, and a person without fear is a dangerous thing. But this is meant for you. There's no doubt. As soon as Mr Tillinghast told me about its powers, I knew you'd just love it."

Van Shaw crossed her arms so she wouldn't reach for the necklace. She didn't feel mesmerized, but she was undoubtedly curious. "What powers?"

"Put it on and see." Gloria knelt and extended her other hand through the bars. "Here, I'll put my hand in the mouth of one of your dogs, and if you don't like what happens next, he can bite it clean off. Will that do as proof that I mean you no harm?"

"Very well," Van Shaw answered stiffly. She was unaccustomed to negotiation. Hers was more often the path of the ultimatum, the intimidation, the demand. She'd always found the constraints of her position a comfort.

There were limitations, but there was also security. Lately, though, she had to admit… those constraints were beginning to chafe.

One of her mastiffs stepped forward and opened its jaws wide, nestling Gloria's arm inside, past her wrist.

"What a good girl you are," Gloria murmured, gazing at the dog with obvious admiration.

Van Shaw snatched the pendant from the woman's other hand and looked at it closely. Then she held it out and let the other two dogs sniff it. Yes, definitely some occult power there… but nothing that was a threat to the Lodge. She grunted.

Well, why not take the thing? She hadn't agreed to give Tillinghast anything in exchange, and, indeed, her oaths were so powerful that she could not be compelled to do anything that would hurt the Silver Twilight Lodge anyway.

*But Tillinghast is right,* the back of her mind whispered. *Sanford is not synonymous with the Order.* She chose to ignore that.

"How does it work?" Van Shaw asked.

"Just put on the necklace and let the pendant touch your skin." Gloria was using her free hand to stroke the head of the dog that held her other hand in its mouth, and the dog seemed to *like* it. The hound's pleasure washed into Van Shaw through their connection and made her more favorably disposed to the woman, too.

Van Shaw draped the chain around her neck, then tucked the little silver symbol inside her dress, to touch her skin, and–

She stumbled, and the dog closed its jaws, but just a fraction. Van Shaw got her equilibrium back and stood up... to stare at herself.

To stare at *both* herselves. One version of her, the original, stood on the grounds of the Lodge, surrounded by her hounds. But there was a second version of her standing on the other side of the bars, beside Gloria, wearing Van Shaw's dress, with the same silver chain around her neck.

Van Shaw felt a brief flare of panic. The Cult of Cain had made horrible duplicates of people, copies that hid subtle deformities, and they often killed the originals, allowing their dark doppelgangers to replace them in society, but this wasn't the same sort of duplication. The other Van Shaw was still her – she could see out of that woman's eyes, she could look through the bars at herself, and see herself looking back, and–

She closed her eyes – all four of them – and took deep, calming breaths.

"You're doing really well," Gloria said conversationally. "Most people sort of fall over and writhe at first. They don't know how to handle two sets of senses, and two bodies. But Mr Tillinghast said you do something a bit like this anyway – that you can control your dogs like they're your own limbs, see through their eyes and smell through their noses – so you'd probably get the hang of using the pendant more quickly. What do you think, Sarah? You have the golden gift of bodily bilocation now. You can be in two places at once. One of you can stay on the Lodge grounds, fulfilling the terms of your oath, and the other body can go... well. Anywhere."

Sarah opened all her eyes. "What's the range?" she whispered.

"Mr Tillinghast says you shouldn't leave this plane of reality, and he can't guarantee the amulet's effectiveness if you go beyond the orbit of the moon, but otherwise…" She shrugged. "Feel free to take that long vacation you've always wanted."

Sarah Van Shaw lowered her head for a moment. Where would she even go? To a warm beach to look upon the sea? To a fine hotel, to order room service, and eat it in bed, wearing a plush robe? To a spa, to take the healing waters, and wash off the long years of psychic grime?

*I could go anywhere*, she thought, and that was the point, wasn't it? She could go anywhere, without forswearing her oaths in the process. "What is the price for this gift, Gloria?"

Gloria removed her hand from the dog's mouth. "First, right now, I'd just ask you to arrange a meeting for me. But in the future… well, we might want you to open a door for us. Or two. With the understanding that we don't want to harm the Order. We want to *improve* the Order."

"I… can do that," the warden replied.

Sanford met Ruby in his private dining room, as it was past time for his own dinner. She came in carrying a glass of tempranillo and sat in the chair on his right. "How has *your* evening been?" she asked. "Because mine has been… Tillinghast-tastic."

"Please don't ever say that again." He cut off a sliver of veal, chewed, and swallowed. "But I confess I have been similarly preoccupied. The man is toying with me. I am certain he means me harm."

"He wants to take you off the board entirely," Ruby said.

Sanford raised an eyebrow. "You met with him already? And he told you this directly?"

"I did, and he did. He said he wants to neutralize you, because you could pose a threat to certain long-term plans he's got going. He also wants me to acquire something from your vault for him."

"Oh, does he? Something in particular?"

"The Ruby of R'lyeh," she said.

Sanford frowned. "But... I have in my possession objects of true power. That gem is just a curiosity. Very old, yes, and some believe its origins are non-terrestrial, but I've never discovered any use for it."

"What's R'lyeh mean, anyway? Some dead king or something?"

"Mmm, no. It's a city, supposedly, sunk long ago beneath the waves," Sanford said. "I don't know if the ruby is even really from there. If R'lyeh actually exists, I don't think anyone knows exactly where. Whatever can Tillinghast want with the thing?"

"He didn't really tell me why it's important," Ruby said. "Just something about the gem allowing freedom of movement in some place where movement is difficult. But anyway. Can I have it?"

Sanford blinked at her. Something so straightforward could hardly be called treachery, but it was certainly *impertinence*. "Can you *what*?"

She sipped her wine and gave him an insouciant smile. "I figure, you can give me the jewel, which as you say yourself is pretty much useless to you, and I can give it to Tillinghast, and then he's assured of my loyalty, and that puts me in a position to find out what his plans are."

He put his fork and knife down carefully. "I am not in the habit of giving away objects of value, Ruby."

She rolled her eyes in that insufferable way she had. "It's an investment, Sanford. You're not the only man who likes subjecting his employees to tests of skill and loyalty. Tillinghast is going to keep me at arm's length unless I can prove myself useful to him. Don't you want to know *why* he wants to neutralize you?"

"Very much," Sanford admitted. "I will consider your proposal. Though I dislike the implications, I can see the merit. Now. Tell me everything. How did you come to meet with Tillinghast?"

Ruby delivered her report in a straightforward and thorough manner. Though it often pleased her to play the part of a flighty flapper, she was, in her way, almost as professional as Sanford himself. When she finished her account, he nodded, his mind racing with plans and interpretations and assessments. "I'll dispatch a couple of Seekers to keep an eye on Tillinghast's shop," he said. "Once they catch sight of the man himself, they'll pursue him doggedly. I've sent Altman to find the Dyer woman, and we'll watch *her*, too, since she seems to be his–"

The door to the small private dining room opened, and Sarah Van Shaw entered. It was a bit odd, seeing the warden inside the Lodge. She had rooms here, but as far as Sanford knew, she never slept, exactly. The dogs slept occasionally, instead. "What is it, warden?"

Ruby turned in her chair and gave Van Shaw a wave, which the warden ignored. She wasn't convivial by nature, and she looked at both of them, stone-faced as usual. Sanford felt a prickle of unease in her presence after their contentious interaction on the grounds earlier. Not his finest moment. He needed to do better, to be better, to play at the top of his game, until this Tillinghast was… well, yes. *Neutralized.*

"A woman has come to the gates, asking to meet with you," the warden said. "She says her name is Gloria Dyer. She claims to be a representative of one Mr Randall Tillinghast."

Sanford ground his teeth. Damn this Tillinghast. Was he playing more games? Did he know Altman was searching for Gloria, and had he chosen to send her here directly in order to tweak Sanford's nose? "I'll speak to her outside," Sanford said. "Under no circumstances is she to be permitted onto the grounds."

"I would never allow anyone who threatened the sanctity of the Order to enter this place," Van Shaw said.

Sanford dropped his napkin on the table and stood up. "Ruby, you should stay here. We don't want Dyer to know you rushed straight to me after your meeting with Tillinghast."

Ruby shrugged. "As you like. I'm supposed to be spying on you, so I doubt she'd be too surprised, but I've had plenty of Gloria Dyer's company for one day."

Sanford strode through the Lodge, the warden at his side. "She is unarmed?"

Van Shaw shrugged. "She might have a knife or a pistol, but the dogs don't smell anything magical in her possession, nor did they get any sense that she means the Order harm. The dogs are a bit crude when it comes to sensing intentions, but they can detect malice."

"Be on your guard, nonetheless. I wish I'd brought my sword stick."

"She seems to be an ordinary woman, hired to run errands," Van Shaw said.

"Nevertheless, we must be vigilant."

"Eternally," the warden replied.

They passed through the anteroom of the house, out onto the porch, and up the front walk, where Dyer idled on the street beyond the gates, smoking a cigarette and looking up at the moon. She turned when they came near and graced them with a smile. "Mr Sanford! What a delight to see you again."

"How may I be of service, Miss Dyer?" Sanford kept his tone politely neutral.

"My employer says he sent you an invitation to meet today, but you never replied, nor did you arrive at the appointed time and place, so I've been dispatched to… follow up, I suppose? He was under the impression that you wanted to meet with him, so he was a bit surprised when you failed to–"

"I regret that, due to circumstances beyond my control, I received his invitation when it was already too late to accept it," Sanford said.

"I can scarcely believe any circumstances are beyond your control, Mr Sanford!" Dyer chirped. "But my employer thought something of the sort might have happened. He sent me to deliver a new invitation in person, and to take him your reply personally. He'd like you to come tomorrow morning, at 10 AM, to his shop in the Merchant District."

The Merchant District? But Ruby said his shop was on the Northside… had she lied to him? Or was Tillinghast still on the move? Perhaps he'd suspected that Ruby might tell him about the shop, and this was just another mind game, to keep Sanford off balance? He refused to let himself *be* unbalanced. "I'll need to go inside to check my appointment book," he said blandly. "Please wait a moment." He turned and walked back up the cobbles, to the porch, and inside, the warden following.

Once the front door was shut, he turned to her. "Find two Seekers with surveillance training and have them follow Dyer, without letting her notice them. I want to know where she goes and what she does, even if it's just home to bed. Arrange for another shift of competent help to replace them in the morning."

The warden nodded and glided off. Sanford paced around the foyer for a few minutes, long enough to plausibly check his book and for the warden to bark her orders, and then returned to the gate. The long grasses on either side of him rippled as the unseen hounds paced him. The warden *was* with him, then, in a way. "10 AM is acceptable," he replied. "I am pleased that Mr Tillinghast agreed to an appointment."

She dimpled, delighted by his reply as she was by all things. "My employer tells me he was going to reach out to you anyway, and you simply beat him to it! He believes you have business interests that may occasionally overlap with his own, and he wishes to discuss how the two of you might best navigate any moments of friction that might consequently appear."

"How very thoughtful of him," Sanford said. "I look forward to our rendezvous immensely."

"I'm sure the sentiment is returned," Dyer said. "Shall we send a car for you?"

"Just the address is fine," Sanford said.

Dyer was ready with a card, with the address printed right there, in black type. Sanford did his best to keep his face calm when he read the street name and number. The location was indeed in the Merchant District, in a storefront that Sanford knew to be empty and available to let… because it had once housed Huntress Fashions, the shop owned by his former Seeker Diana Stanley. Did Tillinghast know about Sanford's personal connection to that address? He couldn't possibly. Could he?

Who *was* this man, and why had none of Sanford's inquiries about Tillinghast among the loose occult brotherhood that spanned the Western world returned anything in the way of useful information?

"I'll take my leave of you, then, Mr Sanford," Gloria said. "Sleep well and have the sweetest dreams."

Sanford looked at her for a long moment, then said, "The same to you, Miss Dyer." He turned on his heel and returned to the Lodge, his mind boiling with orders, plans, stratagems, and contingencies.

He was surprised to discover that, in addition to his apprehension, he also felt invigorated. How long had it been since he'd sparred with someone who might truly be his equal? A long time, and back then, being his equal was a lot easier.

Tillinghast would learn the magnitude of the error he'd made by setting his sights on Sanford. When this business was done, perhaps Sanford would have a replica of Tillinghast Esoterica and Exotics constructed in one of the Lodge's basements, to serve as a trophy.

# CHAPTER ELEVEN
*Stolen Moments*

Ruby yawned, leaning in the doorway of a closed shop in the Merchant District. She'd been ready to call it a night, maybe go draw a hot bath and then head to bed early, but no, Sanford had come stalking back into the Lodge after meeting Gloria and commanded her to go take a look at Diana Stanley's old shop and see if there was any sign of habitation. Apparently Tillinghast wanted a meeting there in the morning, and Dyer claimed that was the location of his shop, which Ruby knew to be untrue… unless he'd changed locations again so soon. He'd need a deft and speedy moving crew, but he had money, and money could buy time. "If Tillinghast *is* there, alert me immediately," Sanford had said.

Ruby really hoped he wouldn't be. She'd never get any sleep if Sanford decided to do a middle-of-the-night raid on the old man. Though an immediate and decisive conflict *would* end this situation, one way or another, and that would be nice, wouldn't it? Ruby was already sick of maintaining divided loyalties, and keeping two sets of stories and motivations straight in her mind was going to get tiresome fast.

She observed the dark shop across the street for a while, alert to any glimmer of light. Her friend Diana's high-end clothing store, Huntress Fashions, had once occupied the bottom floor, but Diana had sold off her stock before she left town, and now the pretty picture window presented only nothingness. Diana's old apartment was upstairs, and if this was Tillinghast's new home base, he might be living up there, but those windows remained dark, too.

Ruby took a circuitous route that led her to the alley behind the shop. Picking the lock on the back door was a breeze, and she was inside in moments. Last time she'd been in here, this was the back room for a bustling business, but now it was the lair of dust bunnies. She prowled through the rooms on the lower floor, the streetlights outside providing just enough illumination to allow her investigation, but there was nothing to find. Tillinghast hadn't set up shop here. Nobody had. This was a place in waiting. It didn't even remind Ruby of Diana, anymore, and that was sad. Ruby hadn't even gotten a postcard from her in a while.

She ghosted up the dark stairs, making her way by feel, and emerged into the small apartment above. Tillinghast wasn't there, either. Nobody was. She checked the bedroom, bathroom, and small sitting room, and there was nothing in the place at all but an old wooden stool by the kitchen counter, which Diana probably hadn't bothered to take with her and the landlord hadn't bothered to remove.

Ruby stood in the empty kitchen and gazed around at the hollow space where a person had once lived. She had… well, not *fond* memories of this place, but she had memories, anyway. She'd sat in that living room, when there were chairs in it, and conspired with her compatriots to rob Carl Sanford's vault. And now she was working for Sanford. While also ostensibly working against him. She opened an empty cabinet and looked inside. "How do I get myself into these situations?" she asked aloud.

"It's a tough old world for us professional gals," a voice said, and Ruby spun, ready to fight or flee, but then she recognized the voice. It was Gloria Dyer, suddenly sitting on the other side of the counter on that lonely stool, the white of her smile visible in the faint streetlight filtering in through the windows. She must have been in the bedroom, or lurking in the shadows.

*I'm getting rusty*, Ruby thought. Normally she had a good sense for whether a property was occupied or not. She crossed her arms, feigning nonchalance. "What are you doing here, Gloria?"

"A little advance preparation for tomorrow's meeting with Mr Sanford, of course," Gloria said. "I suppose that's why *you're* here, too." She clucked her tongue. "Mr Tillinghast expected this, of course. He said you weren't really on the level yet – that you weren't a true double agent, but only pretending to be. You've got some residual professional loyalty to Mr Sanford. It's understandable. My employer hasn't actually paid you those vast riches he promised you yet, after all. You can't buy someone without paying them. Would it help if I promised you he was good for the money? He's paid me enough."

"I'm not loyal to Sanford," Ruby said. "I'm loyal to *me*. I have to walk a careful line here, Gloria. You want me to spy on Sanford, and that means I need to stay close to him, and *that* means I have to play the good little underling. He sent me to find out if Tillinghast was here, so I came. But if Tillinghast *had* been here, I would have asked him – what do you want me to *tell* Sanford I found?"

Gloria shook her head, a shadow of movement. "I can't read minds, Ruby, but I can read people, and I'm not convinced. But that's fine, really. I'm not the one who needs convincing."

"So how do I convince Tillinghast I'm on his side?" *Especially because I'm not, particularly*, she thought.

"Tut, tut, as your Mr Sanford would say. You misunderstand, Ruby. You're the one who needs to be convinced. To truly join us. To stand on the right side of the conflict to come. Money is a great motivator, but it can be fickle – there are so many ways to get paid, after all. So Mr Tillinghast has sent me to offer you something more… unique." She slid a small, faintly glowing object across the counter.

Ruby squeezed her eyes shut and turned her face away, cold terror gripping her guts. "Please don't do this. I'll help. You don't need to snare my mind like you did with Tick. I am on your side, I promise–"

"Mr Tillinghast has no desire to ensorcel you," Gloria said, her voice uncharacteristically stern. "As I believe he told you. You're no good to him with your wits addled."

Gloria hadn't been present for that conversation. Did Tillinghast tell her everything? If so, he was a more forthcoming employer than Carl Sanford.

Gloria's voice regained its customary warmth. "Just look, please. You'll like this, Ruby. You'll *love* this."

Ruby compromised with her fear by opening one eye, then opened both. "Oh. It's just a watch." That glow wasn't some magical mind-snare, but a radium dial, the numerals and hands of the watch illuminated faintly green.

"It's a Gruen Guild Tank watch. Silver case, Swiss jewels, leather strap. A beautiful piece, isn't it?" Dyer's voice was nearly reverent.

"Sure, but... Tillinghast thinks he can secure my undying loyalty with a watch? Even a nice watch? I'm not that cheap, Gloria. I'm honestly a little insulted."

"It's not just a watch, dear. It's a relic."

Ruby frowned. "What do you mean, a relic? It's got a radium dial, so it can't be more than, what, ten years old–"

"It is, in fact, new this year," Gloria said. "But that doesn't mean it isn't a relic. As you and Sanford use the term, relics are objects imbued with unusual properties that seem, to the mundane among you, to be magic. They are found in the ruins of ancient civilizations, because only ancient civilizations knew the trick of creating such things. But Mr Tillinghast knows those secrets, too. Every strange object with mysterious properties, discovered in the foundations of a fallen temple in a deep jungle cave, had to be brand new at some point, didn't it? This, Ruby, is a relic of the future." Gloria tapped the crystal of the watch with one fingernail.

"So, what mysterious property does this watch have?"

Ruby was curious despite herself. Tillinghast could really make such things? That was a lot more than Carl Sanford could do.

"You mentioned a story you liked to Tick. Was it 'The New Accelerator,' by Herbert George Wells?"

Gloria hadn't been present for that conversation, either, and neither had Tillinghast. She'd known Tick was in thrall to the latter, but did Tillinghast's underlings give him reports that thorough? Ruby would have sworn Tick was barely even listening to her. Or… could Tillinghast somehow see through the eyes of those he'd charmed, the way Sarah Van Shaw sometimes seemed to know what her hounds could see?

"I recall," was all Ruby said.

"This is *your* New Accelerator." Gloria picked up the watch. "Not a potion, but a relic. It tells the proper time, but if you twist this dial, and set the clock back, say, five minutes…" Gloria briefly blurred, and then vanished. Ruby gasped, and then someone tapped her on the shoulder. Ruby spun with a shriek, and Gloria was standing behind her, smiling, holding up the watch at eye level, its dial glowing. "Then *you* get to spend five minutes accelerated, while, for everyone else, only a single second passes. When the watch catches up to real time again, you re-enter the regular flow of chronology. You can only set the watch back an hour, at most. I don't know why. But during that hour, everyone and everything around you are frozen in time. You can accomplish a great many things in a stolen hour, can't you? You should let the watch rest between excursions. Mr Tillinghast says repeated uses too frequently will, how did he put it, 'damage the springs.'" Gloria took Ruby's hand, placed the watch in her palm, and folded her fingers closed. "Now you've got time. All the time you need."

"I don't believe it." Ruby stared down at the wonder in her hands. She'd held artifacts before, but those were all stolen property, en route to new owners, and none of them had any obvious use, besides making your skin crawl, or giving you a sick dizzy feeling if you stared at them too closely. This was a miracle, and it was *hers*? "It seems..." She strapped the watch onto her wrist and held it close to her face so she could see the workings. "I turn this dial here?"

Gloria nodded, and Ruby twisted the knob, setting the watch back by five minutes.

At first, she thought nothing had happened. Gloria was still standing there, attentive and solicitous... but then she realized the other woman wasn't breathing anymore. "Gloria?" she said, but the woman didn't respond, or blink, or move at all, however minutely.

Ruby circled around her, but Gloria didn't react. When she stopped moving, Ruby realized the room had become completely silent, apart from the ticking of the watch, which now seemed to toll as loud as church bells. She felt as if her ears were muffled with cotton. Was it *true*? A dizzying elation built in her. With a power like this, she could do... she could do anything!

Ruby went downstairs and stepped out the back door, into the alleyway. She gazed at a brown leaf hovering suspended in midair, and that convinced her of the truth of the trick, more than anything else. She cast about and found a round pebble on the ground. Ruby picked up the stone, held it at eye level, and dropped it. But the pebble didn't drop. When she opened her hand, it simply hung where she'd released it, suspended in space and time.

She laughed in delight, and found more pebbles, hanging them in the air at various heights all around her, forming a spiral. *This could be a new art form,* she thought wildly.

And then the sounds of the world returned, the wind roaring suddenly loud in her ears, and the pebbles she'd suspended all fell and hit the ground with a *rat-a-tat* clatter. She started to wind the watch back again, but then stopped herself. She didn't want to damage the springs. This was a miracle, and miracles should be respected.

She went back inside, up the stairs, to find Gloria seated at the counter again. "How long did you spend in between?" the woman asked.

Ruby was out of breath, though she'd scarcely exerted herself. Her mind was awhirl with possibilities. "Just five minutes. To test it out."

"You should wait a while before using it again," Gloria said. "Especially since I just stole a few moments, too. Mr Tillinghast says overuse can wear down the springs... though I doubt they're *literally* springs... and it's best to let the mechanism rest. Give it eight hours or so between uses, and it should remain functional indefinitely. Otherwise, he provides no guarantees. He hopes the watch, and all those stolen moments, will give you joy." Gloria paused. "He also hopes, and he isn't usually this blunt, that the watch will buy your loyalty."

Ruby stared at the glowing hands of the watch. With something like *this*, the things she could do – she could clean out jewelry stores, she could rob banks! Such inelegant jobs weren't very interesting, but they could provide her with the funds to give her true freedom.

"And lest you see this watch as a ticket out of town and into a whole new life," Gloria said, as if she *could* read Ruby's mind, "Mr Tillinghast says to remind you that what he gives, he can also take away."

Ah. Of course. You wouldn't give someone a tool – potentially a weapon – this powerful unless you could exert some level of control over it, and, thus, over the wielder. "It's a transaction, then," Ruby said levelly. "I serve Tillinghast, and I get…"

"Time," Gloria said. "All the time you need."

What had Sanford ever done for Ruby, anyway? Certainly nothing this good. *He saved your life*, a treacherous voice whispered. *He forgave your trespasses against him. He offered you a partnership.* No. He'd used her, and allowed her to use him in return, when they had a common goal – that was all. Tillinghast was probably a monster, but wasn't Sanford a monster, too? Why should she care which monster was in charge? At least Tillinghast shared his magical relics instead of hoarding them away in a vault, to brood over in solitude.

A vivid sense memory rose up in her mind: the stink of the swamps, the flicker of torches moving through the trees on all sides, the buzzing clouds of mosquitoes, the ground squelching underfoot as she fled with that Horror In Clay clutched to her chest. That was what happened *last* time she accepted a commission from Tillinghast. But… this was different, wasn't it? She was in Arkham, a city she knew well, not a cult-ridden swamp in a lightless place far from her comfort zone. And this time… oh, this time, the reward made the risks worthwhile.

"Tell Mr Tillinghast I accept his offer," Ruby said.

"He never doubted for a moment you would." Gloria rose from the stool. "Tell Carl Sanford that the shop and the apartment were empty when you arrived. It's not even a lie. Isn't it nice when you can get through the day without telling any lies at all?" She gave a little wave and disappeared down the stairs.

Ruby stared at the watch. Eight hours. Just eight more hours until she could feel that rush of power again. And she'd stay in the world between the moments a *lot* longer than five minutes, next time.

Altman was doing the same old bit again: sitting in the dark in an armchair in Gloria Dyer's tastefully appointed living room, a kukri unsheathed across his lap.

He hadn't been there all that long when the front door opened, and the woman came home. "Hello, Mr Altman!" she called, before the door was even shut behind her. "I'm going to make some coffee. Would you like some?" The light in the kitchen came on. He could see Gloria, across the breakfast bar that divided the kitchen from the living room, bustling about.

*Her total lack of surprise rather spoils the effect, doesn't it?* Altman reached over and clicked on the lamp beside the chair anyway, illuminating himself, in all his considerable menace. Gloria didn't even look over at him.

Altman decided to give in gracefully. "Coffee would be nice." He rose and went to the breakfast bar, setting down his curved knife with a decisive clank before taking a seat on one of her padded, high-backed stools.

"Let me guess," Gloria said. "You're here to force me at knifepoint to take you to Mr Tillinghast."

"I intended to ask politely first," Altman said. "Though the knife was meant to be visible during the asking. So, not quite knifepoint. Just… knife adjacent."

She brought out a bizarre contraption that looked like a piece of lab equipment, or perhaps an hourglass, on a wooden stand. "My Silex siphon. Isn't it a beauty? They started making these ten years ago, can you believe it? But with the war and all, they didn't take off with the public right away. I suppose you still boil your coffee on the stove, Mr Altman? Let me assure you, filtration creates a far superior brew. You will be *astonished*. Ideally you should grind the beans fresh for every pour, but I ground too much this morning, and that's almost fresh, so I might as well use them up…" Gloria turned to the stove and began heating a kettle.

"I appreciate the hospitality, but I'm afraid, after we've had our coffee, I'll need to take you with me." He closed his hand on the knife and prepared to fling himself to the floor if Gloria moved with any speed. Letting your adversary have access to a pot of boiling water was a good way to get all the skin on your face bubbled off.

But she turned slowly, and faced him, arms crossed over her bosom. "You should call your employer for an update. My phone is just over there." She pointed. Altman didn't turn to look.

"Why should I do that?"

"Because I've seen Carl Sanford more recently than you have, Mr Altman. You were sent to find me, and I was sent to find him. Your employer didn't let me into his Lodge. He spoke to me at the gate, like I was the Fuller Brush Man interrupting him at dinner time! He's terribly rude, isn't he, your Mr Sanford?"

"He... has a lot on his mind," Altman said.

Gloria sniffed. "So does Mr Tillinghast, but he's always polite, and as I represent him, I am polite, too. I would have invited you in, if you'd waited on my doorstep like a reasonable person instead of letting yourself in. Though you didn't damage the door. I appreciate that. At any rate, I have already arranged a meeting between our respective principals, so there's no need for you to wave your blade at me. You go make your call to confirm, and I'll get the coffee ready."

Altman nodded. "Hand me your purse first?"

"Rude," she said, but she obliged.

He checked the purse and found everything you'd expect to find in a handbag, and nothing you wouldn't – no gun, mainly. Then he rose, backing up, keeping his eyes on Gloria until he was out of range of boiling water or a hurled kitchen knife. He'd searched her kitchen, and the rest of the house when he arrived and was confident she didn't have a gun stashed away anywhere else, either, or at least, not where she could get it quickly.

He picked up the phone and spun the dial. He still wasn't used to this direct calling business, with the automatic exchange – he always expected to hear an operator when he picked up the handset, like the old days. But the automatic exchanges were preferable for the sort of business he did anyway. You could never be sure an operator *stopped* listening after she connected you, after all.

He reached the Initiate who was serving as Sanford's secretary this evening and told her who he was and what he wanted. A few moments later Sanford picked up and began speaking immediately. "Altman, good, you can come back. I found Gloria without you, and there's a meeting arranged for the morning. I've got a couple of Seekers following Gloria, and we'll pick up Tillinghast, too, tomorrow. Once we've got a proper handle on his whereabouts, we can consider our options to eliminate him. Come on back to the Lodge."

"All right…" Altman began, but the connection died. Sanford had hung up on him. *Rude, indeed,* he thought.

He put his knife away and returned to the counter, where Gloria placed a delicate china cup brimming with coffee before him. "At least have a taste of this before you run back to your master." Gloria sipped at her own cup, then smiled at him across the brim. "Tell me, Mr Altman. Do you think of yourself more as a loyal person, or as a practical one?"

# CHAPTER TWELVE
*Men of the World*

After Ruby returned and gave her report, Sanford dispatched a couple of Initiates to watch the deserted shop throughout the night. If Tillinghast appeared, one of them was supposed to race back to the Lodge and inform him immediately. He had a late meeting with Altman to discuss strategies, then went to bed in his rooms at the Lodge, where he slept fitfully, and had unquiet dreams.

No alarms or alerts disturbed his slumber. He woke with the dawn, had his breakfast in his private dining room, checked in with the warden and with Altman, and then sat in his office, impatient and unable to concentrate. He should have told the Initiates watching the shop to send him regular updates instead. Finally, at 9 AM, he called Altman and had him bring the Bentley around. The trip from French Hill to Diana's old shop in the Merchant District wasn't a long one, but they paused before they reached their destination, a block to the west, because he recognized one of the Order's cars, with two Initiates sitting alertly in the front seat, parked in front of the *wrong address*. "Go see what those fools are doing!" he snapped at Altman, who pulled over the car and obliged.

Altman leaned into the driver's window, scowled, and looked down at a piece of paper the Initiate showed him. Altman shook his head, sighed heavily, and returned to the Bentley. "They wrote down the wrong address," he said as he slid back behind the wheel. "Right street, wrong number."

"But *I* wrote down the address for them!" Sanford exploded.

Altman's eyes met Sanford's in the rearview mirror, and he shrugged. "Maybe they copied it down for some reason. Maybe the ink got smudged. Either way, they've been watching the wrong place all night. I told them to pack it in. Shall we head for the proper shop?"

*Did I write down the wrong address?* Sanford thought. Surely not. He'd been tired, certainly, and distracted, but he was *good* at the details. No, no, it had to be Tillinghast again, his continuing campaign of disorientation, to make Sanford doubt himself. But how? How had he done it – wait. The card. The card! Sanford had copied down the address from the card Dyer gave him, and perhaps the *card* was enchanted, and had altered the street number between his first look and his later one, and Sanford simply hadn't noticed, and jotted down the number as written without realizing it had changed. Yes. That was it. It *must* be it. The alternative was… was not to be borne. "Yes, yes, onward," Sanford said.

They traveled another block, then parked on the street. There were a few people out and about, doing their shopping, but none of them seemed to notice that Huntress Fashions had changed. The picture window was now blocked off with a black curtain on the inside, and the window in the front door was soaped over.

Altman and Sanford emerged from the Bentley and walked up to the shop. A notice on the front door, neatly printed, said, "By appointment only. Entrance in rear."

"He wants us to come in from the alley?" Sanford said. "Why?"

"Privacy?" Altman speculated.

"Or it's an ambush. You go first, and make sure it's safe."

Altman nodded and disappeared around the side of the building, while Sanford tried in vain to see anything beyond the edges of the curtain in the front window. Altman returned a moment later. "It's all clear. And this is definitely the right place."

"How do you know that?" Sanford followed him toward the back alley.

Altman said, "You'll see."

"I don't want to *see*, I want you to *tell me*–" But then Sanford saw.

The unassuming back door of Diana's shop had been replaced with a door of ornately carved and polished dark wood. A square window of white stained glass was set at head-level, with a green triangle that contained an eye in the center. Some sort of occult symbol, but Sanford couldn't immediately place it. There was a copper doorknob, but

Sanford was loath to touch the thing. A brass plaque set into the bricks beside the door said:

*Tillinghast Esoterica and Exotics*
*Rare Books and Curios*
*By Appointment*

"He set all this up overnight?" Sanford said. "Ruby reported none of this!"

"She could have missed the back door and the plaque," Altman said. "If she went in the front. He might have put up the curtain and all in the wee hours."

"Or Ruby is in league with my enemies," Sanford said darkly.

"Or that," Altman agreed. "But I'm not sure why she'd lie and say the place was empty, when you were going to see it occupied in a few hours anyway."

Sanford nodded. Tillinghast might well try to turn Ruby against him… or Tillinghast could be trying to make Sanford *think* his people were traitors. Sowing distrust could be just as effective, in the long run, and it was a lot cheaper.

"Try the door," Sanford said.

Altman turned the knob, and didn't catch fire, or get electrocuted, or dissolve into a slurry of deliquescing flesh. The door swung inward. Hadn't the old door opened *outward*? Altman stepped inside, and a moment later said, "You have to see this, sir."

Sanford entered and found himself profoundly disoriented. He'd been in this shop before, when it was

Huntress Fashions, but Tillinghast had transformed the space. The back room was no longer separated from the front, but opened into a single space, the dark wood floors scattered with rugs, and brass lamps glowing softly here and there. Tall shelves hid the walls, and even the curtained front window, and those shelves were filled with books and scrolls and curiosities that serially snagged Sanford's attention until he forced his gaze away. Glass museum cases dotted the open spaces, with even more precious objects under glass. "This seems wrong," Sanford said, gazing up at the ceiling. "The interior dimensions don't seem to match the shop as I remember it."

"You've got some spaces in the basement that don't strictly adhere to the laws laid out by Euclid," Altman pointed out. "Is it so surprising that Tillinghast can toy with space, too?"

"But you have no idea the resources I expended to make those little wrinkles in reality possible," Sanford murmured. "To use such power for a *shop*..." He had begun by underestimating Tillinghast, and revised his opinion of the man considerably upward in recent days, but was it possible he was still undervaluing the strength of the man?

Sanford moved through the shop, toward the long counter at the back. The counter was a glass case, with marvels within, but there was something else on top of it, a glass dome like a bell jar, and beneath it...

"The Grail of Dreams." A man appeared behind the counter, emerging from a dark curtain that Sanford hadn't even noticed. He was a bit older than Sanford, and the word that came to mind was "elegant," from his perfectly cut gray suit to his perfectly manicured white beard to the perfect emerald stickpin in his tie. "A lovely piece, isn't it? It came into my possession only recently. I'm Randall Tillinghast."

"Carl Sanford," he said, and knew he should be taking this moment to thoroughly assess his adversary... but he couldn't take his eyes off the Grail of Dreams. It was a large goblet carved of shimmering black stone and looked almost exactly like the replica Sanford had acquired... but this one seemed to bend the light around itself, subtly distorting the very air in a way that couldn't be accounted for by the mere curvature of the glass dome that covered the relic. He stepped close and flicked the dome with his fingernail. "I recently made arrangements to acquire this very object. You were quicker off the mark."

"We are men of similar tastes, it seems," Tillinghast said with understated bonhomie. He raised an eyebrow and nodded. "This must be your associate, Mr Altman. Gloria has told me so much about you. I'm pleased to make your acquaintance in person at last. I'm pleased to meet *both* of you."

"Are you?" Sanford tore his eyes away from the grail, though he'd wanted the object for decades, since first reading about it in certain forbidden texts. The translations regarding this object were all a bit suspect, but the overall thrust was that the grail could make your deepest dreams become reality. With power like that, Sanford would be able to turn *anyone* to his cause, and his influence would be unparalleled. And now this man, this interloper, had the grail instead. Did Tillinghast even know the true power of what he possessed? If he did, would he have it on display so casually?

"I am… reasonably pleased to make your acquaintance." Tillinghast made a great show of looking at the watch on his wrist. "You are slightly early, which is, I suppose, better than slightly late, but neither is really ideal. Still, I can make accommodations for the vagaries of life. May I offer either of you refreshment?"

"No." Sanford met the man's hooded, somehow reptilian eyes. "What are you doing in Arkham, Tillinghast?"

"This and that." Tillinghast leaned over the counter, casual as any shopkeeper passing the time with a chatty customer. "Meeting with you, just now. And may I say, what an honor it is! You are the great Carl Sanford." His voice was filled with reverence. "The magus of the Silver Twilight Lodge, the most modern and powerful of secret societies. Your direct influence extends up and down the Eastern Seaboard, and your network of connections and allies and sycophants covers this continent and much of Europe besides. You are a renowned summoner – I've even heard it said that you possess your own shoggoth, an example of that protean species from the Antarctic? They say you consort with wise women from beyond the stars, and that the foundations of your Lodge extend deep into the earth and onward into realms beyond. You are renowned not just as a scholar and master of the esoteric arts, but as a collector of relics and artifacts from ancient civilizations – even prehuman ones. As a humble collector of esoterica myself, well, it's truly a pleasure to be in the presence of such a luminary." He straightened and pressed his hand to his chest as he made this final pronouncement.

"How do you know all that?" Sanford demanded, shocked at the man's easy recital of some of his greatest secrets.

"Oh, people talk." Tillinghast waved a hand airily. "There's no such thing as secret knowledge if more than one person knows about it. Surely you know that as well as I do. As soon as I set my sights on Arkham, everyone said, 'You simply must meet Carl Sanford, nothing of any consequence happens in Arkham except by his leave.' But, if I may... that's why I wanted to meet you, sir. My associate Gloria tells me that you were most eager to meet *me*, and asked her to set up a meeting for that purpose. Not realizing the gift I had her present already contained an invitation." He shook his head ruefully. "It was all a bit of a farce, I'm afraid. The sort of comic misunderstanding that could have been easily avoided if I'd only been a bit more forthcoming with my employee. I have learned my lesson there." He spread his hands wide and looked solemn. "But here we are, at last, with our mutual desire for a tête-à-tête satisfied. May I ask, then, why you wished so ardently to make my acquaintance?"

Sanford resisted the urge to reach across the counter and grab the man by his tailored Italian lapels. "I came to tell you to leave Arkham immediately, before I have you removed."

Tillinghast cocked his head and affected bewilderment. "Have I offended you somehow, sir?"

Sanford clenched his fists and growled. "You came to my city and interfered with my business. You charmed my harbormaster, you stole that grail, you sent a madman to pilfer the *Pnakotic Manuscripts*–" He almost added, "You asked Ruby to spy on me," but he wasn't supposed to know that, so he sputtered into silence instead.

Tillinghast sighed, like a put-upon parent dealing with a recalcitrant child. "To respond to these allegations in order... I did not realize he was *your* harbormaster, and I see no reason we cannot share him. I am happy to assist you in your endeavors, where that assistance does not work against my own interests. As for the grail, I wanted it for my own reasons, and while it's true that I scooped it out from under you, that sort of thing happens all the time in business. I am sure there will be many future business dealings where you get the best of me instead. So it goes. With regards to the *Pnakotic Manuscripts*, I wished to check something in my own copy against the earlier translation the university held, but the archivists rebuffed me, so I had no choice but to take other measures. Once I was finished, I gave the manuscript pages to you as a gift, which hardly suggests I bear you any ill will, sir."

"You are meddling in my affairs," Sanford said. "My *dear friend* Sheriff Engle would be interested to hear about your little exploits down by the docks."

Tillinghast brightened. "Ah, yes, the sheriff! I met him, not long after I came to the city. Did you know he's an avid hunter? Birds, mainly, I think. I gifted him with a bird call I picked up from an estate sale. It used to belong to the last priestess of Artemis, and it has the most remarkable ability to summon prey of any kind, not just waterfowl! He was most grateful."

Sanford couldn't speak. The sheriff was a longtime loyalist, bought and paid for, and Tillinghast had compromised him, too?

"There's no need for us to threaten one another." Tillinghast plucked a handkerchief from his pocket and dabbed at a spot on the glass counter, as if his mind was only half on this conversation. "We are both men of business, and men of the world. Let us simply tend to our individual affairs, and when our interests overlap, we can address any complications on a case-by-case basis. I'm unsure why we should ever come into conflict, however. We have so little in common. I am but a humble shopkeeper, a buyer and seller of trinkets, and you ... what is it you do again? Manage a social club, or something of that sort?"

Sanford seethed but held his tongue.

Tillinghast shrugged. "Well. I'm sure your work is very important, and I don't want to impose upon your time. We are both busy men, and if we need to communicate in the future, I can always send my Miss Dyer to talk to your Mr Altman–"

"What is it you want here?" Sanford demanded. "Why have you really come to my city?"

Tillinghast leaned across the counter again, a twinkle in his eye, and beckoned Sanford close. The magus leaned in, though drawing so near to the man felt like putting his face next to a poisonous snake. "You don't get to know," the proprietor whispered in his sand-on-scales voice.

Sanford drew back, as if slapped. "Tillinghast. I assure you that I *always* find out what I want to know."

"Not all secrets are meant for your apprehension, sir," Tillinghast replied, standing again at ease. "Some I must keep for my own. I'm sure you understand. Secrets shared are secrets spilled, after all, as we discussed earlier." He touched the side of his nose and winked. "I hope we've come to an understanding. I don't intend to leave Arkham until my business here is done, and *you* don't intend to leave Arkham at all, and so we must learn to coexist. What other choice do we have?"

*War*, Sanford thought, but he hardly needed to say it. Tillinghast knew. "What other choice, indeed."

"Before you go, could I interest you in any of my little trinkets? I don't know if I have anything to attract the eye of a connoisseur of your stature, but–"

"The grail." Sanford did his best to keep his voice calm. "You are correct. You got the best of me on the deal. But since we are businessmen, let us do business. I want to purchase it from you. Money is no object."

"I agree," Tillinghast said. "Money is no object to me at all. But, alas, I'm afraid the grail is not for sale. I am holding it in reserve against certain potential eventualities. But that doesn't mean we can't do business. I understand you possess many items, the most valuable of which is doubtless the gem known as the Ruby of R'lyeh? I'd be very interested to purchase that, and for more than it's worth. Would you consider, perhaps..." He punched a button on his cash register, reached into the drawer, and removed a ten-dollar bill. "This much? I won't even ask you for change."

Sanford quivered with rage. "You – you *cur*. I will be the end of you. All that you have, I will take from you, until you are left only with ashes."

"Spoken with the weight of prophecy," Tillinghast said. "Albeit from the wrong mouth." He put the money back in the drawer and closed it. "I'm sorry we weren't able to reach an accommodation. Do come back if you change your mind."

Sanford started to reach out, meaning to seize the man's throat, but there was something in those half-lidded, lizardlike eyes that gave him pause. *He wants me to do it,* Sanford thought. *He's goading me.*

Carl Sanford could not be goaded. He chose his own path. It was ever thus. "Good day to you, sir. I would advise you to stay clear of my operations in the future."

"I would advise you to stay clear of mine, too," Tillinghast said, "but I'm afraid before long they'll be too vast and all-encompassing for *anyone* to avoid. But we'll deal with all that as and when the time comes."

Sanford turned stiffly and marched toward the rear door, Altman trailing after. He refrained from slamming the door on his way out, but it required great effort.

"Did that go the way you hoped?" Altman said when they were back in the car.

"It was… informative," Sanford said. "The opportunity to size up an opponent in person is always welcome. He's very sure of himself, isn't he? Smug. Arrogant, even."

"He is that," Altman agreed.

"He certainly has resources." Sanford gazed out the car window at the bustling shoppers. "But I suspect they are chiefly financial. He has wealth. But I have wealth, too… and I also have an organization. Perhaps Tillinghast has made inroads with local law enforcement, but we know plenty of people who work the other side of the street. I think it's time we reach out to some of our less savory contacts."

"What did you have in mind?" Altman asked.

"The usual sorts of things," Sanford said. "Theft. Arson." He smiled faintly. "Assassination. In that order, I think. I want Tillinghast to see that I've taken everything he has, and burned everything I didn't want, before I consign him to the ultimate darkness."

"You don't usually jump to murder so soon," Altman said.

"People are often more useful alive. Even one's enemies can be tools, in the right circumstances. But Tillinghast…" Sanford shook his head. "When you have rats in the walls, you don't try to tame them, and you don't relocate them to live peacefully in the country. You kill them. Reach out to the O'Bannions. They can find us a talented firebug, and a professional killer."

"You don't want me to take care of the pest removal?" Altman said.

"We were just seen emerging from the man's shop. It's better if the two of us steer clear of him, visibly at least, until this… unpleasantness is taken care of. Ruby can handle the theft, though. I want that goblet. And sending her on that errand will serve as a loyalty test."

"She's only loyal to her pocketbook, I think," Altman said.

"You misunderstand Ruby," Sanford said. "She's motivated by money, yes, but she's also sentimental, in her way. She has a romantic view of her profession, and thus of herself. We were comrades in arms against a shared threat, not so long ago, and that buys me a modicum of extra grace from her… but she knew Tillinghast before she knew me, and if there's more to their relationship than I realize, I'd like to find out before it's too late. Head back to the Lodge. We have preparations ahead."

They drove away from the Merchant District, and Sanford gazed out the window, at the familiar buildings and the bustling shoppers. He recognized several of them, because he knew everyone worth knowing in this city, and numerous others besides. They were *his* people. Not his family, but more like… his flock. The shepherd protected his flock, defended them against thieves and wolves at great personal risk, and rounded them up when they strayed… because to do otherwise would be a waste of their wool and meat.

A woman emerged from a millinery, adjusting a blue hat with a large feather in the brim, and Sanford squinted at her. She was the very *image* of Sarah Van Shaw, but wearing a more fashionable dress than the warden ever would, and of course, Van Shaw only left the Lodge in rare instances, under Sanford's orders – certainly not to buy a fancy hat. Where would she even wear such a thing? He almost told Altman to stop the car… but then he saw the woman's face, and her warm smile, and decided he must be mistaken.

He couldn't remember ever seeing the warden actually smile like that.

# CHAPTER THIRTEEN
## *Null-Time*

Tillinghast had assured Ruby that the hounds guarding the Lodge wouldn't notice the magic in her watch and devour her the second she stepped through the gate, but she'd still approached with trepidation. In the end, the warden had waved her past without a word, seemingly distracted by greater matters, and the hounds hadn't even shown themselves.

Now Ruby was down in the basements, though she wasn't supposed to go there without Sanford, and didn't much like going there *with* him. She knew the secret routes, though, and no one had ever been able to keep her out of places where she didn't belong. A few higher-level members of the Lodge were down there going about their inscrutable business, but there were no shortages of dark corners and side passages to duck into when they came too close.

She followed a familiar path along wood-floored

corridors, past indifferently whitewashed walls. Some of the deeper levels of the basement were more changeable, even labyrinthine, but this level was relatively stable, and she knew which turns to take. She made her way past the empty cell where the Scholar from Yith had once been held. Sanford had moved her, apparently, and the unsettling sigils of binding on the walls had been painted over. Ruby didn't mind missing out on a reunion. Talking to that alien mind wearing a human face profoundly disturbed her. Ruby only stole property. She'd never stolen someone's entire life.

In time, she reached the corridor that led to Sanford's vault, but instead of a stretch of hallway, she encountered a solid wall. Ah ha. Sanford had mentioned improving his security after last year's unpleasantness, and this must be part of the change: he'd cut off access to the vault entirely.

Or... had he merely *pretended* to cut off access? Ruby moved her hands over the wall, inch by inch, knocking with her knuckles, and found no hidden doors. Something more mystical, then? Was it a real wall, or a mere bafflement of the senses? She'd come across a few security measures like that, in her past exploits as a cat burglar of the occult, and knew a trick or two that might serve her here.

She closed her eyes and felt her way across the wall again, and this time, her hand went right through a patch of empty air. She opened her eyes, and saw her arm seemingly reaching into the wall, her hand vanishing up to the wrist in the plaster. Ruby tugged, and her hand even *felt* trapped by wood and lathe – that was a potent illusion. She closed her eyes, pulled her hand free without difficulty, and then felt around, discovering a rectangular opening about four feet high and three feet wide.

Sanford had put in a false wall, with a small opening off-center to allow passage, and then cast a glamor to hide the portal. Clever. Ruby crouched and walked through the tunnel, keeping her eyes firmly closed – having her hand trapped in a wall was one thing, but her *head*? She waved her arms around cautiously as she went, encountering close walls and a low ceiling for longer than she would have expected – Sanford had put in a passage of some length. She just hoped there weren't traps, but surely he used this route himself and wouldn't want pits or spikes in his way? Her calves were cramping from her unnatural posture by the time her flailing limbs ceased to make contact with the tunnel walls, and she risked cracking open one eye.

She was in the familiar corridor, the gleaming metal vault door at the far end, with open doors standing halfway down the passage on either side of the hall. She looked behind her to see a seemingly solid wall. She closed her eyes, reached back, and found the opening was accessible from this side, too. Ruby breathed a sigh of relief, but when she opened her eyes and saw the closed-off corridor restored to illusory solidity, a prickle of claustrophobia touched her heart anyway. Her mind knew she wasn't trapped in here, but her body didn't know it.

Ruby sniffed the air. She picked up the faint chemical whiff of the guardian shoggoth she knew protected this vault and listened for the *slurp* of the creature rousing itself in one of the rooms on either side of the corridor. Nothing. Was the hideous thing sleeping? *Could* it sleep? She'd fled the assault of that loathsome blob of eyes, mouths, and gooey pseudopods before, and had no desire to reunite with it, either.

So she set her watch back an hour, and stopped time. Or, more accurately, sped herself up, so that everything around her seemed frozen – at least, that was how the New Accelerator in the Wells story had worked. Though in the story, rapid motion had caused the user's clothing to catch fire, because of the friction of cloth against the air, and the accelerating agent had taken the form of an elixir, not a watch. A chronometer was more suited to that other Wells story, *The Time Machine*. Did Tillinghast have a trinket that allowed you to move through time, too? Such a thing didn't seem possible, but then, she'd seen a lot of impossible things. Hadn't the Scholar from Yith claimed to hail from some distant era?

Ruby was wasting her hour of perfect freedom on idle thought. She took a step forward, gingerly, wary of the shoggoth, and couldn't resist peering into the dusty storerooms on either side of the hallway that served as the creature's lairs.

Both rooms were empty, apart from a broken crate in one and some shards of glass in another. Was the shoggoth inside the vault, then? Surely not. Its slimy bulk would damage the valuable relics Sanford kept there. She investigated, looking for trapdoors and secret hatches, but the only sign she found of the monster was a puddle of sticky black residue in one corner of the left-hand room. Maybe the creature had died. Maybe Sanford didn't know what to feed it; perhaps it required a diet of more than interlopers and acolytes of the Order who failed to pass their tests for advancement.

She approached the vault door, as impressive as any bank's, shining steel and seemingly impregnable. But she'd broken into this vault once, and been ushered in as a guest another time, so she knew how to overcome its defenses. There was a combination dial, but there were also pressure points hidden on the door, and Sanford had changed the pattern since her last visit... but she had time, and after fifteen minutes of pressing her ear to the metal and examining the residue of minute finger-smudges, she unlocked the door, and swung it open.

The interior was lushly carpeted, the walls lined with shelves, with a single chair sitting in the center. Nothing else. The shelves should have been full of objects of power or value or both, jewels and scrolls and statuary, a magic mirror on the wall, a sea chest on the floor that hid access to a secret escape tunnel...

But the shelves were bare, the mirror was gone, and the false chest had been removed, the access hatch beneath it filled in with concrete that formed a rough, ugly rectangle in the midst of the beautiful carpet. "You sneaky bastard," Ruby muttered, turning around in the empty space. Sanford had increased the security around his vault, but it was all misdirection, because he'd emptied the vault anyway.

She had no idea where he might be keeping his relics now, including the Ruby of R'lyeh. She had a very fine replica of the jewel in her pocket, left on her doorstep last night by Gloria Dyer. Ruby had planned on doing a straight swap, since Sanford seemed reluctant to hand the real thing over willingly, despite Ruby's persuasive arguments. Now she'd have to report her failure to Tillinghast, which wasn't a conversation she relished the idea of having. She was sure she could track down Sanford's new hiding place, in time, but extracting information from the magus was going to be a delicate business, what with him so (justifiably) paranoid lately.

What a waste of her magic! She'd expected to dodge a shoggoth and commit a daring daylight robbery, and instead, she'd just taken a boring tour of a basement. Ah, well. That was the business, wasn't it? Brief intervals of excitement punctuating long stretches of waiting, watching, and wool-gathering. She made her way back through the illusory passageway and on to the upstairs areas of the Lodge, checking her watch as she went.

She had another half hour of acceleration… so she might as well ransack Sanford's office and see if she could find any useful information. She made her way to his study, pausing to admire the statuelike Initiates frozen in mid-bustle on the upper floors. The big chair behind Sanford's desk was awfully comfortable, and she was able to pick the locks on his desk drawers and rifle the contents easily enough. She found a calendar of appointments, all marked up with initials and notes so cryptic she couldn't decipher them, and a bank book that showed the inflow of Lodge dues (vast) and the outflow of Lodge expenses (somewhat less vast, but still impressive), and some reports from Sanford's financial advisers (now *those* were thieves), but no diary, nothing about the construction of a new vault, and no notes that gave away any juicy secrets.

The man didn't seem to write down anything important. Either he kept all his secrets in that overstuffed mind of his, or he had a real office hidden away in the depths below the Lodge.

She sighed and spent the remainder of her hour of null-time weaving among the frozen cooks in the kitchen, helping herself to snacks. The last five minutes she spent in the foyer, sitting on a bench and staring into the unmoving flames of the fire. That was by far the eeriest thing she'd seen in null-time: the fire gave off no warmth, and the tongues of flame didn't flicker. She couldn't take her eyes off the strange sight.

Then sound and motion rushed back: the tick of the clock, the crackle of the flames, the distant barking of a dog, and the movement of the Lodge occupants beyond the door. Ruby shivered. Next time, she'd take better advantage of the miracle. She just needed to figure out how.

The front doors opened, and Sanford and his pet thug Altman walked in. The magus did a double take when he saw her. He must have been having a rough day, to let his mask slip enough to show actual surprise. "Miss Standish. I was just going to call for you."

She shrugged. "I thought you might, so I decided to make myself available."

"You mean you decided to avail yourself of a free breakfast," Sanford said.

She shrugged again and paired it with a grin this time. "There's also that."

Sanford turned to Altman. "You can go make those... arrangements we discussed." The other man nodded and headed into the Lodge, head like a block of wood and an expression to match. *He* sure was a bundle of fun, wasn't he?

Sanford offered Ruby his hand, and she accepted, rising from the bench. He frowned. "New watch?" he commented. "A Gruen Tank, if I'm not mistaken? Quite chic."

Ruby snorted. "A gift from a gentleman who misunderstood my level of ardor. I was going to sell it, but I tried it on first, and I rather think it suits me, don't you?"

"Your taste is always impeccable, Miss Standish."

Ruby caught his gaze lingering on the watch for a moment too long, and she imagined his calculating, suspicious thoughts: of Tillinghast's free hand with gifts, even checking to see if the watch face flickered with eldritch light, and that paranoia was as dangerous as carelessness, in its own way.

Well. Perhaps she was projecting her own thoughts on him to an extreme.

Sanford inclined his head toward the door. Clearly, he'd decided the item was perfectly ordinary. "Let's talk in my study. I have a new job for you."

They reached his office, and Sanford sat in his chair, his frown deepening, and then minutely adjusted a few of the items on his blotter. "The Initiates know they aren't meant to disturb the contents of the desk when they clean."

Ruby had been careful during her snooping, but not careful enough, apparently. The man had eyes like microscopes. "It's so hard to find good unpaid labor these days." If the lowly Initiates were allowed to tidy up in here, no wonder Sanford didn't keep anything interesting on the premises. He probably did have a secret office where he kept the real ledgers and minute documentation of all his schemes, but how would she ever find it? The deep basements sprawled beyond any rational understanding of space.

Sanford didn't acknowledge the barbed comment, but simply folded his hands on the blotter and fixed Ruby with a sharp eye. "I want you to steal the Grail of Dreams."

"Haven't we already tried that?" Ruby said.

"Tried, and failed, though I acknowledge that was my fault, not yours. I provided you with incomplete information."

Ruby was taken aback, and not sure she quite hid the fact. Sanford's words had sounded perilously close to an apology, or at least an admission that the magus was less than perfect. Such statements didn't come naturally to Sanford, which meant... what? Tillinghast had him shaken? Or was he trying to ingratiate himself with Ruby? Could be both, she mused. "Nobody could have seen Tillinghast coming," she said, deciding to meet conciliation with conciliation. "He's like one of those fogs that rolls in off the sea out of nowhere. You close your eyes for a minute in sunshine and open them to find yourself lost in the mist."

Sanford nodded in acknowledgment, and then waited.

She leaned back and crossed her legs, pondering. "You know where the grail is now?"

"It's in the man's accursed shop... which is, indeed, located in the former site of Huntress Fashions."

Ruby shook her head. "I was *in* there just last night, it was all dust–"

"Tillinghast must have come in the dead of night with a team of laborers. I'm sure the Dyer woman could have organized such a thing with trivial ease. I set watchers to keep their eyes on the shop overnight, but they were Initiates, and they became confused, or else something confused them, and they watched the wrong site, and so didn't note any comings and goings. I have had people watching the correct address since I departed, however, and no one has left the place since. After nightfall, I want you to break in and take the grail, and anything else that looks particularly valuable."

Ruby nodded, wondering how she was going to navigate this mare's nest of conflicting loyalties. "I thought I was supposed to be ingratiating myself with Tillinghast? When he finds out the grail is gone, he's going to suspect me straightaway."

"That doesn't matter anymore," Sanford interrupted. "The time for subtlety has passed. In fact, you'll be accompanied tonight by an expert in the field of… fire insurance."

She blinked. "You're sending an arsonist to burn down Diana's shop?"

Sanford sniffed. "Tut, tut. There's no place for such misplaced sentimentality, Miss Standish. Diana is long gone, and I doubt she has many fond memories of Arkham, for her shop or otherwise. I'm going to burn down Tillinghast's shop, and if he's sleeping upstairs, he can burn with it – or escape, and face death in another form. I have grown tired of his treacherous and insidious presence, worming his tendrils of influence throughout my city, tweaking my nose as if he possesses some immunity from consequences." Sanford placed his hands on the desktop and said, with blank finality, "I am going to burn him out."

Ruby nodded. "I see. What if I don't like this job, Sanford?"

"You are free to say no," Sanford said. "I will not retaliate against you. Though I would recommend, if you choose to leave my employ, that you also leave Arkham. You have a history with Tillinghast, and I don't want you to go running to him when you find yourself in need of another job." He stroked his neat beard. "But I don't see why you'd decline, unless you have some fondness for Tillinghast? I'm not convinced you'd bother to save me from a fire, if Tillinghast were the one sitting across from you, proposing a similar plan."

She scowled. "I saved you from worse than a fire, and you know it. Don't be offensive. I'll go and get your stupid cup. But I'm not keeping some arsonist company. Firebugs give me the shivers. Send him on his own, after I've come and gone."

Sanford bowed his head, then gave a small nod. "To demonstrate my good faith, and my hope for the fruitful continuation of our relationship, I agree to your terms."

Ruby rose. "If that's all?"

"What else could there possibly be?" Sanford mused.

"He's desperate for that grail," Altman said. "You weren't there in the shop. You didn't see him. I've never known Sanford's composure to crack like that. He was breathing heavy. Practically panting over it! I think it's not even the object itself so much, though he wants that, too… it's the fact that Tillinghast scooped the grail out from under him. That's why he doesn't just want to steal it back. He wants to destroy everything Tillinghast has, and Tillinghast, too."

Gloria Dyer sat beside him in the front seat of Sanford's Bentley, parked out back of Hibb's Roadhouse, where Altman had earlier made arrangements for arson and execution. "I don't think Mr Tillinghast would like that," Gloria said. "Something must be done."

Altman shook his head. "Not by me." During their recent conversation, Gloria had convinced him to help Tillinghast in exchange for certain promises, but he'd negotiated hard limits on what he was willing to do. He would pass them information, and further their agenda when possible, but he would not endanger himself in the process. "I can't stop Sanford. Not without making him suspicious, and if he's suspicious, he might kill me. He might do *worse* than kill me. I swore my oaths to the Lodge, not to Sanford, but the man doesn't make any distinction between the two. Some of the things I've seen in the basement... there are people who betrayed him in far pettier ways, years ago, who are *still* down there." Why had Altman agreed to help this woman and her infernal boss? She'd made him promises, the kind of promises that would change his life for the better forever, but only if her side won. Altman hadn't worked for Sanford long, but he'd worked for him long enough to know that losing wasn't something that happened to the magus often, if ever.

"He's got a basement full of oubliettes?" Gloria said. "I can't imagine those do much for the property values."

Altman shuddered. "Oubliettes would be better. When

you put someone in an oubliette, you forget about them, and they just die after a while. Sanford doesn't forget." Altman stared out at the weathered boards of the dilapidated saloon. "Sanford remembers, and he gets revenge."

"Sanford won't be getting much of anything, pretty soon," Gloria said. "My employer appreciates the tip-off, but it's hardly necessary. Mr Tillinghast deliberately goaded Sanford, hoping he would take rash action. Everything is proceeding just as he anticipated."

"The magus is a lot more formidable than you seem to think," Altman said. "My brother told me stories, and I've seen a few things in my months under the man's wing. He's survived attempted coups before. The people who tried to overthrow him are the ones in the basements."

"I understand," Gloria said. "And my employer understands as well. We are prepared for resistance."

"It's just…" Altman cut his eyes toward Gloria, then looked away. Maybe it was foolish to reveal his misgivings, but what if Gloria could actually reassure him? "What you promised me. It only works if you beat Sanford. Really beat him. You can't just topple him. You have to take him off the board entirely. I'm not convinced you can do that."

"Then why did you agree to our terms?" Gloria seemed genuinely curious.

"Because I'm not convinced Sanford can beat *you*, either, and it seemed sensible to hedge my bets. I'm not going to move against him openly, though, or even defy his direct orders, because if Sanford *does* win, I want to remain in his good books. But… I'll do this much. I'll tip you off about his plans. And I'll slow things down when I can. Ruby is going to come after dark to steal anything from the shop worth taking. The arsonist I hired, Gas-Can McGann, will start splashing his namesake around once she's done. I don't know who O'Bannion is sending to kill Tillinghast, but I told him I needed his best, and with what Sanford's paying, that's what we're going to get. If Tillinghast survives until morning I'm honestly not sure what Sanford will do. But he's got powerful relics, and other things, down in that vault, and if he comes at you with those, he'll be a lot harder to stop than a team of hired criminals. If the mundane approach fails, I think Sanford is going to escalate matters."

"I see. I suspect that Mr Tillinghast will, nevertheless, decline to die. Burning up in a fire in order to avoid greater problems in the future doesn't seem like a sound strategy."

Altman groaned. "Yes, I know, it's just… things are going to get ugly, Gloria. Be prepared for that."

"I am prepared for anything. That's why Mr Tillinghast employs me. Don't worry about a thing. Nothing to come will reflect badly on you, at least, not until Sanford is neutralized. You have my promise." She patted him on the arm, then slid out of the car and disappeared into the night.

Altman considered going back into the roadhouse for a drink, or ten, but instead, he cranked up the engine, and returned to the Lodge, to tell Sanford that everything was arranged.

# CHAPTER FOURTEEN
*Sleeping Dogs*

Sanford finally found Sarah Van Shaw, who was out patrolling the grounds again, peering at holes in the ground. "Warden!" he bellowed, his patience fully expended on greater matters. "Why haven't you tracked down the person who delivered that accursed package?"

Van Shaw rose and turned to face him, and she was... smiling? In an abstracted, faraway manner, but yes, it was definitely a smile, as foreign on her stony face as a flower blossoming on an ice floe. "I did, at least as far as I could. I left a note on your desk with my findings."

There *had* been notes on his desk, quite a few, but he'd assumed they were messages from the pretty blond Initiate who acted as his secretary. He'd been neglecting his usual duties, skipping meetings and failing to return calls, as Tillinghast took up more and more of his attention. "I didn't see them," he snapped. "So you might as well tell me now."

The warden nodded her head in acquiescence. "One of the newer Initiates, a Mr Detwiller, found the package just outside the front gates." Van Shaw wasn't looking at him, but past him, gazing so intently at nothing that Sanford nearly turned to look over his shoulder to see what captivated her so much. "It bore an engraved card that said, 'For Mr Carl Sanford, care of the Silver Twilight Lodge,' and though the box was unusually damp, Mr Detwiller believed it had simply been caught in the rain after being left carelessly outside by a courier. He brought it in and left it on your desk." She pursed her lips. "We have had a frank and thorough conversation in the garden shed, in the company of two of my hounds."

Sanford didn't shudder, but someone else might have. The shed was a ramshackle wooden construction, hidden out back among the trees, and while it did indeed hold various gardening implements, it held other implements, too – ones Van Shaw had proven adept at using more than once. Even to be in the presence of those tools, some allowed to rust and others distressingly gleaming, had a tendency to concentrate the mind. The Lodge had very few repeat offenders when it came to trespassing. Most were simply scared away, but those who'd committed more serious offenses, with more malicious intent, would never have to fear anything ever again. Van Shaw was not just warden, but groundskeeper – and not just groundskeeper, but gravedigger.

She went on. "The Initiate now knows, in the future, to bring any such packages to me for inspection first. I believe I made the point forcefully enough. I have also made arrangements for him to be lightly disciplined by a Seeker in one of the lesser sanctums, though you may, of course, choose to alter those instructions."

Sanford shook his head, scowling. "No, that's fine. So there was no conspiracy with Tillinghast, then? No snakes loose in our henhouse?"

"I believe Mr Detwiller acted all in all innocence," Van Shaw said. "His crime was foolishness, which is serious enough, but there was no treachery there. Beyond that, I cannot say. If you wish me to test *all* the Lodge members for loyalty, that can be arranged, and the results can be definitive, but the process will be time-consuming and not pleasant."

"Thank you, warden, but I think a more targeted approach will suffice." Sanford should have been reassured that Tillinghast didn't have spies inside the Lodge, doing his bidding... but of course, he still might. He just hadn't used them for the gambit with the package. Which might mean he was saving them for bigger, better, nastier things. Still, killing the shopkeeper should have a chilling effect on the loyalty of anyone he'd coopted, Sanford thought. "Carry on, warden. We'll talk later."

"As you wish, master." She went back to staring at the hole in the ground, but Sanford was almost certain she wasn't looking at anything so much as simply lost in her own thoughts. As he walked away, she let out a little sigh, but not a put-upon one, or a disappointed one. The sound indicated... contentment? Van Shaw was stoic, as a rule, but not content.

He shook his head as he returned to the Lodge. He

couldn't worry about his warden's peculiar emotional state right now. He was supposed to have lunch with the mayor, and he really shouldn't put the blowhard off again. For all Sanford knew, Tillinghast had sent his honor some little bauble, too, and that was a connection he couldn't bear to see poisoned.

Sanford endured a thoroughly tedious lunch in the lavish dining room of the Excelsior Hotel. The chop was properly cooked, but the conversation was decidedly underdone. The mayor spent most of the meal greeting his donors as they passed by – the hotel restaurant being a popular destination for local lawyers and businessmen – and delivering the usual bland half-promises he exhibited in lieu of conversation, but Sanford saw no sign the man had been ensorcelled. Sanford even mentioned Tillinghast, and suggested the mayor might take a look at the status of his business license and lease agreements. "I've heard rumors that an unlicensed amateur electrician is rewiring his shop. It's shameful the risks people take to save money, isn't it?" The mayor promised to look into the matter, as he always acceded to Sanford's requests, but showed no reaction to the interloper's name. Sanford was provisionally reassured.

After extricating himself from the mayor's hearty farewell handshake, Sanford strode toward the lobby… and stopped dead when he saw Sarah Van Shaw emerge from the lift, wearing a hat with a feather bobbing in the brim, and a blue dress that made her look ten years younger than usual. A moment later he realized she was also wearing makeup, and delicate shoes with heels, instead of her usual black boots.

Sanford hadn't become head of the Order and the ruler

of Arkham's magical community by being easily shocked, or indecisive in the face of a sudden challenge, so he walked straight up to the warden, noted the brief flash of utter horror on her face, and then took her firmly by the arm.

"My dear Sarah," he murmured. "Perhaps you'll join me for a drink?" He steered her toward the hotel bar, and she came along, unresisting and without speaking a word.

Sanford deposited her in a back booth, shook his head at the questioning look of the bartender, and then sat down across from his errant associate. "Why have you deserted your post, warden? Now, in this time of trouble, when we are beset by the machinations of a devilish outsider who is *proven* to mean us harm?" He was furious, so much so that he could feel a vein throbbing in his temple, but he was also astonished. The warden never left the Lodge, except under the most pressing circumstances, and certainly for nothing frivolous.

She bowed her head. "Master… I just… I needed some, some time to myself–"

"I can't believe I need to say this," he seethed through clenched teeth. "As the head of the Silver Twilight Lodge, I invoke your oaths of loyalty and obedience, and demand that you answer me truthfully."

Van Shaw slumped back in the booth, her posture limp and defeated. "I have not deserted my post." Her tone was flat. "I am there even now, doing my duty, as diligently as always." A spark of defiance flared in her eyes. "And so, you have no cause to reprimand me, master. My oaths are fully upheld."

"What do you mean you're – wait." Sanford fished in his

vest pocket for a pair of pince-nez spectacles with bluish lenses. The glasses weren't as powerful as his Hermetic Mirror, being unable to pierce illusions or differentiate between malicious and beneficial magic, but like the topaz loupe he kept in his desk, these lenses could reveal the presence of the unseen.

He peered through the spectacles and saw a silver thread attached to the back of Sarah Van Shaw's head, trailing away across the room until it disappeared into a wall, leading in the direction of the Lodge. "Is this some form of bodily bilocation?" Sanford said. "Do you mean to say you've created some sort of mystical homunculus, and you're using an astral connection to operate it remotely, sharing in its senses and sensations?" He shook his head. "This is impressive magic, warden, and far outside the scope of your usual abilities. What exactly are you using this newfound freedom *for*?"

"To sleep in a feather bed," she said, voice sharp and full of snarls. "To take a hot bath for as long as I like. To wear something soft, to drink something bubbly, to feel pretty! I am a person, master. I am more than just a guard dog, bred to obedience!"

Sanford was taken aback. Van Shaw's loyalty to the Lodge was absolute. Indeed, it was magically compelled, the result of a complex ritual that had granted her numerous privileges and powers in exchange for her fealty. Sanford had never sensed even a hint of dissatisfaction in her manner before. "What brought on this tantrum? And how did you come to develop this power, anyway? Did you – no." The answer was obvious and as chilling as a sword of ice to the heart. "Was it him? Tell me the truth, warden. Your oaths command you. Did Tillinghast give you this power?"

Van Shaw shook her head. "I've never met the man."

"Then how–" He pounded his fist on the table. As if he could be undone by semantics! The fact that the warden was trying to slither away from telling the whole truth was disturbing enough. "Was it the woman, then? Gloria Dyer?"

The warden nodded, a sour look on her face.

"You *know* she is his creature!" Sanford had to restrain himself from shouting. "How could you betray the Order this way?"

"I have done *nothing* to betray the Order." Her voice was ferocious and certain. She crossed her arms and fixed him with her steeliest gaze, but Sanford refused to be intimidated by an underling, not even the warden. "I am guarding the Lodge right now, as always."

"You have betrayed me by consorting with my enemies." He wanted to kick over the table, and though he resisted that urge he couldn't help himself raising his voice. "And I *am* the Order, warden!"

"I know that you believe that," Van Shaw said calmly. "You might wish to berate me more quietly, master, lest you draw unwanted attention to yourself."

The impudence! The temerity! "What did Dyer give you?" Sanford said. "What bauble did Tillinghast use to enchant you? Tell me! As long as I am head of the Lodge you *will* obey me."

"As long as you are, I will," she murmured. The warden reached into the neck of her dress and drew out a pendant with a little silver charm dangling from the end.

Sanford reached across the table, lighting quick, and yanked the chain off her throat. Van Shaw gasped, wailed, and then vanished, without so much as a puff of smoke. Her dress collapsed, empty, and her hat landed upside down on the table, the feather crushed beneath. The silver thread vanished into the wall, like a line being reeled in.

Sanford hadn't expected a result that dramatic, and he looked around to make sure no one else had witnessed the disappearance. Fortunately, the bartender was busy with a customer at the far end of the room, and there were no other patrons nearby.

He looked at the charm in his hand. It was the symbol for Gemini, the twins. That made a certain amount of sense, symbolically speaking. Sanford was briefly tempted to put the necklace on. Being in two places at once could be quite useful.

But this charm came from Tillinghast, and his gifts had hooks hidden inside them, just like a fisherman's bait. It might not work for him, anyway. The shopkeeper seemed adept at tailoring his gifts solely for their intended recipients. Sanford put the charm in his pocket instead, rose, and left the hotel bar.

He could scarcely believe the *warden* had turned on him. The warden! If someone with her years of loyal service could be compromised, then no one was safe. And how had Tillinghast won her over? Had he done something to her mind, or simply made her an offer she found irresistible? Sanford hadn't realized Van Shaw was unhappy. The thought had never even occurred to him. Why would it? He never thought of her as a person. She was a fixture of the Lodge. You didn't wonder if your furnace was unhappy, or your icebox; you only cared if they worked or not. And right now... she didn't work.

He had compelled her to answer him honestly with her oaths, but that didn't mean she'd told him the whole truth, and indeed, she'd proven a willingness to dissemble. She might be working against him even now!

Tillinghast was a worm, crawling through Sanford's life, rotting it from the inside out.

He stopped at a phone booth and called the Lodge, demanding to speak to Altman, who answered quickly. "Have the warden seized and locked up downstairs," he said without preamble.

Altman paused for only a moment, and then, with his usual practicality, asked, "What about her dogs?"

A fair question. Even the fearless feared those hounds. "Tell her you are acting on *my* orders, with the authority of the head of the Lodge, and she will know the truth of your words, and her hounds will not interfere."

"All right," Altman said. "Anything else?"

A sudden inspiration struck him, irresistible. "Yes," Sanford said. "Tell O'Bannion we won't need his... pest control specialist. I am going to take care of the last part of the job personally."

"Are you sure that's a good idea, sir?"

"It's *my* idea," Sanford said. "So of course it is."

Just after nightfall, Ruby checked in with the watchers Sanford had set to spy on Tillinghast's shop. They confirmed that no one had entered or left the premises all day, by front or back doors. They reported seeing a light go on upstairs, and glimpsing a moving figure through the windows, so Tillinghast was presumably puttering around, maybe having dinner, if the old lizard did anything so mundane.

Now it was full dark, and Ruby had to go and steal from him.

She'd tried calling Gloria to give her a warning about the night's plan, but the woman hadn't answered, probably out running more errands for her boss. Ruby was going to have to play this situation straight, and as the magus commanded. If Sanford's plan succeeded, and Tillinghast fell, well, then she'd pretend her loyalty to Sanford had never faltered. And if this theft-fire-murder gambit didn't succeed, she'd have to find a way to get the grail back to Tillinghast later, along with the Ruby of R'lyeh, probably. What a mess. That was the problem with double-crosses – they got you all crossed up.

Ruby emerged from the shadows, dressed in grays and blacks, almost like a shadow herself. Her area of expertise was upper-story work, climbing onto rooftops and unlatching high windows from the outside, ghosting in and out of museums and lavish homes and jewelry stores. Sending her to break into a shop on the ground floor of a building was like getting Babe Ruth to bat cleanup in a neighborhood sandlot game. The fact that the owner of the shop was home made it slightly more dangerous, and the fact that she was secretly *working* for the owner even more so, but they were minor difficulties for someone with her skills.

And, in truth, she didn't even need her skills, because

she had her New Accelerator. Ruby stopped just outside Tillinghast's back door and set her watch back an hour. The sound of the breeze cut off abruptly, and she grinned, thrilled by the power, and the secret. She was like a ghost now – a sort of *time* ghost. "Ruby the Zeitgeist," she muttered. She could think of worse nicknames.

Her lockpicks made short work of Tillinghast's door, and she breezed into the shop. Once inside, she stared around the dim space in amazement. Everything looked exactly the same as it had when she visited Tillinghast's earlier location, in Northside. The man must have a fanatical level of attention to detail. Even the rugs were in the same positions on the floor, and the merchandise on the tables and shelves were arranged just as she remembered, too. Did he have a diagram he made his workers follow as they unpacked?

She shrugged, dismissing the issue as irrelevant, and did a quick circuit of the shop. She shone her flashlight around without hesitation. There was no danger of passersby catching a glimpse of her light through a window, after all, when she was safely ensconced in null-time.

The Grail of Dreams was there on the counter, just as Sanford had said it would be, underneath a glass dome. The grail looked just like the fake she'd acquired at the docks, a cup nearly a foot high from base to rim, cut into elaborate facets, made of some black stone that seemed to drink in the light. This one had an indescribable *something more* to it, though – not a shimmer, not a glow, but just a presence, like it was more real than everything around it, somehow made of a different order of matter.

She'd been in the presence of relics before – real relics, old ones, not things like the watch Tillinghast had made for her – and so the sensation was unpleasantly familiar. Looking at the goblet was like gazing into an abyss of deep time, where hideous old things still dwelled.

Speaking of time, hers was ticking away. Ruby opened her capacious leather bag and set it on the counter, then reached for the glass dome.

"Hello, Ruby," Tillinghast purred as he stepped out from the curtain behind the counter. "Have you come to do a little after-hours shopping?"

She stared at him, wide-eyed, as frozen as *he* should have been from her vantage point in null-time.

Tillinghast leaned on the counter and cocked an eyebrow at her. "Oh, I see. You're surprised I can perceive you, since I should be stuck in the unflowing flow of time right now, hmm? Did you really think I'd give you a weapon you could use against me, Ruby?" He clucked his tongue. "As soon as you activated the watch, I knew, and I chose to join you here, in between moments. I'd hate for you to get lonely. It can be so *very* lonely, stuck in this timeless time. As you may learn, to your dismay, very soon."

She started to step back, but he darted his hand across the counter and grabbed her wrist, tight as a manacle, and held her in place. "Explain yourself." The gentility in his voice was wearing away.

"Sanford sent me to steal the grail," she said. "I couldn't refuse him, not without giving myself away and getting locked up in the basement. He has people watching me, watching the shop, right now!" She tried to pull away, but his hand might as well have been made of stone. "I tried to call Gloria to tell her I was coming, but she didn't answer! What was I supposed to do?"

"You could have returned to Sanford empty-handed and told him the grail wasn't here," Tillinghast said reasonably. "That you sought it and could not find it."

It was Ruby's turn to cluck her tongue. "This isn't just a test, Mr Tillinghast. It's a loyalty test. Sanford is suspicious of me. He's suspicious of everyone, lately. If I came back empty-handed, he'd never believe me. He'd lock me up in a cell in the Lodge basement and start asking questions, and he has ways of compelling truthful answers. I've been in one of those cells before, and I don't relish the idea of revisiting it."

"Oh, dear! A cell!" Tillinghast shook his head. "You should have accepted the captivity and trusted that I would set you free when I gained my ascendance over Sanford. Because you see, Ruby... I can trap you somewhere *so* much worse than a cell." He dragged her closer to him and put his face near hers. Ruby noticed that the whites of his eyes were actually a sickly yellow. "I can strand you in null-time. To live forever among the statues of your fellow humans, never again to hear a human voice, never again to feel a loving touch. I have that power. That is the cell where *I* can imprison you, Ruby: a prison of time itself."

"No," Ruby whispered, her wonderland transformed into a realm of nightmare. Slipping between moments was only a miracle if she could decide when it started, and when it stopped. Fleeing a cult in the swamps was paradise in comparison: at least in that situation there was the possibility of escape.

"If you are disloyal to me, you are useless to me," Tillinghast said. "And if you are useless to me, why should I allow you to be useful to anyone else, especially my enemies?"

"No, please, Mr Tillinghast, I *do* want to work for you. I'm grateful, I was just scared, I made a mistake, you can see that, can't you?" Ruby knew she was babbling, but her horror at the thought of being stranded here was so great she couldn't stop herself. She had no doubt Tillinghast could do what he said – that his gift had always held this trap within it, from the very beginning.

"I believe you." Tillinghast released her and returned to leaning easily on the counter. "Because I see the fear in your eyes, and fear is a great motivator. Far greater, in my experience, than gratitude. Never forget that I can strand you in null-time whenever I wish, Miss Standish. Even if you toss the watch into the sea, that won't save you. You have been touched by this timeless place, you see, and its mark is upon you. Its *stain* is upon you. I can send you here and bring you back any time I wish, with a snap of my fingers." He snapped them then, and the air changed, the sound of wind whistling around the gutters revealing that time was flowing again. Another snap, and the sound ceased, and Ruby whimpered. Did her watch even possess this magic in itself, or was it simply a prop Tillinghast used to fool her as he imposed his own power over her? The latter seemed horribly likely. That would explain why the dogs hadn't been troubled by her wearing the watch into the Lodge.

"Will you serve me?" His voice was scales sliding over sand.

"Yes," she whispered, but though she was bowed, she was not broken. "But why? Why are you doing all this? You're a collector of relics. Why do you have your heart set on casting Carl Sanford down? Why try to take over the Lodge at all? Do you just want to loot the treasury?"

"Your *former* employer, Carl Sanford, asked me something similar this morning." Tillinghast half smiled, amused. "Why am I in Arkham? What do I want here? I told him that it was my personal business, and not for him to know. I am tempted to tell you the same thing, if only to remind you of our relative positions in this relationship... but the truth is, I like you, Ruby. I've liked you ever since I sent you to steal that statue from those swamp-dwelling degenerates, and you acquitted yourself so admirably. So I will tell you, in the broadest possible outlines, why I am here. I am undertaking a Great Work. Do you understand?"

"You're doing some kind of ritual?" Ruby said.

Tillinghast nodded. "There are various Great Works. For the Hermetic mystics, the Great Work was the eradication of unconscious desire, and the consequent acquisition of total self-knowledge." He waved a hand. "I achieved *that* ages ago. Those cretins who follow Crowley, the Thelemites, have their own Great Work, meant to unify the self with the universe, until there is no longer any division between the two – to merge ego and nothingness." Tillinghast scoffed. "Such a desire demonstrates a profound lack of understanding regarding the true nature of the universe, but never mind. My Great Work is unique to me, however. I seek not to change myself – for how could I improve upon perfection? – but instead to change the world, Miss

Standish. There are those who would stand in the way of my ritual, if they ever apprehended its scope. Carl Sanford is one such."

Tillinghast spoke with such venom that Ruby realized he hated Sanford, which meant he saw the magus as a genuine threat.

Tillinghast went on: "Despite Sanford's frequent traffic with otherworldly forces, he is profoundly attached to this world as it is currently constituted, because he enjoys his power, and wealth, and prestige, and privilege, and he loves this city. He would rightly consider my plans a threat to the status quo, and he would endeavor to stop me."

"But… what is the ritual going to do?"

Something to Arkham? She thought. Or to the *world*?

He showed his teeth. "You'll see. *Everyone* will see. My ritual is delicate, and thus vulnerable to disruption. I cannot properly begin the Work until Sanford is removed from the equation. Moreover, he has resources that will be useful in the course of my work, and he will hardly share them willingly. So he must be removed." The shopkeeper sighed. "Sadly, he has many defenses, both magical and practical, that make simple assassination difficult. To neutralize him, I must first remove all those things he values: his power, his wealth, his prestige, his privilege. His employees. His allies. His house, and its many interesting basements. His *everything*. I have been poking, and poking, and poking at him, to unravel his composure, to make him act rashly, to tempt him into committing an error. When he inevitably does, I will send him into exile, and even if he survives that, he will have nothing to come back to." Tillinghast's eyes seemed to shine. "Is that a sufficient explanation, Miss Standish?"

"Yes," she croaked. "So... removing Sanford isn't even the point? It's just the prelude to something else?"

"A bit like stripping the old paint from the wall before applying a fresh coat, yes." Tillinghast grinned, wolfish. "Wouldn't your magus be outraged to know that my campaign against him is the equivalent of removing a stone from my shoe before setting out on a long walk?" He slammed his palms down on the counter suddenly, making Ruby jump. "So! Let's discuss how you can help in my efforts. Come upstairs with me. I don't have a good knife down here, and I'm going to need a little bit of blood for the next part. I'm afraid I don't have any of my own to spare, so..."

# CHAPTER FIFTEEN
*Armed and Armored*

"What's all this, then?" Altman asked. He'd tracked Sanford down to that strange office in the basements, the one he'd stolen from his early rival and kept in situ as a trophy.

The magus set an assortment of metal strongboxes, drawn from drawers and secret panels, on the desk. He then opened them up, one by one, to reveal an assortment of oddments, one to each box. There was a pale pink ring segmented like an earthworm; another ring of gold, with a chip of broken tooth instead of a gem in its setting; a tiepin in the form of an undulating eel; cufflinks in the shape of tiny cubes, one of ebony and one of ivory; a pocket watch with its silver case elaborately decorated with spirals and other geometric figures; and a bracelet that seemed to be made of scores of tiny metal keys wired together.

"I do not go into battle without armor and arms." As he spoke, Sanford slipped on the rings, clipped the pin to his tie, tucked the pocket watch into his vest, and then, with some effort, fastened the cufflinks into his sleeves. "These are items from my collection of relics, and they provide personal security, among other things. I used to have a ring that could shield me from certain death, but, sadly, I used that during the unpleasantness last year. I'm glad I did, of course, or I wouldn't be here now, but I still keenly feel its lack."

"It's a shame my brother didn't have a ring like that," Altman said. "During the unpleasantness."

Sanford grunted. "He wouldn't have used it anyway. He would have insisted I take it, instead. Your brother was devoted to the Lodge... and devoted to me, which is the same thing, of course. He was willing to die for the cause." The old man looked at Altman levelly. "Are you?"

"How about I just stick to killing for the cause?" Altman replied. "I'm more use to you that way than I would be dead."

The magus shrugged. "Fair enough. You are not your brother, but you have still proven yourself invaluable." Sanford put his hand on Altman's shoulder, and Altman bore it, though he wanted to shake it off – not so much because of discomfort over his betrayal, though that was a factor, but because he didn't know what those rings Sanford was wearing could *do*. "It's time to go to the shop and smoke out Tillinghast. Then, once he's seen his building turned to ashes, his precious things reduced to rubble... I'll finish him."

"What exactly do you plan to *do*, sir? Just shoot him down in the street?"

"Oh, I'll stab him, I think," Sanford mused. "With my sword cane."

"You can't murder a man on the streets of Arkham!"

Altman protested. "We should at least take him somewhere more private first. I can see you might not want him in the basements, but there's always the warden's shed–"

"Every moment that serpent lives, he drips his venom!" Sanford shouted, suddenly furious, and it took an effort of will for Altman not to cringe away. "Tillinghast has already taken my warden from me. I won't give him a moment to take anything else. The Initiates will ensure there are no bystanders nearby, and if anyone *should* see us, we'll deal with that later. You can always stand as my witness, and say Tillinghast went mad and attacked me, and I was only defending myself." He waved an impatient hand. "These are just details, Altman. They aren't important." Sanford picked up his cane from where it leaned against the desk and tucked it under his arm. He checked the time on the unusual pocket watch, then grunted and returned it to his vest pocket. "Let us make haste."

Altman had promised the Dyer woman he wouldn't interfere with their plans for Sanford – that, and providing information, was the only price he had to pay for the rewards he was promised – but what did "don't interfere" mean, exactly? Did driving Sanford across town to murder Gloria's employer count as interference?

Well, Altman could hardly refuse. The magus was in a murderous mood, and Altman wasn't convinced he could best the man if it came to blows. Sanford was older, and less strong in a purely physical sense, but he was also craftier… and now, armed and armored. It was better to go on playing the loyal lackey for now. "I'll get the car ready, sir."

•••

Before they left the Lodge, Sanford stopped by the warden's cell. He looked through the metal grate set in the door and found her standing perfectly still in the center of the small, grimy room, her hands clasped in front of her, her eyes fixed on Sanford… or maybe just staring at nothing, with Sanford in her eyeline. "Sarah," he murmured. "I never expected you, of all people, to turn on me."

She didn't reply. She seemed to be waiting. "What are you waiting for?" he demanded. "What do you expect to happen? Do you think your hounds will save you? I think you'll find that your oaths to the Lodge will prevent them from–"

"I am waiting for a change," Van Shaw said, voice calm and uninflected. "Everything changes, master. The poet said, 'No life lives forever, and dead men rise up never, and even the weariest river winds somewhere safe to sea.' Have you forgotten?"

"I have seen dead men rise up," Sanford snapped. "And another poet said, 'With strange aeons, even death may die.' I think you'll find *I* won't die until it suits me, and while I live, you will regret your betrayal."

"I never betrayed the Silver Twilight Lodge," she said. "I cannot, any more than I could choose to stop my heart from beating. I simply came to believe you were no longer the best choice to rule the Lodge. Because you care only for yourself, Sanford."

"I *am* the Silver Twilight Lodge!" he shouted, shaking the barred window. "The Order was just another milquetoast mystery cult before I made it into something great! What did you think we were *doing* here?"

"Discovering great and hidden knowledge, and preserving it," she said. "And I am confident that work will continue when you are… gone." A half smile touched her lips, and Sanford drew back, as if scalded.

"I know I haven't been… warm with you, warden, but your nature hardly invites warmth, does it? You exist to fulfill your function, like a lock on a door. Should I have brought you little fairy cakes and tea? Given you the occasional holiday?" He scoffed.

"That would have gone a long way toward cultivating a degree of personal rather than institutional loyalty, yes," the warden said. "But it's too late now. Are you off to kill Tillinghast?"

"He's the *first* one I'm going to kill, yes," Sanford said, voice heavy with menace.

"Go on, then." She made a gesture with her fingers, like she was flicking away a fly. "I wish him luck." The warden turned her back on him and looked at the rear wall of the cell instead. The bloodstains didn't seem to disturb her at all.

Sanford bit back the retorts that occurred to him. He was wasting time here. Altman was waiting upstairs with the car. He'd deal with the warden later. Perhaps death was too kind. He could exile her through one of the many doors in the basement, the ones that led to *other* places, and let her attachment to the Lodge slowly sap her will and weaken her, until the denizens of those realms could best her. Yes. That was tempting.

He turned and strode down the hallway, cane clicking on the weathered hardwood floors. Forget the warden. She was a symptom, not a cause. Tillinghast was the problem. He was the tumor, the canker, the source of all this decay. Once the shopkeeper was cut out of Arkham, the rot would stop spreading, and Sanford would be able to repair the damage done.

He found Altman in the Bentley, idling on the curb in front of the Lodge, and slipped into the backseat. They drove on toward the Merchant District... but Altman pulled over to the side when a fire truck rumbled past, and Sanford spat a curse, leaning forward. "Follow that truck, damn you!" he said.

Altman obeyed, and soon Sanford spied a glow in the evening sky. "It's burning already? That damnable firebug was supposed to give Ruby time to get the grail first and burn the shop later! What sort of idiot did you hire, Altman?"

"The best idiot available, sir," Altman said. "Gas-Can McGann is a professional. I don't know what happened."

They got as close to the fire as they could. The city had put up barriers in the street a block away, and a disheveled city policeman held up his hands when the Bentley approached. Altman parked, and Sanford climbed out of the car and stomped toward the barrier.

The officer blathered something at him, but Sanford ignored him, craning his neck to see the damage. The building that had once held Huntress Fashions was still mostly intact, and only smoldering now, the pumper truck sending gouts of water in through the broken display window up front and the smaller windows on the upper floor. The fire hadn't spread to the rest of the Merchant

District, which was a mercy. They were so close to the river that everyone worried about flooding, so losing the shops to a conflagration would have been a cruel irony.

"Was anyone hurt?" Sanford demanded. "Did the shopkeeper make it out?"

"What shopkeeper?" The policeman was a rangy young Irish man, glaring and pugnacious. "The building's been empty for months, and there's nothing to burn inside but dust. We figure a tramp broke in to get out of the weather and dropped a cigarette on a bundle of rags or something."

"No, that's not… there was a new shop there, just today."

The policeman looked at him like he was dotty and patted him on the arm. "It's all right, gramps. You must be thinking of some other shop. I heard from the boys with the hoses, and they said there's nobody and nothin' in the place. Don't worry so much. We got a report about the fire fast, and it didn't spread. No real harm done, as long as you don't own the building, but maybe you do, huh, driving a car like that? But there's always insurance."

Sanford scowled. Had Tillinghast outfoxed him *again*? "Was there… did you see a girl? Anywhere around here?" Ruby hadn't been caught in the fire, apparently, which was a mercy.

The cop shook his head and smirked. "Looking for a girl, huh? This ain't the right place for that. Why don't you head over to Hibb's Roadhouse?"

Sanford turned and stalked back to the car, where Altman stood leaning against the fender, watching the smoke rise in gray curls against a black sky. "We should find the Initiates. They must have seen what happened."

Altman nodded, and they set out walking around the block, through alleyways, and finally up a lowered fire escape ladder to the roof of a building diagonal from Tillinghast's burning shop. That's where the Initiates had set up their observation post, with clear lines of sight on every exit, and even a partial view into the upper windows of the shop.

There were two figures standing at the low wall that bordered the rooftop, watching the fire, and Sanford felt a surge of irritation. They should have called, curse them. The Initiates on duty now were named Marlowe and Darrow, or Darling and Marley, or something like that – one was a penniless public defender, and one was the idle child of wealthy parents, though Sanford couldn't remember which. It hardly mattered. Your position and power in the world outside the Lodge was irrelevant to your rank inside it – there were Guardians of the Black Stone who scrubbed toilets for a living, and Initiates who ran banks, and within the Lodge, the former could order the latter around at will.

No one could order Sanford around, inside the Lodge or outside it, but he was an exception in so many ways.

He stormed across the roof, slamming his cane down with every step, and they turned to face him–

It wasn't Darrow and Marley. Or rather, it was *one* of them, the rich boy with the unhealthy pallor, but the other was Ruby. And she was holding a bulky leather bag in her arms.

There was a handkerchief wrapped around one hand, as if she'd hurt herself. Had she been injured while escaping from the burning building?

"Sanford!" she said. "I wasn't expecting to see you here. We just sent Dartmouth to call the Lodge and tell you about – well, everything."

"I am here now, so you may tell me directly." He spoke with great dignity, trying not to stare at the bundle in Ruby's arms. He shouldn't jump to conclusions. It could be anything. But it could also be the object of his ardent desires.

She sighed. "It was unexpected, Sanford. I broke in like we planned, didn't have any trouble there, and I found the grail, right where you said it would be. I nicked it and stuffed it in my bag, but before I could snatch up anything else, I heard movement upstairs. I knew Tillinghast was still there – well, I *thought* so, anyway – and it sounded like he was coming downstairs. I thought he'd heard me and figured I'd better scamper. I made it out the back, and off down the block, and the next thing I knew, the building was on fire. I don't know if your arsonist was extra eager to get started or what, but I shook a leg before the fire brigade showed up. Then I made my way up here, met with the boys, and, well, you're pretty much caught up." She shrugged.

She had it. She had the Grail of Dreams, right there, against her chest? Sanford wanted it... but not as badly as he wanted something else. Not *quite* as badly.

"Where is Tillinghast, then?" Sanford seized Marley or what have you by the lapels and shook him. "You were supposed to be watching, but he is gone, and the shop is empty!"

The young man's eyes were as wide as serving platters and

his mouth hung open, slack. "We did watch, Mr Sanford, I mean, master! We even saw him, or somebody anyway, through the windows upstairs, moving around every once in a while! He was in there, and he didn't come out the front *or* the back door."

"He must have gone *somewhere*, you worthless—"

"Tunnels, probably," Altman said mildly.

Sanford let the boy go and turned on his bodyguard. "What did you say?"

The thug shrugged. "There are tunnels all over Arkham, aren't there? French Hill is more tunnels than dirt underneath, as I understand it. Even over here in the Merchant District, there have to be, what, old smugglers' tunnels from colonial times, and soldiers' tunnels from the Revolutionary War days, and the bootleggers are always digging new ones, aren't they? Tillinghast probably slipped in and out of the shop through a tunnel in the cellar, and moved his stock in and out that way, too. He could have come out by the river, or in the basement of a neighboring building, and loaded all his goods on a truck without our bright boys on the rooftop seeing a thing."

Sanford frowned. "That is possible," he allowed. And more comforting than the idea that Tillinghast could move his shop, and himself, around by magic. Such things could be done, but meddling with occult portals and eldritch passageways was a dangerous business. Things lurked in the dark between places, and magic doors didn't always open where you wanted them to. Traversing such paths could twist your mind, as well, which was why Sanford preferred to take mundane journeys by car or train or ship. "I don't suppose we'll be able to get inside the building to confirm your theory anytime soon."

Altman shrugged. "Maybe Tillinghast escaped that way, and maybe he did it some other way, but what does it matter? The point is, Tillinghast is loose, again, and he probably suspects you're the one who tried to burn him out. I'm a little worried about how he's going to react to that. The Lodge is vulnerable right now, especially with the warden locked up…"

"Wait, why is the warden locked up?" Ruby interrupted.

Sanford cut them both off with a slash of his hand. "All right. We'll return to the Lodge, and make sure everything is secure. Then we'll figure out our next steps. Perhaps you'll have to go out to abduct the Dyer woman *again*, Altman, and actually succeed this time, hmmm?"

"I am at your service, as always," Altman said.

"Ruby, you can ride with me. Initiate, go home. You did a serviceable job." The foolish boy beamed at that. Any attention at all from the magus was better than praise from anyone else, Sanford knew.

He went down the fire escape, more slowly than he'd gone up it, and the others followed. Ruby managed the descent just fine with the bag slung over her shoulder. He desperately wanted to snatch it from her, tear it open, and look upon the bounty inside, but that would be undignified. There was time for all that once they made it back to the Lodge.

Besides, there was something delicious about the anticipation. Tonight hadn't gone entirely as planned, with setbacks and disappointments aplenty, but at least he'd gotten his hands on *one* prize.

When they made it back to the Bentley, the barriers were gone, and the cop was, too. The fire department had put sawhorses around the half-burned building, but there was nothing else in terms of security. Sanford was seized with an urge to go inside, find the basement, look for Tillinghast's secret tunnels… but Altman the pragmatist was right. There was no real reason to do so.

Plus, Sanford was a little afraid he wouldn't find any tunnels, and then he'd have to accept that Tillinghast's mastery of the occult surpassed his own. Sanford couldn't have spirited away an entire shop and himself in the blink of a magical eye, after all. Tillinghast, his superior? That was a thought that could not be borne. Sanford was the best there was, or ever had been. Simon Magus was a minor talent, John Dee was a dabbler, Agathodaemon was an amateur, Paracelsus a putterer. They all paled next to what Sanford had achieved in the realm of the mystic arts. He would not be dethroned by some… some *shopkeeper*.

He slid into the back of the Bentley with Ruby, who still clutched the bag close to her. As Altman drove them back to the Lodge, he leaned over and murmured, "Is it the real thing? You're sure? Not another replica?"

"This one is different." Ruby swallowed. "I can't really describe how, but the fake grail was just a big cup, and this one… it's something else. Something more. It's like it takes up more space than it should, or it's bigger than it looks. It sort of thrums, only without making a sound…" She sighed, clearly exasperated with the limitations of language, an experience that Sanford found all too familiar. He'd seen the real grail himself, noted how it seemed to distort the light around it, and how its presence seemed greater than mere physicality would suggest. Ruby was describing the same qualities. "I don't know what the cup does, but this is the cup that does it." She hesitated, then said, "What *does* the Grail of Dreams do? Why are you so keen to have it, anyway?"

Sanford's instinct was to brush her off – knowledge was most valuable when it was hoarded, after all – but she'd served him well, proven her loyalty, and was the only person tonight who hadn't disappointed him, and that list included himself. "The literature is unclear, the translations a bit suspect as usual, but overall... the grail makes dreams come true. The line I remember best is, 'The world of your dreams will be realized, and you will dwell there forevermore.' Now, it's possible that it means *literal* dreams, and not figurative ones, which could be dangerous."

Ruby shuddered. "I dream about my teeth falling out and people chasing me with torches through a swamp. I don't need to dwell in those, thanks."

"Indeed not. But I have schooled my mind over the years and am an adept lucid dreamer."

"What kind of dreamer?"

"Lucid. I am aware of the dream when I am dreaming. I don't believe it's real, as so many do when they slumber. No, when I dream, I do so consciously, and thus, I am capable of shaping the dreamworld to suit my own desires. It's quite entertaining. We are as gods, in our dreams, you know. I can teach you a few techniques, if you'd like to learn. It's just about building the right habits. My skills should give me an advantage if the grail really *does* interact with the holder's literal dreamscape."

"What are you planning to dream *about*, then?" Ruby said.

"Oh, I have so many dreams." Sanford smiled. In truth, he intended to do a great deal of research before he tried to use the grail at all, and he would start small with careful experiments. He'd known too many occultists who'd dabbled in the unknown and died, or been mutilated, or vanished, or *almost* vanished, leaving only a pair of smoking boots and a set of false teeth behind. Those fates were not for him.

They got to the Lodge and went inside, Sanford leading the way to his office. He pointed to his desk, and Ruby put the bag down on it. Then she drew back to stand with Altman by the door.

Sanford looked at the bag, resting where the sodden package from Tillinghast had so recently sat, and felt a triumphant burst of glee. Yes, Tillinghast was still a toad in Sanford's garden, but stealing the grail from him was a win, and Sanford would celebrate it. He'd put the grail away in a safe place, with the other relics he'd cleared out of his no-longer-invulnerable-vault. But first, he had to get a look at the thing. He unzipped the bag and looked inside.

The Grail of Dreams was there, standing upright – assuaging his deep-seated fear that he'd find a carved wooden copy or something inside the bag – and it still darkly thrummed. Something was different about it, though, or maybe he hadn't noticed this detail last time, in Tillinghast's shop. "There's something in the bottom of the cup."

Sanford turned on his desk lamp and moved it over, so the light shone down into the vessel. "It looks like… a little blood, still fresh. Why didn't it spill in all that jostling around? I wonder if the grail has preservative properties. Some of the literature suggested that a minor sacrifice was required to make the grail work. This may be a remnant of the last ritual."

Ruby and Altman said something, but their voices were far away and strangely inaudible. The grail was still *thrumming*, and no, it wasn't a sound, or at least, not one you heard with your ears. It was a song in the mind. It was singing: *yours, yours, I'm yours, I'm yours, I belong to you, I belong with you, take me, take me, take this up and let it be yours.*

Sanford reached down to pick up the grail, watching his hands as if they belonged to another person entirely. He wouldn't normally handle a relic like this so cavalierly, with bare hands and no precautions, but there was something about it, something that drew him, something that entranced him, and he simply had to touch the cup to his lips.

*The grail is my bauble*, he thought, horror bubbling up in his mind. *Tillinghast has given me the object of my desire, and that means–*

Sanford's hands touched the grail. He lifted it free of the bag, and up, and pressed the cold stone rim to his lips. Would he drink the blood? He didn't even feel disgust. He just felt a sort of mild curiosity.

Something warm broke over the chill of the stone, and wet his lips–

And then the world was transformed into swirling prismatic black.

# CHAPTER SIXTEEN
*New Management*

Ruby screamed, or tried to, but Altman was right there, clamping a hand over her mouth and shushing her. "Be quiet!" he hissed. "You'll alert the Initiates! We can't let them know what happened!"

She wrenched herself away and spun to glare at him. "Let *them* know what happened? We don't even know what happened!" She circled the desk, staring at the Grail of Dreams like it was a venomous serpent. The grail had fallen on its side when Sanford, well, "dropped it" wasn't quite right, was it? It was more that the hands holding the grail had disappeared, along with the person those hands were attached to. The blood wasn't trickling out, though. In fact, peering into the cup, the blood seemed to be gone entirely. Had Sanford actually tasted that blood? How hideously intimate.

Back in the apartment over the shop, Tillinghast had taken a small silver knife and cut the back of Ruby's hand, painless as a razor slice, and then directed her to let the drops fall into the grail. Her hand shook as she complied. He hadn't cut her deeply, but the fact that he'd cut her at all was ominous. What if he felt moved to cut her again?

"Amateurs often slice the palms of their hands when they need blood for a ritual," the man said conversationally. "It's a foolish thing to do. Human palms are full of veins and muscles and all sorts of important components, and they're terribly sensitive to pain as well. Plus, every time you flex the hand, you risk reopening the wound. Whereas the back of the hand, if you don't cut too deeply or slash across the tendons, will provide ample blood without limiting the use of the hand much at all." He watched the blood flow, then whipped out a handkerchief and offered it. Ruby took it, careful to avoid touching his fingers with her own, and wrapped the cloth around her wound. "Now that the blood is in the cup, the grail is... active. Don't touch it with your bare hands, or any other part of your flesh, for that begins the ritual, and you will feel a particular compulsion to complete it. The next person to touch this object should be Carl Sanford. And, believe me, he won't be able to resist doing so." Tillinghast beamed at her. "See? You get to steal the grail after all, and thus prove your loyalty to Sanford, and still serve me, all at the same time. Isn't that elegant?"

"What will happen to Sanford, when he touches the grail?" she asked.

"Why, his dreams will come true. Or someone's dreams, at any rate. Oh, don't worry, it won't kill him. I wish he could be so easily killed! That would make this much easier.

Though also rather less entertaining, and I do so love to be entertained. Killing a man is much less fun than removing the stones from the foundation of his world, one at a time, and watching that world crumble."

"You and I have different definitions of fun, Mr Tillinghast. I like taking in a show or playing cards with the girls, myself."

"It would be, as they say, a funny old world if we were all the same." He clapped his hands. "Get your gloves on – or your glove, I suppose the handkerchief will do for your other hand – and put the grail in the bag. It's best if you go on your way and deliver it to Sanford." The old man's eyes twinkled. "There's about to be a terrible fire here."

"What about all your stock?"

"What stock?" he asked, and shooed her away.

When Ruby went down the stairs, she was astonished to find that Tillinghast's wares were all gone, and the shop was as empty as it had been the day after Diana's departure from Arkham. Even the screens and shelves and curtains were gone. She hadn't been upstairs for *that* long – how had he cleared the space so quickly? Ah, but Tillinghast had given her the New Accelerator, and if he had one such relic, he might have others, and Gloria or some other employees – or *retainers* – of Tillinghast's could have been flitting away in null-time for hours while she was bleeding in Diana's old kitchen.

She hurried out the door – the *old* door; even Tillinghast's new one, with the sigil of the eye, was gone now – and into the alley. If Sanford's arsonist was watching, she didn't see him. But then there was a crash of breaking glass, and a great *whump!* and when she looked back, fires were dancing in the windows upstairs. She clutched the grail, wet with her blood, primed for its terrible work, to her chest, and–

"–the hell did he *go*?" Altman said, snapping Ruby back to the present. He was leaning over the desk, glaring down at the grail like he could dissolve it through the force of his will. "I don't see any scorch marks, or any, ah, residue, so I don't think he spontaneously combusted. Was he transported someplace? Is he, what, inhabiting one of his own dreams now? Is that what the grail does? Lets you bodily travel into your own mind?" Altman made a sour face and shook his head. "Sounds like a living nightmare to me. Why did he even touch the thing?"

"Maybe Tillinghast planned this." Ruby spoke slowly, gathering her thoughts. She had to tread carefully now. Altman was loyal to Sanford and probably the closest thing to a friend the old man had, even if they'd only known each other for a few months. She sometimes thought Sanford forgot this man wasn't his *first* confidant named Altman. Though to be fair, the brothers Altman were similar in appearance and demeanor, and to be scathingly accurate, Sanford tended to view most people as basically interchangeable anyway. The point was, she didn't want to give Altman any reason to doubt her. She had no doubt he was an experienced and remorseless killer. "This whole thing could have been some kind of ruse, you know? Maybe Tillinghast let me steal the grail, knowing how badly Sanford wanted it, and set the fire himself. Maybe the grail was even enchanted, like the other gifts Tillinghast has been passing out, and Sanford was drawn to touch it."

"That could be," Altman said. "He's normally more careful. When we found that wet box on the desk, we took it to an operating theater and treated it like an unexploded bomb." Altman reached down for the bag, which the grail was still on top of, and wiggled the leather around until the grail settled back inside it again, then swiftly closed the bag around it. He nodded firmly and stepped back. Ruby had to stifle a laugh. Altman was a man of action, and he needed to *act*, or at least feel like he was doing something useful.

He looked at her and said, "We should try to find him, right? We could ask the Scholar downstairs where he went. She knows things."

Ruby shrugged. "It seems like Sanford would have asked her about the grail already, but we can try if you like." What Ruby really needed to do was get out of here and wait for Gloria to contact her. Her old boss was gone; long live her new boss. She wasn't any happier about serving Tillinghast than she had been about Sanford – less, really, since Sanford had only ever threatened to kill her, not strand her in null-time – but Ruby was essentially a realist.

And she might still actually get that big payday Tillinghast had promised, once his Great Work was finished. He was the sort of person who liked to wield the carrot *and* the stick. Though she had to wonder if money would be worth anything after his mysterious ritual was complete.

Altman picked up the bag with the grail. "Can't leave this lying around," he muttered. "Let's find a safe place for it, anyway." He led Ruby through the warren of passageways, down a secret staircase, and into the depths of the basements. Ruby wondered how deep those subterranean levels really went. She was sure they took up more space than there was room for, geographically speaking, and she'd heard rumors that some of the doorways led to places not strictly of this earth, though the same rumors said they couldn't be traversed easily, or without Sanford's leave.

"Who's in charge, while Sanford is ... away?" Ruby asked. "There must be a chain of command. There are all those levels, Initiates and Seekers and the other ones, so who's the vice president of the Silver Twilight Lodge?"

"The Keeper of the Red Stone?" Altman said it like he was asking her, not telling her. "I think he's the highest-ranking member of the Order after Sanford, but he's never here. His whole job is traveling the world chasing down leads and looking for artifacts. He was here recently, simply to replenish his supplies, but I think he left again. After that, I'm not sure. There's the warden, of course, but she's locked up now..."

"Why? Van Shaw *is* the Lodge, practically!"

"She betrayed Sanford," Altman said. "She took a bribe from Tillinghast. Some bit of jewelry that gave her powers she didn't normally have."

Ruby started to touch the watch on her wrist, and then made herself stop. So, the warden was on *her* side? Maybe she should try to set the woman free. "What kind of powers?"

Altman grunted. "I don't really know the details. You know how Sanford is when it comes to filling people in.

What matters is he caught her, took her new toy away, and locked her up. I don't have high hopes for her life expectancy." He paused, then bowed his head and leaned heavily against the wall. "Then again, if the magus is gone… I don't know who's going to pass judgment on her. There are a few Knights of the Stars in the city, including myself, and we're fairly high up in the hierarchy. At my initiation ceremony, the others were annoyed I was given that title when I hadn't gone through the ranks properly like they all had. But they don't strike me as leaders. They're enforcers, like me." He shook his head. "It's not like Sanford encouraged us to think about what we'd do without him. The very idea of the Lodge without him is supposed to be impossible. Worst of all, we don't know who we can trust. If Tillinghast got to the warden, who else has been compromised? Who else has betrayed the sacred brotherhood of the Order?"

Altman looked so stricken at the idea that Ruby couldn't think of a single thing to say.

*Am I laying it on too thick?* Altman thought. "The sacred brotherhood of the Order" – he sounded like a recruiter for a college fraternity. But he couldn't give Ruby any cause to doubt his loyalty. She'd proven her own devotion to Sanford by bringing in the grail, even if she *had* been acting as an unknowing dupe for Tillinghast in the process.

Ruby knew a lot of the other people in the Order, and if she started pointing fingers and declaring that Altman had turned on the master, some of them might believe her. Even though she didn't have any official status in the organization, she'd been around longer than Altman had, and accusations from her would at the very least cause a commotion. He needed to keep things together here until Tillinghast did... whatever he was going to do... to seize power, now that Sanford was gone. He just wished he knew *where* Sanford had gone, and how long he was going to be there.

Altman stopped. "Wait. Shouldn't there be a door right here?" He was confronting a blank wall.

"I haven't been to visit the Scholar since she was trapped in that nasty old cell," Ruby said. "You tell me."

"I'm sure I... maybe we took a wrong turn at the last branch." He backtracked, and Ruby followed, and then she touched his shoulder.

"Altman, this is different, too. The passageway that led to the vault should be right here, and there's just plaster now. Maybe it's an illusion." She closed her eyes and moved her hands all over the wall, methodically touching it from the floor to the highest extent of her reach, then shook her head and faced him. "That's an actual wall. What's going on? Could the floor plan be changing?"

"Sanford said he'd instituted various security protocols, after the business with the Cult of Asterias," Altman said. "He never told me what those protocols *were*, exactly, but he said he didn't intend to let anyone run rampant through his Lodge again."

Ruby groaned. "Let's see what else has changed."

The answer was: a lot. There were still plenty of twisting corridors and T-junctions and dingy hallways, but none of them seemed to lead anywhere; worst case, you hit dead ends, and best case, you ended up looping back to where you started. All the doorways to the various chambers, ritual sites, theaters, storage areas, libraries, and mysterious liminal spaces were gone. The basement was all hallways and no rooms now.

They retreated back upstairs, baffled, and found the dining room full of two score Lodge members, all loudly talking over one another and gesticulating furiously. "What is the meaning of this?" Altman boomed, silencing them. He outranked everyone there, and they all bowed their heads and touched their chests in the Lodge salute.

One of them, a rabbity fellow that Altman recalled as one of Sanford's archivists, stepped forward. "We were all working downstairs, and then we… well, I got lightheaded, and sat down, and closed my eyes for a moment, and when I opened them again, I was here. I must have been somehow transported through time and space…"

"You walked," one of the cooks announced flatly, leaning on the counter in the pass-through between the kitchen and the dining room. "I watched the whole lot of you stumble in here, eyes closed. I think you was sleepwalking."

One of the Initiates who served in the dining room nodded her head rapidly. "It was like watching a line of ants head for an apple core on the lawn! They came single file and sat down in neat rows and then a second later they all woke up and stood up and started yelling."

"Are we under attack?" the archivist said. "I heard something like that happened last year. Where's the warden? Where's the master?"

"No one is under attack!" Altman shouted. "I'm Carl Sanford's head of security, and he has me testing a new security protocol in case of enemy action. It worked perfectly. That's all. It's late. You should all return to your homes, or your guest rooms upstairs."

"But I work the graveyard shift," one of the basement people objected. "My work can only be done under the dark of the moon–"

"The moon will be dark again another time," Altman said firmly. "All of you, go home." They meekly obeyed, and when the dining room was empty, Altman sat down at the long table. Ruby joined him, and Altman put his head in his hands. "I had no idea there were so many people underfoot in the evening. I guess in the basements it doesn't much matter if it's day or night. It's all the same down there." He yawned hugely. "*I'm* tired, though. I could use a night's sleep before it gets to be morning again. Maybe Sanford will return, and all this will be settled before I wake up."

"I don't imagine Sanford will be back anytime soon," Gloria Dyer said, strolling into the dining room with a smile. She wore a pink jacket over a white shirt and a pink skirt and carried a pink purse to match; even her pumps were pink. "How lovely to see both of you!"

Altman rose and glanced at Ruby, who was gaping at the woman. "How did you get in here?" she demanded.

Gloria beamed. "I opened the gate. I followed the path. I opened the front door. I walked through that ghastly foyer. I strolled into the house, and heard your voices, and came here. It's so strange. No horrible dogs snarled at me, no imperious women barred my way, and the door wasn't even locked. Aren't you the head of Carl Sanford's personal security, Altman? I must say, you're falling down on the job."

Altman glowered and drew himself up. "You. What have you, I mean, what has Tillinghast done with Sanford? Answer me, or I'll drag you down to the basements and... and..."

"Oh, settle down, Altman." Gloria put her purse down and pulled out a chair for herself, then sat at the table with her hands clasped before her. "Go pour us some brandies, would you? We're all friends here."

"What – what do you mean?" Ruby said.

"I mean, *I* work for Tillinghast." She touched her breastbone. "And *he* works for Tillinghast." She pointed at Altman. "And *you* work for Tillinghast." She pointed at Ruby. "Have you two been circling around each other, trying to prove your loyalty to Sanford?" She laughed like tinkling bells. "How funny. Well, there's no need for all that now."

Altman and Ruby stared at each other for a moment, and then Altman looked away. What had Tillinghast promised Ruby? It couldn't be the same thing the old man had promised *him*. Only one person could have that prize. "Brandies. Right." He went to a sideboard and began making drinks.

"A splash of soda in mine please!" Gloria called.

He returned, awkwardly holding three glasses, and passed them out. Gloria took a long sip of hers and made a sound of satisfaction. Ruby didn't touch her own, and Altman wasn't thirsty.

"You all did beautifully tonight," Gloria said. "Well, you didn't have much to do, Altman, but you stayed out of the way, as promised, and Ruby, you were magnificent. Tell me all about it. Did Sanford snatch the grail out of your hands the minute he saw you?"

"No," Ruby said, and recited the events of the evening in an emotionless and bare-bones way, up to the point when Sanford vanished. "He didn't fade out, or anything, it was more like a soap bubble popping. Just there, and then gone."

"I've never seen anything like it," Altman said. "And I've seen a lot of things. Where did he go?"

Gloria shrugged, seemingly uninterested. "You'd have to ask Mr Tillinghast. Sanford has been dispatched on a long vacation to distant climes, is all I can say."

"But... is he trapped in his own dreams?" Ruby said.

"Oh, the translations he read weren't accurate," Gloria said. "How can a person crawl inside their own mind?" She leaned forward, twinkling and conspiratorial. "To be honest, I think Mr Tillinghast commissioned forgeries of ancient texts and put them where Sanford's agents could find them, to get the magus interested in the grail. It certainly worked out well, didn't it?"

"But Sanford said he first read about the grail long ago," Altman said. "Does that mean... has Tillinghast been plotting to take down Sanford for *years*?"

"My employer keeps his own counsel, but I don't get the sense he rushes into things," Gloria said. "He's a planner, and he thinks long-term, and he enjoys savoring his triumphs."

"This is his triumph, then?" Ruby said. "So I can collect my pay and leave town now?"

Altman was astonished. They'd bribed Ruby with nothing but money? Didn't she know what Tillinghast could do? Did she really have such a profound lack of imagination?

"You know better," Gloria said. "Mr Tillinghast needs to take control of the Silver Twilight Lodge, and seize its treasures for his own, especially something called the Ruby of R'lyeh. At least, those are his immediate concerns. He'll have other errands for you two as well. Your contracts are a bit open-ended, by design. But don't worry, you'll both get everything you've been promised, and I'm sure they'll bring you nothing but joy in the end."

"I'm sure." Ruby glanced at Altman. "What did Tillinghast promise you, anyhow?"

He hesitated, and the thief snorted. "Come on. Gloria already knows, and it's not like I'll think less of you. Let's compare compensation packages and see who got the better deal."

"I get the Silver Twilight Lodge," Altman admitted. "When Tillinghast is finished with it, I'll take Sanford's old job."

"Sanford's old *everything*," Gloria said. "Mr Tillinghast has a team of lawyers and bankers and, I'll be honest, document forgers working on making everything all legal and official. What once belonged to Carl Sanford will soon belong to him, and when he's done with his business in Arkham, Mr Tillinghast will have no need for a bunch of deeds and titles and safety deposit boxes and bank accounts, and he'll sign the lot over to Altman. Then our wandering mercenary will finally be able to put down roots." She patted his hand and beamed at him.

"That's just Sanford's *stuff*," Ruby objected. "That's not the Order."

Gloria preened. "Oh, the loyalty oaths sworn by every Lodge member at the level of Seeker or above will pass to Altman, too, when he becomes leader of the Lodge. Though I've suggested he might want to require new oaths, with altered wording. To ensure a more personal sort of loyalty."

Ruby frowned. "What do you mean, personal?"

"The Seekers, the Knights, all of them, they swear to defend and protect the Order," Altman explained. "That is, the Silver Twilight Lodge as a whole. Not Sanford himself."

"That's how we were able to get the warden on our side, despite her formidable oaths," Gloria said. "We showed her that Sanford wasn't the right man to lead the Lodge anymore, and that someone else could do it better."

Altman nodded. "Same with me. I couldn't burn down this building, I couldn't loot the treasury, and I couldn't murder all the Initiates, because those would be crimes against the Lodge, and those are forbidden by the oath I swore before the other Knights, upon that stone, in that circle. But I could turn on Sanford, personally, because..." He scowled. "Why should *he* get to be a little god here? What makes him so noble and important?" Altman slammed his fist down on the table, dormant rage bubbling to the surface. "He let my brother die!"

Ruby nodded, seemingly undisturbed by his outburst.

"Sanford's not a good man, exactly. Not a bad one, either. His moral compass points to true north, but truth north, for him, is the prosperity and safety of Carl Sanford, first, and the Silver Twilight Lodge, second, and maybe Arkham itself, third. You think you'll do a better job as boss, Altman?"

"I won't send good men into dens of cultists to die, that's for sure," Altman said. "Maybe I'll get this Lodge to do all the things it *purports* to do. Charitable acts. Civic duty. Strengthening the fabric of Arkham society."

"You're the charitable sort now?"

Altman didn't like the way Ruby was looking at him like he was some interesting and new species of beetle. "Why not? I've seen what happens when men are desperate, evil, grasping, and greedy. I've never been in a position to do anything to make the world better. When I run this Lodge, when I run this *city*, I'll be able to do a lot more, and I will. What? Do you have something to say to me, Standish?"

"The shift from murderer to philanthropist is quite a leap, is all," Ruby said.

"Says the thief," he sneered.

She shrugged. "I steal things. You snuff out lives. I've got no illusions about myself. Until five minutes ago, I would have said you didn't have any about yourself, either, but, well. People do insist on surprising you, don't they?"

"What did they give *you*?" Altman demanded. "A bag full of cash?"

"Sure. The deal is, I get enough money to set myself up independently for life. Plus a piece of magic to make that life infinitely easier and more interesting, and that's all I have to say about it."

Altman grunted. "I don't see why I should–"

"Enough, children. Don't squabble." Gloria didn't raise her voice, but there was none of the usual suppressed laughter in her voice. "Mr Tillinghast is on a timetable. He has a Great Work to commence. He is currently busy shepherding the legal side of his assumption of Carl Sanford's estate. Your former magus will be found dead in a fiery car wreck soon, or, at least, a corpse fitting the general description will be found in his Bentley, wearing the burned remnants of Sanford's clothes, and that will be good enough for our pet coroner. Sanford's will, to everyone's surprise, will name Tillinghast as his sole heir, and steps are being made to... expedite the transfer of his estate."

"But Sanford isn't dead, is he?" Ruby said. "What if he comes back?"

"People *do* sometimes come back from the place where he's gone," Gloria said. "But they're seldom sane when they return, and Mr Tillinghast has taken steps to ensure that Sanford will not find a warm welcome there. If I were giving odds on his return, you wouldn't want to take the bet. Now. I told you what Mr Tillinghast is doing. Here's what *I'm* doing." She rose from the table. "I've been sent to see to the physical aspects of the estate. To check out the Lodge, from top to bottom. And I mean the *very* bottom. He wants me to inspect the basements, and find Sanford's hidden vaults, and the Ruby of R'lyeh, and you're going to help me."

Altman and Ruby looked at one another. Ruby shook her head minutely, and Altman grimaced.

"About the basements," he began.

# CHAPTER SEVENTEEN
## *The Doom That Came to Sanford*

The swirling blackness parted, and Sanford found himself sprawled on his back, arms and legs flung out, staring up at a sky the color of a purple bruise. That sky was threaded with pulsing veins of white that he would have called lightning if they hadn't been constant, merely dimming and brightening in pulses rather than properly flashing.

A sharp stone dug into his spine, and he winced as he rolled over and got to his knees. He was atop a heap of gray rock – a pile of rubble, more like – and tiny triangular pebbles tore at the knees of his trousers. He rose unsteadily and leaned against a fragment of chest-high freestanding wall. "Where the deuce am I?" he muttered. It crossed his mind to call for help, but shouting in strange places could bring strange responses. Better to be quiet until he figured out where he was, and what was happening.

His memory was strangely fuzzy. Ruby had succeeded, and brought him the grail, and then... yes. He'd touched it, and been mesmerized. Tillinghast had set a trap, and Sanford had walked into it. He cursed himself. Had he been drugged by the contents of the cup, and transported to this place? Or had he been transported here by the grail's magic? Either way, the most pressing questions were, where was he, and how could he get back?

He looked over the top of the wall, trying to make sense of this bizarre landscape. He'd seen the aftermath of zeppelin raids during the Great War overseas, city centers turned to rubble and cinders, and this was a bit like that… but much worse, and much less fresh. This might have been a city, or part of a city, but now it was a ruin, and an ancient one to judge by the trees that grew up from the devastated plazas and building foundations. The plants didn't look healthy – they were leafless and covered in patches of leprous white mold – but they were big and well-established.

He clambered down his rock pile, then walked up a slope, planting his feet carefully to avoid slipping on the scree, until he found a section of intact stone staircase, the risers just a bit taller than comfortable, and climbed them to what must have once been the upper floor of a building… or a balcony, or a landing, or something else. Now it was a jagged platform about ten feet across and twenty feet up, and it gave him a better view of his surroundings.

The city, or what remained of it, spread in all directions as far as he could see. Though "heaps of rubble" was the predominant theme, that level of devastation was not uniform. There were numerous holes in the ground, ranging from the size of manholes to large enough to swallow a car, and many were smoking, or at least exuding yellowish vapors. He saw a half-melted statue of some sort of immense lizard emerging from the rocks nearby, though all he could make out clearly was its spiny tail. A dome, broken like an egg, stood silhouetted against the sky to his left. It might have been shining gold, once, but was now speckled with either mold or the guano of flying animals. Off in the distance there were more freestanding sections of wall, some of them gleaming white marble, allowing Sanford to guess at the likely perimeter of whatever city once stood here.

"No point staying here," he muttered, descending the stairs. He knew his situation was dire, but his mind skittered away from the full implications. He resolved to move forward, one foot in front of the other, until he gathered more information, and then… and then… he'd know how to proceed. Yes. Of course. He wasn't truly lost. He was just temporarily unclear on his precise location.

He set off in the direction of the nearest significant chunk of wall. He didn't have his cane, and sorely missed it. He didn't usually need the stick to walk, but landing on those stones made his body ache abominably, and he limped through the wreckage.

After a time, he reached a stretch of nearly clear road, and realized he was walking on mud-streaked onyx. A devastated city, with streets of onyx and… was it granite? He'd read about such a place, hadn't he? If he were in the Lodge, he could go to his library and look up the details. He could almost picture the volume he'd read about this city in: it had a black cover, with silver engraving, but he couldn't quite bring the *title* to mind.

He sighed. He'd learned long ago that trying to chase down an errant thought only made it flee deeper into the recesses of the mind. Better to focus on putting one foot in front of the other and let the back of his mind sort through the detritus of his decades for a useful morsel.

He stepped over the remnant of a fallen arch, and into the foundation of what must have once been a vast structure. There was something white gleaming off to one side, and he changed his direction to investigate. After all, he didn't know where he was, or where he was going, so what harm could a detour do?

The white object proved to be the remains of a great throne made of ivory. He hadn't realized that ivory could melt – it couldn't normally, could it? Whatever doom had befallen this place must have been of an uncanny nature.

Doom. Why did that word seem to resonate in his mind, apart from its accurate description of his current circumstances? He concentrated, but nothing came into focus. No matter. He looked at the chair closely. There were lions carved on the arms, but like medieval depictions of the beast, they didn't much resemble actual lions – more like someone had carved them based on a secondhand description of a lion at best.

Or else… the lions in this country were a different sort than those elsewhere. Sanford sat on the slanted fragment of the throne's seat that remained, and for the first time, allowed himself to confront the fact his mind most wished to avoid: this did not look like any place on Earth.

Oh, it *might* be on Earth; there were secret valleys, deep caverns, and mysterious hollows, and some of those might suffer under such an outlandish sky, but on balance, he didn't think so. Tillinghast had tricked him with the grail. Charmed him into putting the cup to his lips, and then sent him to some distant realm, beyond the back of the stars, or in between the conventions of ordinary geometry. He'd poisoned the chalice. Or else... perhaps Sanford hadn't understood what the grail did, not really. He drank from it, and found himself here, and this was no place he'd ever dreamed before, in a doomed city.

Dream... doom... why did those two words seem to go together?

He rose and sighed and set off again. The air smelled of dust and damp mold, but at least it wasn't freezing cold, only chilly, and his suit jacket was good wool. He walked through the remnants of what might have been houses, or manors, or shops, and he avoided the miasmic holes. They looked like they could be *dens*, and he had no desire to see what creatures might dwell beneath this place.

He passed a few scummy ponds, but dared not go near them, a worry confirmed when he saw one of the lakelets begin to roil and bubble. Something long and wet flicked out – a tongue, a tentacle, a fin? Nothing he wanted to trouble himself with. He wouldn't die of thirst, anyway. His segmented ring – the Annelid, it was called, or sometimes the Tapeworm – provided him with the necessities of survival, among other benefits. He did not need to eat or drink or sleep while he wore it. The ring magically stole life energy and took sustenance from the living things around him, a parasitic enchantment for his benefit. If he'd found himself in an entirely lifeless place, of course, the ring wouldn't help, but there *was* life here, of some sort, and he could live on their stolen bounty. The creatures around him would hunger, thirst, and grow weary, while he continued fresh as a spring morning.

Not all the rubble was gray – some of it was shining white, and after scuffing some stones with his shoes, he realized most of them were quartz, but coated in dust and mud to hide their luster. Streets of onyx, bricks of quartz... some memory was stirring in his unconscious, but he couldn't quite grasp it.

He finally reached one of the walls, a fragment that stood almost as tall as he did, though he imagined they must once have soared, judging by the abundance of stone fallen all around him. The wall was decorated with chiseled designs – more lions, and chariots, and other things he couldn't identify.

There was one thing he *could* identify, though, a splash of color that was wildly out of place: a green triangle, messily painted with a brush, and in its center, a red eye. Sanford couldn't stop himself from shouting then, and pounding his fist against the wall. Even here, exiled to this strange place, Tillinghast *taunted* him.

He slumped down and sat, his back to the wall, staring at the horrible ruins before him. He'd brought this on himself, hadn't he? His life was a Greek tragedy, and he'd been brought down by the most obvious of fatal flaws – hubris!

He'd assumed that he could get the best of Tillinghast, even though the man had shown repeatedly that he was playing three moves ahead. Just because Sanford had always triumphed before didn't mean he was *destined* to triumph.

There was no such thing as destiny. The universe didn't care about him, or about anyone else; no one was *meant* to do anything at all. You had to find your own meaning to give purpose to your life. It just so happened that Sanford had always found his meaning in being the smartest, the wiliest, the cleverest, the most informed, and the *best*. Now Tillinghast had proven himself Sanford's better. He'd used Sanford's own arrogance and avarice against him, turned his allies into enemies, and taken glee in showing Sanford the cracks in his world.

The magus in exile closed his eyes and leaned his head against the stones of the wall, under his enemy's eye. He was beaten. He was stranded who knows where, with nothing but a few magical trinkets, and no idea how to find his way home.

But… there had to be a way home, didn't there? If Tillinghast had come here to paint his sigil and then returned home, that meant it was indeed possible to escape this place.

Sanford opened his eyes. He got to his feet. If something was possible, Sanford could do it, couldn't he? He'd even been known to do *im*possible things, after all. Was that hubris again? Well, what of it? He'd already hit rock bottom, quite literally. Pride goeth before the fall, yes, but now that he'd fallen, what harm could pride do him? Or not even pride. Call it… clear-eyed self-regard. Sanford had recently come up hard against the limits of his capabilities, and now he had to admit that he had limitations. But that didn't mean he lacked all resources. Just because he couldn't do *everything* didn't mean he couldn't do *anything*.

It was best to keep moving, anyway, and trying, even if he ended in failure, doomed to wander this bleak place forever. The alternative, after all, was to sit down and become a ruin himself. His despair sang a siren song tempting him toward that option… but there was more than despair within him. There was fury, too, and spite, and resentment, or at least their smoldering embers, and he could feed those, turn them into roaring flames, and let those ill feelings heat the engine of his revenge. Yes! It was something to do, anyway; trying was something to do.

Sanford spat on Tillinghast's sigil, and then followed the wall, trailing his hand against the stone as he went, leaving a line of wiped-away dust, until he reached an opening big enough to step through, and did.

Beyond the wall, there was a lake, deep and dark and vast, so large it might almost have been an inland sea.

But Sanford knew it was a lake, and not a sea, because, with his mind lit by anger, he could suddenly see the title of that book in his library, written in silver on black:

*The Doom That Came to Sarnath*

Yes! The book was a slim monograph, describing a vision experienced by some lunatic or sage (or both). It told of a great city built on the shores of an immense lake, with walls of chiseled marble that stood four-hundred-and-fifty feet high, with streets of onyx and granite, filled with temples and gardens, and palaces dotted with ornamental ponds. But that city was built upon a crime, for the earliest denizens had slaughtered the peaceful, intelligent inhuman creatures who lived in the lake, in order to claim the land as their own. After a thousand years of prosperity, a terrible mist rose from the lake, and the city was destroyed utterly in a night, and none of its denizens ever seen again. When he read that book, Sanford had thought it nothing more than another "lost city of Atlantis" variation.

But he was *here*. This was ruined Sarnath. Except… that couldn't be, could it? According to the text, travelers from nearby lands who'd tried to visit the city reported that nothing of it remained, not even a single stone. Where the city had stood, there was only a vast marsh, populated by water lizards. There was no rubble, no ruin, and no sign of the city that had been. Then was this… the place where the ruins had gone? But where could *that* be?

Some creature scurried past on the edge of the lake – like a rat, but the size of a cat, and when it looked at him, it had a mass of feelers on its face, a bit like a star-nosed mole, but these were *wriggling*, and far more numerous. The thing looked at him with at least as much intelligence as a cat possessed, but something about its gaze was considerably more malign, which was saying something. It scurried away, and that's when the penny dropped for Sanford.

He'd read about *those* creatures, too. He couldn't remember what they were called, but they'd infested an enchanted wood before being driven away by the populace of a nearby city in the Dreamlands, and apparently some of them had ended up here, on the shores of this vile lake. This wasn't Sarnath, or at least, not exactly. This was the *dream* of Sarnath – the half-remembered specter of the fallen city.

Sanford was in the Dreamlands.

He'd read extensively about this world, or collection of worlds. It was supposed to be unimaginably vast, and wondrous, full of strange and dangerous cities, and wise and generous denizens, and vice versa. The Dreamlands were in a space beyond space, in a time beyond time. Visitors had returned with tales of the city of Ulthar, where cats were sacred; the tourmaline spires of Celephaïs; the yellow wooded slopes of Mount Aran; the icy heights of Kadath; the insidious depths of the Underworld...

Sanford had even tried to reach the Dreamlands, in his lucid dreaming sessions, as some were reputed to do, but he'd never found a portal. He didn't have the knack. Some people could visit this realm naturally, especially as children, just as some people possessed the natural ability to see the unseen, or glimpse the future, but Sanford did not have their gifts. There were relics that could let you visit this place in your sleep – he'd spent many years tracking rumors of one in particular, a silver key, and had become so enamored of the legend that he'd even named his personal boat the *Silver Key*. He'd never found the key, though, or successfully found entry to the Dreamlands, though he'd spoken to people who claimed they'd been.

Now he was here, which might have been thrilling, under other circumstances, except that he'd wanted to come here in his *sleep*, sending his mind and soul to explore, while his body was safe in bed! Tillinghast had contrived to send him here in his physical body, which was infinitely more dangerous.

Sanford knew where he was now, though. The nature of the Dreamlands was elusive, the magic wild and unpredictable, but there were connections between this world and his own, and if he could find one, he could return, and take his revenge on Tillinghast for trying to strand him here. Time was said to move differently here, that you could spend weeks or months exploring the Dreamlands, and wake to find only a night had passed on Earth. But there were other stories, of people who spent a single night here, and woke to find they'd been asleep on a hillside for a hundred years, and that the world had moved on. Who knew how time worked when he was here in his physical form?

"Nothing to be done about that," he told the air. "I can't worry about things I can't control. I must focus on those things I *can*."

He walked along the edge of the lake, looking for some sign of anything, really, and finally saw a distant golden sparkle, in the sky. Were there cities in the clouds here, or was it a temple on a mountaintop? Either way, it was a destination, and he sorely needed one of those.

Sanford squelched along the muddy shore, wishing he'd worn boots today instead of his loafers. If he could sail across the lake he could reach the golden city, or whatever it was, faster, but his *Silver Key* was in its boathouse back in Arkham, and there were no helpful ferrymen in the vicinity. He'd have to circumnavigate the bleak body of water, then.

Something stirred in the water, and he paused, watching. What sort of things would swim in the dream of a lake? Probably nothing pleasant.

That thought was confirmed when a figure rose from the lapping waves and stepped onto the shore. It was humanoid, but with something of the fish about it – like a

Deep One, but with a different shape to its frilled head, and a different slouch to its body. The creature was translucent, as if made of icy fog, the edges of its form seeming to swirl, as if it could barely hold onto its consistency.

"Hello," Sanford said, just in case it could speak. He'd interacted with strange entities before but usually on his own terms with the creatures confined to a summoning circle. To encounter one in the wild was more disconcerting, but he resolved to show no fear.

Others rose from the waves, too, and joined the first, standing as if in a choir. They were more toadlike or lizardlike than fishlike, now that he had more of them to observe. Drat it all, hadn't the book talked about these creatures, too? The… denizens of Ib, was it? These were the semiaquatic beings who'd been exterminated by the founders of doomed Sarnath – or they once had been. Their ghosts had risen after a thousand years and laid waste to Sarnath, killing or spiriting away all its people… and now they were looking at *him*.

"I'm not from Sarnath," Sanford called. Was there a language barrier in the Dreamlands? "I'm just passing through. Do you happen to know of a way back to Earth?" They stared at him, faces expressionless, not that he could have reliably read the expressions of the ghosts of a horrible species of toad-monsters anyway. "Failing that, do you know what that golden thing is, over there?" They turned their heads to follow his pointing hand, which gave him a moment's hope, but then they turned their faces back to him, without answering. "Well, then, sorry to have troubled you. I'll just be moving on."

The Beings of Ib stepped closer, their spectral feet not quite touching the mud. They were murmuring, now, and though he couldn't make out the words, he was nearly certain they were angry murmurs. He was not defenseless; he did have weapons on his person. The eel pin on his tie would make short work of this lot... but he could only use that once, and was this threat serious enough? Moreover, these creatures were spectral, which meant the eel might not even faze them.

One of them came closer and spoke, slowly, in words that Sanford *could* understand. "Tilling... ghast... sends... his... regards..."

This was a welcoming party from his enemy, then. It was almost flattering, wasn't it? Tillinghast wasn't comfortable merely exiling Sanford. He had to exile him and *then* kill him. Well, the shopkeeper had a better chance at assassinating him here, that was for sure. It would be difficult in the extreme to kill Sanford in Arkham, the seat of his power, surrounded by a thousand safeguards he'd redoubled after his close call with the Cult of Asterias. He smiled a little at the thought of Tillinghast encountering some of those safeguards soon when he tried to take over the Lodge. Various grim precautions had activated automatically the moment Sanford left the boundaries of Arkham.

Pleasant daydreams had to be put aside for unpleasant realities. "Tilling... what? I'm afraid I don't know the fellow. You've confused me with someone else. No harm done. I'll go my way, and you'll go yours."

The denizens of Ib extended their dripping hands, and some of them held blades. The blades were translucent, too, just like their wielders, but he had no doubt they were sharp enough to cut him anyway.

Sanford didn't want to turn and run – nothing made a monster chase you more than running from it – but sometimes your choices were limited, and you did what you must. He spun and tore off through the Dreamlands, away from the lake, and into the dark emptiness beyond.

The things chasing him howled the name of his enemy as they came.

# CHAPTER EIGHTEEN
## *Retainers Assemble*

"You told me about a magic mirror that reveals truth?" Gloria said. "We can use that to navigate this maze he's made, can't we?" She glared at the white plaster wall of a dead-end corridor on the first level of the basement.

"The mirror is probably behind this wall somewhere," Altman said. "I certainly don't know where."

Gloria paced back and forth. "Axes and sledgehammers, then. The rest of the basements must still exist back there. Let's just smash our way through."

"It's not like Sanford sent a carpenter to build this wall," Ruby said. "He did something magical to rearrange the layout. Smash through the wall, and you could end up breaking through into a tunnel full of ghouls, or, I don't know, a *void*. I really wouldn't recommend it."

"Did you say ghouls?" Gloria shook her head, seemingly more amused than distressed. "This job gets stranger and stranger."

Ruby was amazed at the woman's equanimity, but could see why Tillinghast depended on her. Still, Ruby wondered how unflappable Gloria would be down in the tunnels beneath the hill, with pale arms reaching out from the darkness. Maybe she'd have the chance to find out. She didn't relish the idea.

Gloria crossed her arms. "Listen, you two. This is simply unacceptable. We need to get into the basements – the *deep* basements. My employer does not like failure. Surely someone besides Sanford is capable of figuring out how to defeat this magic?"

"The warden, probably." Ruby didn't particularly want to help, not after Tillinghast's threats, but she'd hitched herself to the vile man's wagon, and she supposed she'd better start pulling. "She has a deep connection to the Lodge, the grounds, and the building, and if anyone can navigate her way through whatever trick Sanford pulled, it would be her."

"Then let's summon her," Gloria said. "Isn't she always lurking about?"

"Sanford caught her… or, her doppelganger, I suppose… in the city," Altman said. "He found out she was working with you, and stole her necklace, and locked her up in a cell." He rapped his knuckles against the wall. "Somewhere on the other side of this. So, it's the same problem with the mirror."

"The Scholar might know something," Ruby said. "But she's back there, too."

Gloria closed her eyes and took a few deep breaths, then smiled. "I am here in a supervisory capacity. You two are the ditch-diggers and water-haulers. I have identified the problem. You two will solve that problem. Or should I interrupt Mr Tillinghast and tell him to come here personally?"

Ruby thought of an eternity in null-time and said, "No, no, we'll figure it out."

Gloria clapped her hands. "Wonderful. Don't take too long. I wonder if there are any little cakes in the kitchen?" She wandered off.

Ruby and Altman leaned against the wall, side by side. *I guess you take whatever allies you can get,* she thought.

"Well?" he said. "Any ideas?"

"No useful ones. The best idea I've had all day is putting my feet in a tub of hot water with Epsom salt. It's after midnight, and I've done a lot of walking, and the dogs are barking–" She snapped her mouth shut, stared at Altman, and then laughed aloud. "The dogs!" She rushed away from him, through the short corridors and up toward the surface.

"What about the dogs?" Altman called, pursuing her.

He caught up with her outside, where Ruby was standing on the path, calling, "Here, boy! Or girl. Or... here, hound!" She whistled sharply and slapped her hands on her thighs.

"They're not really dogs, exactly, I don't think," Altman began, but Ruby shushed him, and whistled again.

The grasses parted, and a single black hound slouched toward them, and looked at Ruby, head cocked sideways. "The warden sees what you see, doesn't she?" Ruby said.

The dog did nothing to confirm or deny that assertion.

Ruby sighed. "Warden, look. If you can hear me. Sanford is out. It's a new era. Tillinghast is taking over. Altman and I… we're on his payroll, too, just like you, and probably for similar reasons." Greed, resentment, fear… there were lots of reasons. "But Sanford did something before Tillinghast booted him out of the Lodge. He changed the whole layout in the basements, and now it's just hallways that don't go anywhere, and we can't reach the deeper levels at all. You're down there somewhere, but we can't find you. If we *could* find you, then we could let you out, and Tillinghast would be happy, and maybe then we could get some actual sleep. I don't know if you sleep, but I sure do."

The hound trotted past her toward the Lodge, and in through the front door, as if it were the most ordinary thing in the world, though Ruby had never seen the dogs beyond the threshold. She whooped and chased after the dog. Altman followed after her, shaking his head and muttering.

"The dog is probably just going to the kitchen to beg for scraps," Altman said.

"Have a little faith," Ruby said. "You're talking about woman's best friend there. Or at least the warden's best friend."

They followed the dog into the dining room, where Gloria was nibbling at a piece of cake while a tired-looking Initiate stood awkwardly at her shoulder, holding a coffee pot by the handle. "Nice doggie!" Gloria said. "What a good puppy. I see what you're thinking, Ruby. Good idea. Let me know if it works."

"How do you know it wasn't *my* idea?" Altman grumbled.

"Women's intuition," Gloria said, and gave Ruby a wink.

The hound led them through the old servants' quarters, to a pantry that hid an entrance to the basements. It trotted down the stairs, and they followed. "Just like hunting boar, probably, huh, Altman?" Ruby said.

"Boar wasn't a thing I hunted," he said. "Following a dog seems like a good way to find a rotting animal carcass, and not much else. Except a lady dog in heat, maybe."

"There's some bloodhound in this breed. I can see it." Ruby followed the dog as it went down one hall, to a dead end… and then backtracked to go down another hall… and then returned to the first one… and then backtracked to go down a *different* hall.

"This is pointless," Altman said. "This animal is stupider than those mice that run mazes. We're going to the same places over and over again!"

The hound did, indeed, lead them back to the first hall, for their third visit, but this time, instead of a blank white wall, there was a blank white wall with a *door* in the middle of it. Ruby almost reached down to pat the dog on the head, but settled for saying, "Good girl!" She turned to Altman. "Do you see? It's a trick with space. You have to follow a certain path in a certain way, and then the opening appears! I knew Sanford wouldn't seal things up forever with no way in. He likes all the little treasures he has stashed away too much." She opened the door, which led to another corridor, and this one had familiar scuff marks on the walls. "Did Sanford lock up the warden in the same cell where he locked *me* up that time?"

"How should I know where he locked you up?" Altman said. "Before my time."

"I bet he did. It's his favorite, because it's the smallest, and there's blood on the wall, and it smells of rat shit." She went down the hall, first following the placidly walking dog, then surging ahead as she neared her destination.

Ruby looked through the grate near the top of the cell door and grinned. Sarah Van Shaw was there, staring at her, standing perfectly upright. "Hello, warden. How'd you like to get out of there?"

"No one has ever cared much what I like," she said. "But I'd rather be elsewhere, yes. You two are in league with Tillinghast, then?"

"'In league' might be putting a little too much pepper on it," Ruby said. "But for the time being we're on his side, yes. It's the only side available at the moment, anyway. We're all friends here, and I'll let you loose. But, ah, I don't have the key. Altman? Do you have a crowbar handy?"

"I have the key," he said wearily, walking up with the dog at his heels. "I took all Sanford's keys from his desk. I don't know what most of them open, but I was the one who locked the warden up in the first place, so I recognize that one." He fitted a key into the large lock and turned it over with a *thunk*, then pulled the door open.

The warden emerged, all dignity, and gazed around the dingy hallway. Her hound pressed against her legs like a child seeking comfort, but she didn't take any notice. "I see Sanford has made some changes." She closed her eyes for a moment, then opened them with a grunt. "Did you kill him?"

"We didn't do anything to him at all," Altman said. "He just… well…"

"He drank blood from a magic cup and disappeared," Ruby said. When the warden stared at her, she just shrugged. "Well, he *did*."

"Sanford set up safeguards." The warden closed her eyes again, gazing at some inner landscape. "If he should ever fall, he wanted to prevent his enemies from gaining access to his treasures ... and weapons. I didn't realize the extent of the enchantments, but he seems to have hidden everything away down here. It's like a maze, and parts of it are opaque even to me." She opened her eyes. "Sanford must be dead." Her voice was as flat as cracking stones. "This wouldn't have happened otherwise."

Ruby suffered a sick twist in her stomach. Could the old man *really* be dead? "Gloria is upstairs, Tillinghast is taking over, but I guess you know that, and she says Sanford is still alive, but that we shouldn't expect him back anytime soon. Or ever. I think they sent him ... away."

The warden cocked her head. "If he left the earthly realm ... if he is in another world ... yes, that would trigger his defenses as surely as his death." She barked a laugh. "That's why he didn't just arrange for this whole building to drop into the Abyss, or for the basements to fill with boiling mud, or even lock things away behind barriers no one could penetrate."

"Because if he ever made it back from some other world, he'd want access to his *things*," Ruby said.

Altman nodded. "That sounds like Sanford. He wouldn't even consider death a certainty, I bet. People come back from *that*, too, sometimes, though not always changed for the better. So we can access the basements again. That's good. I think Tillinghast would have been annoyed if we lost everything."

The warden stared at Altman with those stonecutter eyes. "Do you think this Tillinghast will care for the Lodge, and see to it that the Order prospers, once he takes control?"

"I don't know about that," Altman said before Ruby could so much as scoff. "I think he has plans that Sanford would have fouled up, so he fouled Sanford up first. But he doesn't really want the Order, warden. In fact, Tillinghast promised me, when he left town, that he'd leave the whole thing in *my* hands." He drew himself up and looked Van Shaw in the eye, trying to look commanding, though Ruby could tell it took him some effort. *Like a boy dressing up in his father's clothes*, she thought.

The warden only clucked her tongue. "You help to overthrow the old king, and plot to take his place?"

Altman didn't shrink before her steel gaze, though, which made Ruby respect him a little more, or else doubt his intelligence. "You speak as though that isn't always how these things are done," Altman said. "When the power shifts, you do your best to figure out which side it's going to settle on, and if you've got any sense, you stand on that side. You jumped ship from Sanford, too, as I recall."

"I never had any real loyalty to Sanford. I have loyalty to the Silver Twilight Lodge. Sanford wasn't a good steward, even if he was our founder. I have my doubts about whether *you'll* be a good one, either."

"The truth is, I have my doubts, too." Altman sounded almost humble. Could that possibly be genuine? "Which is why I'd like you to run the Order with me, warden. We'll make all the important decisions together. And I can say whatever oaths on that awful stone in that horrible circle you like, to prove my sincerity. You know more about this organization than anyone else, and I'd be a fool not to want you by my side."

The warden looked astonished, which, on her face, was only shown by a slight widening of the eyes. Then she nodded. "Aye. Seems a sensible way to handle things."

"You two make things so complicated," Ruby said. "I just want a great big pile of money and some magic jewelry."

Gloria Dyer appeared around the corner. Why hadn't Ruby heard the clicking of her heels? "Before you go counting your money," Dyer said, "or handing out crowns and titles, first you must earn them. Our work isn't done. Not until Mr Tillinghast has full control of this place and its relics and libraries and *everything*." She smiled at them, but Ruby thought her expression strained. "Glad to see you're free, Miss Van Shaw. We'll get you a new necklace, but for the time being, we'd prefer you to focus your consciousness and attention here."

"How did you get in here?" the warden demanded.

"She just walked in, because you weren't up there to stop her," Ruby said.

The warden shook her head. "No, I mean here, through Sanford's maze?"

"I came down to see what was taking so long and followed the sounds of your voices."

The warden said, "*Hmm.* When Standish and Altman traversed the secret path to open the passageway here, it must have stayed unlocked. I suppose Sanford's plan was to return and take a leisurely stroll in the pattern he set and open the basements up again behind him. We'll have to do the same. But… well…" A cloud passed over her face.

"What?" Dyer said. "Can't you do it? I thought you *were* the Lodge?"

"I can lead us down," Van Shaw said. "I can sense the passages, because no place in the Lodge may be barred to me – my oaths see to that. But it's not just confusion and dead ends we have to worry about. Sanford may have made… other arrangements."

"Traps?" Gloria said.

"Among other things." The warden sniffed. "But we'll cope with them as and when needed. What would you like to see first, Miss Dyer?"

Altman insisted on going upstairs to get a shotgun, though the women seemed to be of the opinion he was silly to think a firearm would be any help down below. Ruby accompanied him, though, and ducked into Sanford's office, returning with his sword cane. "I saw this scare some ghouls off, once, so I know it's good for something," she explained.

"Do you even know how to use a sword?" he asked.

"I know which end of it to hold, if that's what you're asking." She took up a perfect fencer's opening pose, right there in the hallway, bowed formally to Altman, and then moved rapidly through a series of slashing and stabbing forms with the sheathed stick, her feet moving as quickly as a dancer's, her arms a blur.

Altman drew back in alarm, and Ruby laughed, sheathing

the sword and then leaning on the walking stick. "I had to ingratiate myself with some society girls for a job once, and they were all mad for fencing, so I signed up for some classes. I took to the sport like a duck to water, though I suppose real fighting is a lot different from scoring points in a mask and padded jacket."

"You're a damn sight better with a sword than I am," Altman said. "I never even learned any fancy knife-fighting, though plenty of the boys in my unit liked showing off their moves. I never bothered." He drew his kukri, showing her the curved blade. "The most successful knife fights are the ones where your opponent is dead before they notice you're even armed. The only time I let someone see my knife coming is when I'm aiming to scare them, not kill them. Or at least not kill them right away."

"You don't benefit much from the element of surprise with a sword, as a rule," Ruby said. "Though hiding it in a stick is a good start." She leaned the cane across her shoulder at a jaunty angle. "Shall we see what the warden and Gloria are up to? I doubt they're swapping recipes for Sunday roast."

Those two did a make an odd couple, Altman thought – the bubbly Gloria and the dour warden – but they had a lot in common, didn't they? Both had experience serving as reliably competent lieutenants for powerful men. Would Gloria ever turn on *her* master? And if she did, would she be as successful as the warden had been? Was the current situation really success, or just a pause in the hostilities?

Altman followed Ruby down to the basements, his gun held at port arms, his mind a million miles away. So

Sanford was stranded in another world? What did that even mean? The magus had occasionally mentioned strange places Altman had never heard of – Yuggoth, the Plateau of Leng, the Cold Wastes – but Altman figured they were just remote regions of jungle or desert or tundra. After his time overseas, Altman was well acquainted with the variety of monsters that seethed and slithered on and under the earth, but if there were other worlds… Altman clearly had a lot to learn if he wanted to run this Lodge. He would find everything he needed to know in the hidden libraries, he supposed, if they could regain access. He'd never been much of a reader, but if he wanted to change his life, that was probably the least of the new interests he'd need to develop.

They found Gloria and the warden, still trailed by a hound, walking down a narrow passageway not far from the holding cell. There was a solid wall at the end of the hall, but the wall was receding as the warden walked steadily toward it. It looked like some trick of distance or perspective, but no; the wall was really moving, sliding along backward as if on hidden rails.

"I've had hallucinations like this," Ruby whispered to him as they brought up the rear together. "Only, I haven't had any absinthe tonight."

The wall abruptly fell over backward, leaving a dark opening in its place, but there was no crash of impact. The wall was simply gone. "Look, a stone staircase descending into infinite darkness!" Gloria said. "How spooky!"

Altman joined them at the top of the steps – he could only see the first half a dozen stairs before darkness swallowed them – and peered around at the vast darkness beyond. Was this some huge cavern under French Hill? Or was it just… *nothing*? "I've never seen this part of the basements before."

"We're standing in the *real* basement," the warden said. "The one that's actually under the house, that someone dug out with shovels a long time ago. The rest of the basements, the deeper levels… those weren't built at all. They were made. And that darkness is the place they were made *in*." She gestured at the endless dark. "Sanford – or not Sanford himself, but his adepts – stole empty spaces from all over the world. They took from abandoned mines, lightless caves a thousand feet down, and flooded basements in abandoned towns. They bundled all that space together using strange geometries, and moved it all here, or rather, made it so you could *reach* that concatenation of space from here. Sanford has been expanding the habitable portions of the basements steadily for decades, growing the halls and chambers like mushrooms in a cave, and he hasn't begun to fill this space yet. There are a lot of forgotten places in the world." She took a hesitant step onto the stairs descending into the dark, as if testing for firmness. "It seems he's moved most of the basements farther away, pushed them into the dark. We're lucky he left a stairway to connect us to the rest. Once we reach the deep basements, I can stitch things back together, connect a door in the real basement to a door in the magical ones, and things will return to… I suppose you could call it normal."

"How far down do we have to go?" Altman said. "Through the dark?"

The warden chuckled. "Wrong question, lad. You should be asking what's *lurking* down there in the dark."

"Do you think that horrible shoggoth is down there?" Ruby pulled the handle of the sword cane out enough to show an inch of steel.

"The shoggoth?" the warden said. "I remember you had a run-in with the ma– with Sanford's pet. You nearly pissed your knickers, didn't you? Ha. That thing was just a baby, and half tame besides. That's how Sanford was able to use it as a guardian. There are things locked up in Sanford's menagerie that would eat the shoggoth and consider it an hors d'oeuvre. If *I* was Sanford, and I wanted to make sure no one mucked around with my things while I was away, I'd open up the grim menagerie and let those creatures roam."

"Really?" Gloria sounded more interested than terrified, which Altman thought displayed a tragic lack of understanding. "But surely the monsters would eat him, too, when he came back?"

"Oh, the things Sanford locked up are all afraid of *him*," the warden said. "They've learned."

"We'll just have to teach them to be afraid of us, too, then," Gloria said cheerfully, and strolled down the stairs, as if they weren't a narrow thread of matter connecting the earthly to the unknown.

# CHAPTER NINETEEN
## *The Cold Wastes*

"My first week in the Dreamlands was especially dreadful," Sanford said to the ash-haired sage on the top of the mountain. The magus – now the wanderer – scratched at his beard, which had gotten quite long, and was no longer neatly trimmed, though on occasion he hacked at it with a knife. "On the very day I arrived, I was pursued by the ghosts of the Beings of Ib. Have you heard of them? Frightful creatures."

"They brought doom to Sarnath." The sage didn't have ash-*colored* hair, but hair made of ash, sifting gray flakes down onto the shoulders of his red robe. "Though some say they did not rise up on their own, but were dispatched by–"

"They were certainly dispatched after me," Sanford interrupted. He'd met a few of these sages already, though most were more humanoid, and knew they could go on for hours if you let them start lecturing. "An enemy of mine made some kind of arrangement with the ghosts, and sent them to kill me, or at least keep me by the lake." He nibbled some kind of seed cake and sipped a cup of vile herbaceous tea. Sanford still didn't need sustenance. His ring was supping on the life force of the sage and any living things in the snow outside even now, but there was no reason to be impolite. This man, or man-shaped entity, was going to help him get home. *Finally*.

"And yet you escaped," the sage said. His eyes were just smoking holes in his stony face, but there was no doubt he could see perfectly well. That seeming contradiction would have unsettled even Sanford, once, before he'd spent all these months in the Dreamlands.

Sanford leaned back on a pile of cushions and looked up at the ceiling of the temple. They conversed beneath a dome of stone, with a circular window at the very top, revealing a white sky of blowing snow. It was quite warm and cozy in here, though, despite the lack of a fireplace or stove. The sage needed neither, as he produced ample heat – he was his own furnace, in a way.

"Oh, yes," Sanford said. "I thought, being ghosts, they might have a limited range. Many apparitions are linked with a particular place and can't stray far from their locus of origin. I set myself on a path that led straight away from the lake and ran. The knife-wielding spirits nearly caught up with me, once or twice. I have a spot on the back of my neck where one of them even laid a finger on me, and do you know, that patch of skin is completely numb? No sensation there at all when I press on it. I shudder to think what would have happened if they'd grabbed me… elsewhere."

"You escaped the denizens of Ib. You have traveled far from that place, to reach this one. Have you gained understanding in your travels?"

"Oh, I'd say so."

The sage leaned forward, eyes faintly smoking. The smell of fire and stone reminded Sanford of the night Huntress Fashions burned down. Gods, how long ago had that been? Months, at least. Time was hard to mark in the Dreamlands. "Tell me what you have found."

Sanford had had ample opportunity to reflect on his mistakes, to learn from them, and resolve to do things differently when he made it home. "I have learned that I should take better care of my allies. I have learned that personal loyalty is valuable, and preferable to instilling obedience through fear and intimidation. I have learned that I might, perhaps, in the future, relate to those in my employ with an open hand rather than a raised fist."

The sage frowned. "I am less interested in your personal growth than I am in the sights you saw and the entities you encountered."

Sanford chuckled. "Yes, quite."

The sage looked at him expectantly, even hungrily, and Sanford drew breath to tell the rest of his tale. He found this whole interaction tedious, but that tedium was the price he had to pay for help: the sage collected wisdom, or rather, the sage collected information, and then sifted it for wisdom, the way a panner sifts the contents of a riverbed for gold. Thinking of gold...

"I saw a golden gleam in the distance, and once the Ib were behind me, I set off across the blasted heath toward its source. I followed a spiraling path up a mountain, past these little caves with things living inside them, a bit like ghouls, but paler and with longer limbs. I had to fight them off. Fortunately, I had with me a dagger, made from the fang of an unusually large Hound of Tindalos." He flexed his right hand. The ring with a tooth on it was long gone, transformed into the knife, and subsequently lost. He'd acquired other blades, but none so wondrous. "That sent the buggers scattering for their holes, but didn't give me much hope for finding civilization at the summit. Functioning city-states tend to clear the monsters off their access roads. When I reached the heights, I found an abandoned temple of shining gold. It would have been lovely to loot, back in my world, but it was useless to me here, and infested with more of those monsters. I did find a sort of gondola, though, made of gold, which carried me across a sea of mist to the far shore."

"Yes, and then?" The sage's smoking eyes were showing hints of flame now. Did the fellow somehow *burn* knowledge, to fuel himself? Sanford didn't know, and, upon reflection, didn't much care. As long as he got what he wanted out of this arrangement, Sanford was not opposed to a fair deal. Sometimes that was the best you could do, after all.

The wanderer settled back as comfortably as he could and told the sage about his journeys. After the sea of mist, he reached the shores of the Underworld, where he supposed he must have been all along. Where else would the spirits of a dead city and its destroyers live?

But he recognized the Vale of Pnath from his extensive

research on the Dreamlands, and soon traversed the Sea of Bones. "It's aptly named," he said. "A truly vast plain of skeletal remains, some so ancient they crumbled to powder when touched, and some so fresh there was still meat clinging to their knobs." Anyone else would have died of thirst during his trek, but there was life even in that desolate place to sustain him – the ghouls who dumped their bones there, and the monstrous dholes who swam *under* the bones. "I lost my beautiful dagger in the side of some immense, wormlike beast, but they gave me a wide berth after I slew that one. And you know, I never had any bother from the ghouls at all, just saw them watching me from a distance."

"Why do you think that is?" Smoke emerged from the sage's mouth when he spoke now.

"Who can say?" Sanford shrugged. Privately, he thought the corpse-eaters might have heard stories about Sanford from their cousins under French Hill, and decided it was wisest to leave him be.

"From there I climbed the Peaks of Throk, and avoided the nightgaunts, and found the house of Shuggob."

"I have heard of this," the sage said. "A house of secrets and mysteries. Tell me what you learned there."

"Precious little," Sanford said. The house was a half-decayed manse nestled into a hollow near the summit of those foul mountains. Shuggob was said to be the oldest ghoul in existence, far more intelligent than others of his kind, and receptive to guests… so long as they were respectful. He was rumored to possess a library of arcane lore unsurpassed in any world, and the chance to visit that library was one of the reasons Sanford had wanted to come to the Dreamlands in the first place. But such a prospect was much more appealing in an astral body, when he could return to the waking world at will. If he went there in person, he might become a victim of the elder ghoul's notorious biological experiments. On the other hand, Shuggob also might know the way home. In the end, that was too great a temptation to resist.

"The problem was, Shuggob wasn't home," Sanford told the sage. "I sought entry into his house, and called out for him, but the commotion drew the attention of a passing nightgaunt, and I had to flee. I wasn't well equipped to fend off death from the sky at that point."

"That's disappointing," the sage murmured. "Tales of Shuggob always make good tinder."

"Imagine *my* disappointment. I'm sure the fellow could have pointed me toward the nearest portal back to Earth. But instead, I wandered farther." Sanford explained how he made it out of the Underworld, and continued to search for a way home, coming entirely too close to death at times. He'd been forced to unleash the great eel-thing from his tiepin when he was attacked by a massive shambling nightmare thing in the jungles of Kied. The eel devoured the beast, of course, and now the pin – in his pocket, since he'd been forced to use his tie as a bandage long ago – was in the shape of a thing made of teeth and tusks and tongues. "In Hlanath, I found a portal to the Abyss, which was not at all the direction I wished to go. In Hatheg and Mir, someone offered me a berth on a ship bound for the moon, assuring me that the moon of the Dreamlands and the moon of Earth were one and the same, and surely I could get home from *there*?"

"Couldn't you?" the sage said. "Are they a great distance apart? I have never been to Earth and have heard few tales about it."

"Suffice to say Earth and the moon are separated by a greater distance than I was capable of comfortably traveling," Sanford said. "I had other leads to follow, though. Some ghouls promised to show me a tunnel to a graveyard on Earth, but when I queried for details, it became clear it was a ruse to trap me, kill me, and devour me, so I had no choice but to dispatch them." That lot must not have been close with their cousins under French Hill, or they would have known better.

He went on: "I traded my pocket watch for passage to Illarnek, the great desert city, following a rumor of an explorer from Earth who was said to be living there, but by the time I arrived, the fool had gotten himself stabbed to death in a disagreement over the price of some relics." Those relics proved to be mundane Earth things: a dented teapot, a yo-yo, a ceramic dog. Everything was wondrous somewhere. "In time, I made my way to the city of Ilek-Vad, where I had an audience with the king, a most remarkable fellow who used to live on Earth. I had high hopes, and he was quite friendly, but had no interest in returning to our mutual home world, and he no longer possessed the key that had allowed him to travel easily from one realm to the other." That hadn't been a surprise. Sanford had heard rumors for decades that the Silver Key was on Earth somewhere and had wasted a fortune trying to track it down.

"I have heard of this man," the sage said. "I did not know he still lived. He must be very old."

"He had a snow-white beard down to his belt, so I'd concur," Sanford said. "Being a king in the Dreamlands either leads to a nice long life, or a brutally short one, I suspect. From there, I made my way to Dylath-Leen, and the wise women there told me about a sage who guarded a passage to my world, and so, here I am." He spread his hands.

"Here you are," the sage said. "But you are misinformed. I do not guard a passage to your world. I guard a passage to the Cold Wastes."

Sanford frowned. "The Cold Wastes? On the Plateau of Leng?" The Plateau was known to him, but he'd never realized that dreadful place was connected to the Dreamlands. Perhaps they came into conjunction only rarely? Or the borders shifted? Or maybe it was just a hole in his knowledge. At any rate, he could make his way to Earth from that frozen wasteland... albeit with a whole new set of challenges standing in his way. Still, progress was progress.

"I'm afraid there is no easy passage to your home from here, man. The wise women were mistaken, but from their point of view, one alien world seems much like another." The sage rose and let the red robe drop, revealing a sexless body of black stone veined by pulsing red lines. His eyes were burning bright now, white like the sparks from a fire brought to forging heat. "But it matters not. You have told me many things, Carl Sanford of Arkham of Earth. I have sampled the contents of your mind and memory and found them to be delicious. I will enjoy consuming the rest of you."

Ah. So the sage acquired knowledge by consuming the one who *possessed* the knowledge, then? Burning them and, what, inhaling their memories in the smoke? If only Sanford could have learned things so easily. The wise women might have mentioned this deadly detail, but then, the sage probably had some reciprocal arrangement with them. He must have a network of people spread throughout the Dreamlands to send him the desperate and credulous to sup upon.

Certain death, then. Again.

But Sanford hadn't spent these months searching, striving and surviving just to die here. He leapt to his feet and ran for the door he'd entered the temple through, grabbing for the knob – and hissed, drawing back his hand. The knob glowed red hot, and the door was too stout for Sanford to kick down.

There were no windows, and he couldn't make it through the door to the Cold Wastes without going past the sage, and that seemed a dangerous proposition. Flames were now leaping from the being's eye sockets, and his outstretched fingers glowed like branding irons.

Sanford considered his options. He had a new knife with a blade that glowed and burned, but its heat would hardly trouble this fellow. He could unleash the jungle beast trapped in his pin, and then the sage would be devoured and trapped in its stead. Having a wise one made of flames bound to his will could be useful in the future... but this domed room was small, and the jungle beast was so large it would fill the available space, almost certainly crushing Sanford against the wall and killing him. That was acceptable as a last resort – Sanford would never die without taking his assailant with him – but hardly the best choice.

He had another item, tucked away in an inner pocket, though he wasn't sure what good it could be here. There was very little written about that object, and what *was* written suggested it helped one to "move freely," which wasn't of obvious use in a fight like this. He wasn't sure that item did *anything*, honestly, though perhaps it had some passive effect, offering magical protection in subtle ways. He had made it through all these months traveling in the Dreamlands without being lost or trapped, which he would normally ascribe to his own superior capabilities… but he was a bit humbler these days, so yes, it could be down to the rock in his pocket instead.

He had only two other weapons left, then, and those would be consumed upon use. His hoarder's heart was loath to use either one, but since the alternative was being burned alive, needs must. "Nothing else for it, then," Sanford muttered. After a moment's thought, he plucked the ebony cube of a cufflink from his ragged left sleeve and rolled it across the floor toward the sage.

The cufflinks were in the shape of small dice. The pips on the ebony one were simply black, and thus nearly impossible to see, though you could feel the indentations with your fingertips. The ivory die had white pips of similar subtlety. "Looks like it's bad luck for you, old chap."

The sage looked down at the die, clearly expecting it to explode, but instead, it simply crumbled into fine grains of black dust. "Was that supposed to do something?" Flames burst from the sage's mouth when he spoke, hot enough to make Sanford turn his face away, even six feet apart. "I'm genuinely curious. I'm *always* curious."

"I suppose only time will tell." Sanford reached for the other cufflink. If necessary, it might make a tiny, life-saving difference–

The sage took another step toward him… and then a look of comical surprise appeared on his face, his eyes and mouth forming perfect Os as the floor of the temple collapsed beneath him. He vanished as neatly as if he'd been dropped through a trapdoor.

"Bad luck," Sanford said again, approaching the hole in the floor. You could never be quite sure what the dice would do, as they were, by their nature, random, but he knew the black one would lead to misfortune for his enemies, and the ivory one would grant him a temporary boon, from the minor to the major, depending on which number came up. At least he still had the good luck charm left. He might yet need it.

The temple was cantilevered out over the mountainside, and the sage had fallen straight through to drop about sixty feet to the frozen slopes below. All Sanford could see down there were gouts of steam rising from a hole in the snow. Assuming the sage couldn't fly – which was just an assumption, in this place – it would take him a while to trudge back up to the temple, his flames cooling all the while.

Sanford would be well on his way before then. He quickly checked the temple for anything worth taking, but the sage was an ascetic, and there wasn't so much as a silver candlestick or salt cellar, let alone survival gear or objects of a mystical nature. Knowledge was the sage's sole power – that, and the ability to spray flame from his eye sockets, of course.

The arched stone door at the back of the temple was barred, but not otherwise locked. Sanford wrapped his white fur cloak around his body, then flung open the door and stepped out into the freezing wind. He felt a tingle at the base of his neck that told him he'd left one world for another... though this was a world of nothing but featureless white and stinging snow.

The door slammed shut behind him, and when he looked back, it was no longer visible, either hidden, or actually vanished – which was sensible enough. Various deadly and terrible entities were said to dwell in the Cold Wastes, and you wouldn't want things like those wandering into your warm and cozy temple.

Sanford knew a bit about the Plateau of Leng. It was one of the other worlds he had visited, during his years mastering the mystical arts. He'd even glimpsed the fabled Monastery of Leng once, though a blizzard had prevented his expedition from reaching it, and he'd been forced to turn back when two of his fellow explorers died of hypothermia. They were only Seekers, though, so it was no great loss. He'd always intended to return, better provisioned, but he hadn't yet had time.

But he *could* return, because there was a portal to the Plateau, and indeed to the Cold Wastes, on the deepest level of his subbasement. He even used that portal, occasionally, to exile Lodge members who'd failed him, or put their own interests above his own. Their bodies were doubtless preserved under the snow even now. To think, all along, it held a connection to the Dreamlands! No matter how much he discovered, there were new mysteries to uncover.

He was in a horrible frozen wasteland, yes, but he could *get home* from here. The Lodge's portals to other realms were warded, of course, and couldn't be traversed by just anyone. He could hardly let curious Seekers wander to other worlds at will, and he didn't want monsters strolling into *his* world uninvited, either. But Sanford still wore the bracelet of little keys on his wrist, and those allowed him to access every part of his Lodge, and to open (or close) every passageway from the basements to other worlds.

Salvation was near! But not necessarily *very* near. The Cold Wastes were vast, and largely bereft of landmarks, so it would be difficult to find the particular bit of empty space that held the doorway home. Still, Sanford was tireless, thanks to his Annelid ring... but in the Cold Wastes, the most desolate part of the Plateau, would there be anything alive to draw sustenance from? The monks, perhaps, if the monastery wasn't too far away, and if it didn't magically travel... man-eating spiders, if he walked near some, assuming such things could be robbed of their energies...

"Tut, tut, Sanford," he muttered, hunching against the relentless wind. "Don't be defeatist now." He had to focus. Tillinghast was in Arkham, taking what belonged to Sanford – assuming the shopkeeper hadn't died trying to reach the basements. Also assuming Sanford was returning to a home he would recognize at all. Time ran differently in the Dreamlands, and it could run differently in either direction. Sanford might return ten minutes after he'd left... or ten centuries.

But he *would* return. If he must die, he would die on his native soil. Sanford set off across the snow, and he walked, and he walked, and he walked. There seemed to be no sun in this place, or else, its presence or absence made little difference to visibility or the light level, which was a constant gloom. The far north on Earth had long periods of sun, and long periods of dark, but this place seemed an eternal twilight. The ring tried to keep Sanford's body temperature in the appropriate range for human health, but since there were few sources of heat to steal from here, his teeth were soon chattering.

Then he glimpsed something in the distance. A gleam of light, visible through the snow. He redoubled his efforts, hurrying toward the light, glad he'd traded the handful of coins in his pockets (impossibly exotic here) for sturdy fur-lined boots, and his cloak, back in Dylath-Leen.

Soon he reached the source of the light, and he stared, first in bafflement, and then in understanding. He began to laugh, so hard he had to bend at the waist and brace his hands on his knees, so hard it brought tears to his eyes, only for those tears to freeze on his own face.

The wanderer was standing before a great glass wall, and on the other side, distorted but identifiable, he could see the shelves of a country store for giants – cans of beans the size of houses, lanterns as tall as lighthouses, bags of potatoes as big as boulders. A human figure, but immense, passed across the glass, like a whale in an aquarium, and then moved out of sight.

Sanford was looking through the glass of the enchanted snow globe that Tillinghast had given that objectionable little man at the store. The globe wasn't full of magical snow at all. It simply provided a window onto a fragment of the Cold Wastes. Or… did it somehow *contain* that fragment? Surely not. Tillinghast couldn't be that powerful.

Sanford remembered glimpsing a figure moving in the snow globe, trudging through its perpetually blowing snow. A monk? A lost wanderer? Or even… Sanford himself, glimpsed through a distortion in time?

"I must give that wretched Tillinghast his due," Sanford said. He'd gotten into the habit of talking to himself, in recent months, because good conversation was important. "His baubles are certainly of exceptional quality."

He briefly considered trying to smash the glass, mostly out of spite, and partly out of curiosity. Would breaking the glass shatter the connection? Would it open a tiny portal between the howling wastes and that man's store? Would Sanford be able to pass *through* it? If he did, would he remain tiny on the other side, or return to his proper relative size?

In any case, he had nothing to plausibly break the glass with anyway, so such speculations were pointless. He turned his back on the view of the general store and trudged into the blowing white wind.

Home was near, and he would find it soon, and when he did, he would bring this cold back with him, in his heart, and Tillinghast would be frozen before him.

# CHAPTER TWENTY
*Those Who Fight Monsters*

Ruby had no idea how long they descended into that darkness. The staircase was wide, easily ten feet across, but it felt terribly narrow in that vastness. There were no railings, so they went single file down the center, stepping carefully. No one speculated aloud on what might happen if you fell over the side and went tumbling into all that stolen space. Ruby's personal theory was "just keep falling until you die of thirst," but the back of her mind whispered that such a death would be too merciful – that there must be things down there in the dark, with hungry mouths and grasping claws.

There were landings every few hundred yards, and when they got within a few steps of one, a gas lamp on a pole there would illuminate, spreading a pool of light. Those lamps stayed lit behind them, at least, so Ruby could glance back and see a series of glows rising, rising, rising through the blackness. Breadcrumbs to follow home, if it came to that.

Every third landing was outfitted with a little park bench, as if they were situated at scenic observation points, instead of just overlooking the lightless void. Gloria paused at each landing and gazed out, exclaiming over how *wondrous* and *remarkable* the place was. She was beginning to grate on Ruby's nerves in a way she never had before. Being perky was one thing. Being delusional was another.

There were a hundred steps between each landing, and the light from the lamps covered forty or so, leaving a shadowy stretch to cross before the next landing lit up. The warden was leading the way, or rather, one of her hounds was, with the warden close behind. Gloria came after her, walking with a bounce in her step, enjoying this outing as only someone with no concept of supernatural peril could. Ruby came after her, sword cane at the ready, and Altman walked behind her with his gun, grumbling pretty much constantly.

After several thousand steps, Ruby said, "Are we even *getting* anywhere? I'm sure we passed that same bench twenty minutes ago."

"We are progressing," the warden said from the front of their parade. "The first test is a simple test of patience."

"What's the second test, then?"

The warden was just disappearing into the pool of shadow beyond the reach of the light above. "That remains to be–" she began.

Then a large, lithe shape swooped down out of the darkness above, snatched up the hound, and bore it away. The dog howled, but soon its yips faded away to nothing. Ruby drew her sword and crouched, looking all about her, and the warden dropped, too. Altman cursed behind her, and she dearly hoped he wouldn't discharge his shotgun so close to her head – she'd be deafened, at best, and caught by a stray shot at worst.

"Was that one of the... mi-go, are they called?" Gloria was still standing up, looking around, as if watching for rare birds. "Mr Tillinghast told me about them. He has this cunning little canister he says they dropped in one of their flights here–"

"It was a nightgaunt." The warden's voice was strained, and she hissed, as if in pain. Did her connection to the dogs extend to feeling their agony? "Get down, you fool woman! They'll carry you off, and you'll never be seen again!"

Gloria didn't crouch. "Oh. Mr Tillinghast mentioned those, too. He said they're vile things, truly abominable. No faces, isn't that right? Just blank spaces. No faces means no teeth, at least."

"Their claws will do just fine," the warden said. "I said get down!"

"I don't think crouching will help," Gloria said. "There's no cover here. Perhaps we should keep moving, instead, and more swiftly?"

"I agree!" Altman shout-whispered and jostled against Ruby's back.

"I... there doesn't seem to be a flock of the things," the warden said. "I'm still connected to my poor hound, and it's being carried off. There's some sort of stone pillar where the thing has a nest... they usually travel in swarms. They aren't solitary by nature, but this one is alone. It must be from Sanford's menagerie. He only had one nightgaunt, last

I heard. So he *has* set the beasts free. We must be near the bottom of the stairs, then... but who knows what waits for us?"

"We won't find out by huddling here," Gloria said sensibly. "Listen, Ruby, you should scout ahead. Use your special little trick and see if you can clear us a path."

"I..." She swallowed. "I'm a thief, Gloria, not a monster hunter."

"You're the one who picked up the sword, dear," she said. "Mr Tillinghast will be very grateful, I'm sure."

Ruby moaned. She was really going to have to do this, wasn't she?

"What are you talking about?" Altman said. "If anyone should go ahead, it's me. I have a shotgun. What special trick does she mean?"

"Let a girl have some secrets, Altman." Ruby considered asking for the shotgun, but how would it even work in null-time? She'd be able to fire it, probably, but once the pellets moved away from her immediate vicinity, they'd likely hang in the air, unmoving, and she could end up blowing her own face off if she was standing in the wrong spot when normal time restarted. Better to proceed with the sword.

Ruby moved slowly around Gloria, stepping too close to the edge for comfort. The woman patted her on the back, making Ruby flinch. "That sword is *made* for slicing up monsters," she said. "You'll do fine."

"Warden, how many beasts, monsters, whatever, are in this menagerie?" Ruby paused alongside Van Shaw.

The warden sniffed. "I haven't been down there in a long

time. Locking things up that way, it's not to my liking, but Sanford said it was important for his *studies*. But as I recall, besides the nightgaunt, there's a byakhee – those fly, too – and a child of Abhoth, and one dhole, though it's only about the size of a footstool. There's definitely a crawling one... there was a hunting horror, but it died in captivity, two researchers were poisoned during the autopsy... oh, and the gug, of course, that was one of his first live acquisitions. There's definitely a Leng spider, and a moon-beast. I think that's all. And your old friend the shoggoth is down there somewhere, too."

"I don't know why I asked," Ruby said. "Apart from the shoggoth, I don't know what any of those things you mentioned even are."

"If you see a monster, it's more important for you to kill it than to identify it," Gloria said from behind. "And do it soon. The clock is ticking. My master wants this place under his control by morning, and the night is progressing swiftly."

"Yes, fine, I'm going." Ruby took a breath and stepped past the warden but didn't immediately leave the shadowy stretch of steps. Being in the darkness felt a little safer, somehow, though if the nightgaunt didn't have a face, it probably didn't hunt with senses as mundane as sight anyway. With luck, it would be occupied for a while, eating the hound.

Ruby looked at her wrist, the radium dial glowing in the dark, and began to twist the knobs.

"I still don't understand what she's doing," Altman complained.

"Your understanding is not–" Gloria began, but then Ruby finished turning the clock back, and null-time took hold. There were few sounds in the void, but that only meant the breathing of her compatriots was easily audible, and its absence made the place into a tomb.

She only had an hour, to find and kill whatever beasts down there wanted to find and kill *her*. She drew the sword and left the wooden sheath on the steps, moving swiftly toward the next landing.

Which wasn't illuminated, of course, because she was outside the regular flow of time, and the gas lamp stayed dim. She should have thought of that. But… there *was* light, wasn't there, up ahead? When she peered down the next flight of steps, an end to the descent finally appeared. There was a real hallway down there, the edges of the walls and floor and ceiling sheared-off and visible against the darkness, like a stage set of a room seen from the theater audience. It looked like the other half of the hallway they'd departed from in the world above, and there was a light bulb shining on the ceiling.

Ruby briefly wondered what would happen if she climbed on *top* of that ceiling, and walked across the roof of the corridor, into the dark… but she wasn't curious enough to try it. She hurried down the dark steps instead, and when her feet touched the floorboards, and she finally had walls on either side instead of void, she wanted to drop to her knees and kiss the ground. The hallway turned sharply to the right just a few yards ahead, and she hoped there wouldn't be another maze down here, since she had no hound to help her traverse it.

Ruby walked around the corner, sword held before her – and screamed, dropping the blade and stumbling backward a few steps. There was a huge beast in the hallway, a purple crab the size of a Shetland pony – no, it was a *spider*. Look at its fangs, look at its glittering profusion of eyes! Ruby wasn't one of those people with a paralyzing fear of spiders. She'd had a roommate once who couldn't even smash the things with a shoe, but could only hyperventilate and beg someone else to deal with the menace. But it didn't take an arachnophobe to feel terror at the sight of *this* thing: it was malevolent death on eight legs.

The thing was frozen mid-scuttle, its four front limbs lifted off the ground, their pointed ends aimed at Ruby like spears. The spider filled the hallway entirely, impossible for her to get around … but she wasn't supposed to get around it, was she? She was supposed to kill it.

Ruby bent and picked up the sword. She imagined this spider, moving in real time, scuttling around the corner, up the stairs, launching itself toward them with terrifying speed … it would have killed them all, and easily. Ruby thought she probably would have leapt off the side of the stairs rather than face its clashing mandibles and horrible limbs.

She touched the end of the blade to its abdomen, closed her eyes, and pressed. Despite the thing's chitinous armor, the sword point penetrated with ease – she might have been cutting butter. When she made herself look, the sword had pierced the spider's body fully, point emerging from the back. Was that enough to kill the thing? She wasn't sure, and the idea of the spider scurrying around, wounded and maddened by pain, was even more terrifying than the thought of it healthy.

So Ruby started cuttings its legs off. The result was deeply surreal. She severed the legs as close to the body as she could with swipes of the sword, but the detached limbs still hung in the air beneath the spider, as if attached by invisible threads, until she pushed the dismembered parts aside with the flat of the blade. Ruby couldn't bear the thought of touching the legs with her hands, so she pushed them to both sides of the hallway as best she could. Chopping the legs off was tiring, too, like splitting a cord of firewood with an old axe.

The sword blade was covered with purplish black ichor by the time she was finished, and she swung the blade back and forth to fling off the droplets, which then hung in the air all around her in hideous globules. Ugh. She was clearly still getting the hang of navigating null-time.

The body of the spider hung in the air, now unsupported by its legs, like something one of those surrealists in Paris might have painted. Ruby slashed down with the sword, right through the center of the body, intending to bisect it cleanly, but the thing was just too *big*. The sword only cleaved about two-thirds of the way through its body, but surely that was a mortal wound?

How to proceed, though? The thing was still in the way! Ruby finally got down on her hands and knees and crawled awkwardly underneath the spider, pushing the sword along the floor ahead of her. The back of her brain screamed that she was in danger, there was a predator right above her, there were hideous fluids dripping on her, a great weight was going to crush her – but she pushed on with gritted teeth until she'd reached the far side and regained her feet.

A glance at her watch told her that the whole affair had only taken about five minutes, much less time than she'd believed. The watch was distorting time in one way, and her fear was distorting it in another.

She took a breath, squared her shoulders, and set off down the hall, toward the next turning. Whatever waited for her on the other side would meet the same fate as that hideous spider. It felt a little unsporting to carve up these monsters while they were frozen in null-time... but it wasn't like the beasts would have given up their advantages in size, speed, strength, and hideous mandibles if their positions were reversed.

"You must be the gug," she said when she found a multi-limbed, multi-jointed thing, with mouths shaped like scythe blades, looming in the doorway of a side passage. "You *look* like a gug."

She set about her grim work, and wondered how long this night was going to last.

Altman was tense, watching for monsters, and still bitter that Ruby had been sent on ahead instead of him, when he was clearly the stronger choice... and then Ruby returned, scarcely minutes after she'd left, trudging up the stairs toward them, dragging the point of her sword on the ground. Her clothes were smeared with green and black stains, her hair disheveled, her sword coated in slime. How could anyone possibly get so dirty so quickly? "You're back already?" Altman said.

"I cleared the way." She sounded incredibly weary, and the sword was covered in foul, dripping slime.

"What, you killed everything?"

"I didn't see the shoggoth. But I saw a lot of other things and killed them all. There might be more... but all the ones I found were headed toward us, *hunting* us, so with luck they're all gone."

"How did you defeat the entire menagerie so quickly?" Altman demanded.

"Mr Tillinghast is a powerful friend to have," Gloria said. "He gave her the tools she needed. Is it much farther to the bottom, Ruby?"

Ruby mutely shook her head and started back down the stairs, limping.

Altman heard a flapping sound, and something swooped out of the darkness toward Ruby. Not the nightgaunt again – this was winged, too, but less humanoid. It put Altman in mind of an immense beetle, but with a carapaced head and black teeth. "Down!" he bellowed, and raised his shotgun. Gloria and the warden ducked, and Ruby actually flung herself down full-length on the stairs.

Altman pulled both triggers, and the shotgun kicked hard against him. The sound of the gunshot was swallowed up by the void, without echoes, and the monster – a byakhee, Altman thought it was called – tumbled to land on the steps below Ruby. It thrashed and mewled, a winged monster the size of a Great Dane, until Ruby got up and thrust the sword into its head in a single decisive motion. She looked back up the stairs at him. "Good shooting, Altman."

"Praise from the master monster-killer?" Altman said. "I appreciate it, and I mean that sincerely."

She gave him a little salute, then kicked the byakhee's body until it tumbled off the side and resumed her descent.

After the next landing, the end of the stairway appeared suddenly, like a magician's conjuring trick. Ruby reached the bottom first, and then the warden descended with stately calm, and Gloria with unhurried ease, all preventing Altman from doing what he *wanted* to do – leap down in great bounds to something that at least *looked* like a normal corridor.

When Altman's foot finally touched the floor of the deep basement, there was a gurgling, wrenching sound above him. He turned to look back, sure they were going to be cut off and sealed below that darkness forever, in Sanford's final trap.

Instead, the staircase extending so far above him into the dark distorted, first seeming to stretch out and attenuate, becoming a long thread attaching them to the world above. A moment later, the stairs seemed to compress down instead, like an accordion, the landings overlapping, stairs piling atop stairs... until, after a confused moment, there was only a single flight of a hundred steps, leading up to the hallway where they'd started this journey. The darkness was gone, or at least held back by walls of wood and plaster.

"Sanford's spells are unpicking themselves as we progress," the warden said. "Restoring the original topology of the Lodge. We won't have such a long walk back up, at least."

"Excellent," Gloria said. "If we've reattached the

basements to the upper floors, then we've made major progress. We'll take a look around, unravel any other spatial knots Sanford has left for us, make sure none of the beasts of the menagerie are still loose, and then… we're going to find where the magus hid his relics. We need them, especially the Ruby of R'lyeh. Mr Tillinghast mentioned that in particular. Once that's done, I can give a positive report to Mr Tillinghast." She clapped her hands like a camp counselor about to start a singalong. "Shall we proceed?"

"There are ugly things up ahead," Ruby said, voice still drained of energy. "Consider yourself warned."

She led the way through the basements, and Altman's astonishment only grew. They passed the chopped-up remnants of an oozing spider bigger than himself, and then a heap of slime and limbs that had come from some creature he couldn't possibly identify. Next came a great shell, and the creature that lived inside, like a cone snail but writ large, was sliced to pieces.

Ruby pointed out one of the libraries to Gloria, and said, "Sorry about the mess."

The mess was considerable – the floor was covered in a sort of ankle-deep gray suet, from which emerged fragments of bone and tentacle. It stank like a midden. That had been something *alive*? Altman was aghast, and after all he'd seen, he'd believed himself beyond disgust.

"I'm sure we can have it cleaned," Gloria said.

The operating theater where Sanford and Altman had examined the sodden gift was covered in thousands of dead worms, and a few that still slithered and wriggled. "What happened here?" Altman said.

"A crawling one," the warden said. There was a dog at her heels again – where had it come from? The hound stalked around the room, snapping up the living worms in its teeth. "It's a great horrible lot of worms all working together as one. Looks like Ruby cut it up well enough to break its coherence, but my hound will finish the job. Otherwise, it might re-form, in time."

"You doled out this much slaughter in mere minutes?" Altman said to Ruby.

"Time isn't what it used to be," she said. Why did everyone have to be so maddeningly *vague*? When Altman possessed all the Lodge's occult secrets – well, yes, he'd probably keep them to himself, too, actually.

They walked for what felt like days, and was at least hours. Gloria produced a little notebook at some point, and seemed to be drawing a map, stopping to consult with the warden from time to time. The basements had been restored to their original form, at least as far as Altman could recognize. There was the ritual chamber, with the stone where he'd said his oaths. The vault, now entirely empty, which made Gloria cluck her tongue, even though Ruby had told them to expect it. The archives, the storage rooms, the research labs, the theaters. The only things they couldn't find were the doors to *other* places.

"There should be a dark forest right through there." Altman patted his hand against a doorway blocked up with blank gray stone. "Did Sanford have these doors walled up, or something?"

"He severed the portals to other worlds," Gloria said. "Or else he barricaded them by magic. That's a trifle annoying, but it's of no great consequence. Mr Tillinghast has his own ways of traveling."

"But *I* don't," Altman said. "I'd like to have my magic doors back, thanks, when the Lodge is mine."

"I'm sure once you're head of the Lodge, you'll have the resources to restore them," Gloria said, clearly indifferent to his plight. "Now, what's down this way?" She strode forward, toward a set of double doors that led to a sunken Greek amphitheater where disquieting plays were sometimes staged by a troupe of Seekers.

"Oh no," Ruby said. "Do you all smell that?"

The warden snapped her head up and actually growled, in tandem with her hound, whose hackles were up. Gloria cocked her head, merely curious. Altman sniffed. There was a sort of chemical reek, like too many cleaning supplies mixed together.

And then a bubbling blob of slime the size of a car appeared from a side corridor and jammed itself into the hallway. Its bulk divided their party. Gloria was on the far side, nearer the amphitheater, while Altman, the warden, and Ruby were on the other.

Gloria was shouting something incomprehensible, hidden from view beyond the creature, and Altman and the warden froze, staring at the hideous bulk and its writhing pseudopods.

Ruby just *ran*, instantly, sprinting away from the others without so much as a look back.

Altman gaped after her for a moment, and then lifted his shotgun. "What *is* that thing?" The monster roiled, eyes floating in its body like beans floating in a stew, and horrible sucking mouths opened and closed at random across its form. The thing made a terrible high-pitched sound from those mouths: "Tekeli-li! Tekeli-li!"

"It's a shoggoth!" the warden cried.

"What?" Altman cried. "I thought Sanford's shoggoth was smaller – just a baby!"

"It *was* just a baby. But it's grown!" The warden turned and ran, too, her hound at her heels, and Altman hesitated for only a moment before following. It was hard to imagine firing on that monster with a shotgun would achieve anything other than drawing its attention. As for Gloria… she could run away, too, and they could find each other elsewhere–

But then behind him, he heard a sound that must have been Gloria's final scream, and all he could think was: *Better her than me.*

# CHAPTER TWENTY-ONE
*Ruin*

Sanford pushed through the frigid whiteness, stumbling on the uneven ground, the cold sapping his strength, his will, his everything. His ring could find nothing from which to draw sustenance in this place, and he could feel every month of hard travel, as if he'd only deferred the pain, not avoided it. His muscles ached, and the numbing cold seeped all the way into his bones. Knowing there was a way home somewhere nearby made his suffering worse. He might easily perish here, within strides of a portal, and there would be no marker, no record, no sign that the great Carl Sanford, erstwhile leader of the Silver Twilight Lodge, had breathed his last moments.

"Except for 'Here lies an unremarkable heap of snow,'" he said out loud, grimly.

He staggered another step, kicking through ice-crusted snow, his teeth gritted against the wind. He'd never given up. He wouldn't give up now until his body gave him no choice.

The bracelet on his wrist rattled of its own accord, the profusion of tiny wired-together keys clattering.

He stopped, and turned in a slow circle, arm extended into the wind, until he felt the bracelet tug, and then he walked in that direction, like a dowser following his rod to deep water.

The wanderer walked with purpose through the blowing flakes, following the pull of the bracelet, until he found a boulder the size of a cottage. Yes! That was familiar, a rare landmark in the wastes.

He felt around the boulder until he came to a crack, barely big enough to wedge himself into sideways, but he knew that crevice, and he shoved himself into it hard, even as the stone scraped against his back and chest.

The keys on his wrists jangled, playing the music of his passage, and then...

Sanford stumbled out of the Cold Wastes, and into the deepest basement of the Silver Twilight Lodge. He sank to his knees on the worn wooden floorboards. It wasn't warm down there – the basements were a constant cool temperature, like a cavern – but it was so much warmer than the wastes that it felt like he was beside a roaring fire.

Sanford was *home*. His face ached as he smiled, and he clenched his fists and raised them overhead. Yes. Yes! He would gather his weapons, and muster his allies, and take the fight to–

Ruby Standish came hurtling around a corner into the passageway, holding a sword – *his* sword! – in one hand. She was clearly panicked and didn't see him as she spun and slammed closed a set of double doors at the end of the hall, then shot home the bolts at top and bottom to secure it. How peculiar. The basement should have become a nigh-impassable labyrinth as soon as he left the vicinity of Earth, but then, Ruby always was resourceful.

She turned to resume her sprint, sword held before her like a jungle trailblazer's machete, but after two steps she stopped and stared at him, wide-eyed, for a long moment. "*Sanford?*" she cried. "Where did you come from?"

"Elsewhere." He rose to his feet, trying to present his usual unflappable, dignified self... which was difficult in a filthy suit jacket he'd been wearing for months, under a tattered fur cloak, with snow melting in his eyebrows. "Tell me, dear Ruby. How long have I been away, and what have I missed?"

When she saw the shoggoth, Ruby lost all reason. She sprinted down corridors at random, slamming doors shut when she passed them, hoping to put distance and barriers between herself and the newly immense monstrosity. She'd spared barely a thought for Gloria, or Altman, or the warden, but under the circumstances, it was everyone for themselves. She trusted they'd had the good sense to flee, too, and make their own way through the labyrinthine basements... at least, Altman and the warden might have. Gloria had been cut off from easy escape routes. She was resourceful, but Ruby feared no amount of resourcefulness could have overcome that situation.

Ruby never doubted the shoggoth was chasing after her, though. It knew her. It *remembered* her. And so she'd run, and run, and run.

She almost ran right into Sanford. Ruby didn't even recognize him at first. He was dressed like some sort of barbarian chieftain in a pulp magazine, and she thought he was another monster from the menagerie, so brandished her sword at him.

When she recognized him, she almost struck him down anyway, knowing Tillinghast would richly reward such a decisive act... but she couldn't do it. Killing frozen monsters was one thing, but this was Sanford, and whatever else he might be, he was a *person*. She'd saved his life before, and he'd saved hers. Betraying him in the abstract had been a strategic decision... but striking him now, face-to-face? No. She wouldn't allow Tillinghast to turn her into a murderer. She wouldn't let him. She lowered the sword and let it hang by her side.

That was even assuming the sword could kill him, which was no sure thing. The magus was good at staying alive. Clearly. He'd returned from whatever horrible exile Tillinghast had sent him into. But even though that spoke to Sanford's resilience, and even though it was kind of nice to see him and alive, she really didn't think he could beat Tillinghast... and she had to ally herself with the winning side.

Fortunately, there were other ways to deal with Sanford than violence. He still thought Ruby and Altman were his allies, after all. Ruby was much better at deception than she was at stabbing.

She answered him with an array of half-truths. "After you disappeared, earlier today, Tillinghast sent in Gloria and some thugs to take over the Lodge. The warden is helping them. I don't know why, maybe they're controlling her mind. Altman and I have been trying to stop them. We followed them down hundreds of steps, through a void, and then… Sanford, there are all these monsters down here!"

He actually smiled. "Lovely specimens, aren't they? They're normally locked up in special cages for study, but I made arrangements for their release if I should depart the earthly realm. I don't suppose the Dyer woman got eaten?"

Ruby thought of the shoggoth and shuddered. She hadn't even consciously decided to flee from the thing. Just seeing it again, hideous as ever and so much larger than last time, had short-circuited her mind and activated her legs. "She might have been. I haven't seen her since we started fighting off your pets. It's been chaotic down here."

"That *was* the idea, yes," he said. "What about Tillinghast? Is he here?"

She shook her head. "I haven't seen him." *He's up in Arkham, stealing your life.*

"He's probably making arrangements to have me declared dead, and himself my heir," Sanford said.

That was shockingly accurate. "Why do you say that?"

Sanford sighed. "Because it's the same thing *I* once did, to a man named Alexander Peterman, when I stole his secret society from him. Tillinghast is fond of nasty taunts, I've learned, and doing to me what I once did to another would please him, I think. I may not be the nicest person, Miss Standish – I have no illusions on that score – but I am seldom cruel for cruelty's sake, unlike Tillinghast."

Something slammed into the double doors on the other side, rattling the doors, and Sanford frowned. "One of my beasts, I suppose?"

"The shoggoth, probably," Ruby said. "I don't think it likes me, since I escaped it last time."

"Mmm. I'm not sure they hold grudges, exactly, but they're strange beings, so who knows? I've been feeding it, you know. It's growing nicely. Perhaps it ate those thugs of Tillinghast you mentioned. They don't seem to excrete waste; they just get bigger with every meal." He stroked his long and ragged beard. "Now that I'm home, Ruby, we really must find a way to dispose of Tillinghast once and for all."

Inspiration struck Ruby like lightning out of a clear sky. There might be a way to stay on Tillinghast's good side without resorting to violence. She was much more adept at deception, anyway. "Sanford. I know how to beat him." She put her hand on his arm, moving close to him, and concentrated all her efforts into appearing sincere. She had to sell it to make her plan work. "You have to take me to wherever you've hidden your relics." She glanced back at the closed door. "Assuming we can get there without backtracking."

Sanford raised an eyebrow. "I can go anywhere I please down here. But you think I possess something that can defeat Tillinghast?"

"You do. You've had it all along." Her voice rose with excitement. "It's the Ruby of R'lyeh, Sanford! I pretended to work for Tillinghast, like you told me, and gained his confidence. After you disappeared, he let slip why he wants the gem so desperately – his soul is trapped inside it!" She was wildly confabulating, but if she could find out where Sanford had hidden his treasures, she could steal the relic and make Tillinghast happy. Maybe he'd even forgive her for not killing Sanford when she had the chance.

The doors rattled with another impact, making Ruby flinch. She really wanted to start running away again, but it would be good if she could also be running *toward* something.

The magus took no note of the commotion, so fixed was his attention on Ruby. "*What*?" Sanford's eyes widened. "All this time I've held Tillinghast's life in my hands? I have the Ruby of R'lyeh *with* me!"

"Wait, you do?" That wasn't ideal. Tillinghast would be pleased to get the gem, sure, but he wanted everything, and how could she trick Sanford into revealing the location of his new vault now?

Sanford scoffed. "Of course I do. As soon as Tillinghast made it clear he wanted the stone, I resolved to keep it on my person, lest he send someone to retrieve it. I'm ashamed to say I even doubted *your* loyalty, Ruby, until you brought me the grail." He sighed. "Not that the grail worked out as I'd hoped, either. I'll have to tell you about my adventures sometime. For now..." He patted his filthy suit on the breast. "His soul, eh? That's an old sorcerer's trick. If you keep your soul safely locked away, your body becomes immortal. I had the gem with me when I was exiled, and I've held on to it through travails you can't imagine. I would have thrown the thing into a volcano if I'd known it contained Tillinghast's essence. I'm going to smash the blasted thing now."

Ruby chewed her lip. "I think it's pretty sturdy. You'll need a hammer or something–"

The doors buckled as the shoggoth hurled itself against them in its rage, and Ruby took advantage of the commotion to flinch, pressing herself against Sanford. She was a better cat burglar than a pickpocket, but she was one of the best cat burglars in the world, and she was a *very* good pickpocket. She reached into Sanford's inner pocket, plucked out the Ruby of R'lyeh, and had it tucked away in an instant.

"Sorry." She steadied herself and moved away from him. "We should go and find, I don't know, an anvil and a big hammer or something; surely you've got a horrible armory down here someplace."

"There's no need for all that." She spun and saw Tillinghast leaning against the wall, examining his fingernails.

Ruby gaped at him. Tillinghast *was* here? Had he trailed along after them, waiting for them to clear out the spatial puzzles and the monsters, and following once it was safe? That certainly seemed like Tillinghast's way. Why risk himself when he had retainers to clear the way?

The shoggoth rattled the doors, the wood splintering at the top, but Tillinghast appeared entirely unconcerned, and Sanford only had eyes for his enemy. He plucked the sword from Ruby's unresisting hand and then put himself between her and Tillinghast – an act of casual protectiveness that made Ruby's guts twist. Was it too late to change her mind, and switch sides?

But the pragmatic part of her decided to wait and watch instead.

"I've got your life in my hands, Randall," Sanford crowed, reaching into his suit jacket. The look of puzzlement on his face was brief but heartbreaking, and in less than a second had hardened into a blank hostility. He turned around, his gaze landing on Ruby.

She stepped past him, and around him, and went to stand beside Tillinghast. She took the Ruby of R'lyeh from her bra and handed it to the shopkeeper, who held it up to the light of the bulb overhead and smiled before pocketing the gem.

"I'm sorry, Sanford." She bowed her head for a moment, an uncharacteristic wash of shame flowing through her. She'd really believed she could juggle her relationship with these two sorcerers and keep their competing needs in balance, but down here, in the dark with the monsters, she had to make a final choice. She chose the bigger monster. "I really am. But if I didn't do what Tillinghast wanted… he was going to do horrible things to me."

"And you think I won't?" Sanford's voice was steel and ice.

She bowed her head. "I think you probably won't be able to."

Tillinghast watched their exchange with open amusement.

"Does the Ruby even hold his soul?" Sanford asked.

The shopkeeper threw his head back and laughed. "My *soul*? How droll. My soul. Like some wizard in a fairy story? No, no. That's not why I want the Ruby of R'lyeh at all."

"Then why?" Sanford demanded.

"You don't get to know that," Tillinghast said. "The

magus is now the ignoramus, and you will die that way. I've enjoyed toying with you, Sanford – a bit like tearing the wings off flies, I suppose, but one must take diversions where one can. Ruby, why don't you leave us? If you follow the corridor behind me and take the first two lefts and then a right, you should reach a familiar passage. I'm sure you'll find your way out. The warden and Altman escaped the shoggoth, so I imagine you'll find them heading for the exit, too." He smirked. "Yes, Altman betrayed you, too, Sanford."

"But… what about Gloria?" Ruby said.

"I don't think you'll be seeing her again," Tillinghast said with complete indifference.

Ruby shuddered. She cast one last look at Sanford, but his eyes were fixed on the shopkeeper, and she hurried away.

"It's all come down to this, then." Tillinghast stood with his hands clasped casually before him. "Two great foes, facing off for control of the Silver Twilight Lodge, and for the soul of Arkham itself, in a clash of occult mastery–"

"Oh, do shut up," Sanford said, and threw the tiepin he had clutched in his hand at Tillinghast's feet.

The pin flashed with a burst of green light as it fell, and the hideous jungle beast Sanford had faced in the Dreamlands appeared, enraged. That rage fell squarely on Tillinghast. The thing was bigger than an elephant, so immense it cracked the walls with its bulk, and it lashed its limbs and gnashed its maw at the interloper. "Oh, who's this now?" Tillinghast shouted, voice full of mirth.

*Laugh while you can, old man.* Sanford backed away toward the double doors – the enchantment that had bound the Dreamland creature meant it couldn't harm him intentionally, but it could easily injure him by accident if he wasn't careful. Now the beast would devour Tillinghast… and then *Tillinghast* would be trapped in the pin, the binding enchantments passing to him, and he would be in Sanford's power forever. *I'll drop the pin in a volcano*, he thought. Unlike the false claims about the ruby, the pin really would hold Tillinghast's fetid soul.

Sanford turned to the double doors, splintered by the shoggoth's exertions, and spoke to the thing pressing on the other side. "It is I," he said. "Your master. Kindly back away."

There was a sloshing, slithering noise, and then the shoggoth moved away. He'd trained it to obey him when it was small, and even now that it was so much larger, the residue of that training remained. Sanford wrenched open the bolts, with effort – the door was twisted in its frame – and hauled one of the double doors open. The shoggoth waited patiently beyond, a wall of eyes and mouths and putrid flesh, but Sanford looked upon it with great fondness.

"Are you hungry?" Sanford asked. "I have a few traitors for you to eat." The warden… Ruby… Altman… they'd all turned on him. They'd all bet on *Tillinghast*, over him. They were fools, but the treachery still stung. Tillinghast might have lost the war, but he'd done irreparable damage to Sanford's world in the process and left the sort of wounds that might never heal.

He looked back, expecting to see the great beast vanished and a tiepin in the shape of a dapper little man on the floor, but instead there was a burst of green light, and, impossibly, Randall Tillinghast, strolling forward, wiping off the blade of a silver dagger with a handkerchief. Was the knife an artifact? It wasn't immediately familiar to Sanford, but if Tillinghast had slain the bound creature with it, the dagger *must* possess potent magic.

Unless it was just an ordinary knife, and the magic belonged to Tillinghast inherently.

"That was quite a nasty beast you unleashed on me, Carl," Tillinghast said conversationally. "You brought it back from the Dreamlands with you, I presume? It looks like someone's nightmare. Not mine, of course."

"How?" Sanford began, but it didn't matter how, did it? He pointed, and said to the shoggoth, "Kill him!"

The guardian – *the only ally I have left*, Sanford thought bitterly – slimed past him, contorting its semifluid form to avoid touching the magus with its caustic flesh, and then bore down on Tillinghast, its countless mouths lamenting, "Tekeli-li!"

Sanford could see nothing past the bulk of the writhing shoggoth, but he waited a moment to see if Tillinghast would scream... but he didn't. He laughed, instead. And then the *shoggoth* screamed.

Sanford turned and ran. He began to confront the possibility, once again, that he might not win this fight.

Fine, then. If he was going to lose, he could at least make sure that Tillinghast lost, too, along with those who'd betrayed them. The Lodge belonged to Sanford, and if he couldn't have it, no one else could.

•••

Altman and the warden started back toward the stairs, intending to flee for the upper floors, and were halfway there when Ruby came barreling out of a side passage that Altman would have *sworn* didn't exist a moment ago. "Sanford is back!" she shouted. "And Tillinghast is down here! I think they're fighting!" As if on cue, a great rumbling crash sounded from deeper in the basements.

"We don't want to be in the middle of an occultist duel," the warden said. "Let's get upstairs and wait to see who emerges. Though we might be better off if *both* perish down here."

"As long as we don't," Altman said. "Warden, lead us out."

They traversed corridors, some of which Altman didn't even recognize, and he dearly hoped Van Shaw was using a shortcut. "Nearly there," she said, turning a corner into an octagonal room with a domed ceiling and a black stone fountain in the center, with passages leading off in all directions.

Carl Sanford walked out of an adjoining passage on the left, holding the besmirched sword. He wore a white fur across his shoulders and looked like he'd been through the wars.

"Hello, traitors," he said, standing before the fountain to gaze at them, the same old look of supercilious smugness on his battered face. "Fancy meeting you here. Shall we discuss your grievances before I end your lives?" He slashed the sword back and forth a few times, and the blade began to glow, something it certainly hadn't done for Ruby.

He pointed the sword at Altman. "You, cur. This is how you trample your brother's memory? By turning on me?

What did Tillinghast bribe you with, to make you forswear yourself?"

"He offered me your job," Altman snarled. "You think I want to be a lackey for the rest of my life? Tillinghast is going to make *me* the magus!"

"Tut, tut." Sanford shook his head. "You're a fool. No one can make you into the magus. You have to make *yourself* into the magus. And you simply don't have the experience, Altman… though you have the ruthlessness, perhaps."

He sniffed dismissively and turned to Ruby. "And you… after all we've been through… I really thought we were friends, or as close to friends as people like us could be."

"Tillinghast left me no choice," Ruby said. "He promised me money, sure, but he threatened me, Sanford. It was either take his side, or suffer a fate worse than death." She fiddled with the watch at her wrist, then cursed as it flashed briefly with green light. Broken glass, springs, and gears pattered down onto the stone floor. Ruby rubbed at her wrists, hissing, and said, "No, damn it, too soon…" She looked up, stricken, like her last and greatest hope had just died.

Altman didn't know what Ruby had tried to do, but it had obviously failed. Sanford didn't seem to care either way. He stroked his uncharacteristically unkempt beard, still gazing at Ruby. "Hmm. You had no choice. I can see that. A fate worse than death! Well, you'll be heartened to know the only fate I'm promising you is plain, old, ordinary death. But give me just a moment."

Sanford shifted his stance slightly and looked at Van Shaw for a long moment before sighing. "I knew you were a trifle disgruntled, warden, but really, do you consider this *protecting the Lodge*? I'm going to have to bring the whole place down on your heads, you know."

Van Shaw snarled, stepping forward, and shadows thickened around her. "You dare to threaten the Lodge in my presence?" Her voice was full of snarls, and Altman and Ruby edged away. The darkness gathering around her flashed with sharp whiteness, like the teeth of her hounds.

"I'll dare almost anything," Sanford said, seemingly unconcerned by her transformation. "If I can't have the Lodge, no one can. I'm going to sever the connections between the deep basements of the house, setting these dark chambers adrift in the void, and rendering them inaccessible from the world above. Not that any of us will ever see that world again in any case." He smirked. "Cutting off the magic will cause a certain amount of damage down here… and I'm afraid when the magical foundations are ripped away, a sinkhole or two might open beneath the Lodge house, which won't do the architecture up there any good, either." Sanford clucked his tongue. He actually seemed to be enjoying this! "Don't worry, though, Sarah. You won't live to see the devastation of that grand old house. You'll die down here in the dark like the rest of us."

Sanford rested the sword, point-down, against the wall at the base of the fountain, and Altman reached into his coat for his brother's knife. But then the old man unhooked a bracelet from his wrist, and Altman froze. That bit of jewelry was one of the relics Sanford had taken from a strongbox, and it could do *anything*–

"These are my keys to the Lodge," Sanford said. "Among other places. They open all the doors, and they shut all the doors, and most of all, they keep the walls up, and the geometry Euclidian. I don't have any use for these keys anymore, though, do I? The time of the Silver Twilight Lodge is over." He dropped the bracelet on the ground and stomped on it, grinding his heel down hard.

The very walls around them groaned, followed by a distant roar of snapping wood, like a thousand trees falling in a forest. "We'll all be entombed here together, rather like a pharaoh and his servants." Sanford picked up the sword. "You'll die first, warden. Your betrayal cut me the most deeply."

The shadows around her thickened, and a pair of hounds stepped out of the darkness around her feet, snarling and stalking toward Sanford. He struck a fencer's pose and held the shining sword aloft. "You want me to kill your dogs first? Whatever pleases you, my dear."

But before the magus and the hounds could do battle, Tillinghast walked in from a corridor on the right. He looked like a man out for a Sunday stroll, though there were flecks of gray slime on his lapels. He was carrying a knife, but not by the hilt – he had the blade pinched between his thumb and forefinger. "I'd step back, my friends," he called. "Or don't. It's up to you."

Altman grabbed Ruby's arm and hauled her back into the shelter of the passage they'd come from, and the warden retreated, too. Tillinghast threw the knife, deftly as a carnival performer, but not at Sanford: it flew straight up at the roof of the chamber.

The dagger should have bounced off the dome and clattered into the fountain… but it was clearly no ordinary knife, because it buried itself in the roof of the room instead, vibrating from the impact.

And then the roof came down.

Altman watched Sanford as he looked up, mouth agape, and dropped the sword. He hunched over and crouched down, as if ducking his head could possibly save him from the tons of stone that dropped straight onto him, with a deafening crash.

"My god." Ruby coughed, waving away the clouds of dust sent up by the explosion. "Tillinghast *crushed* him."

Pebbles bounced across the floor, including a perfectly formed white cube that rolled out of the collapsed wreckage and bumped against Altman's boot. He looked down and watched the cube crumble into an undistinguished heap of white powder. Altman lifted his gaze at the pile of huge broken stones that covered Sanford and nodded. "No getting out of that."

"The tethers are tearing loose!" The warden shook Altman's arm. "Sanford really did cut us off! The deep basements are being ripped away from the world above! We have to hurry!" She set off running toward one of the room's many exits, her hound in tow, and the others followed suit.

Altman didn't see Tillinghast anywhere and wondered if he'd be trapped down here. Altman hoped so. The old man had basically cheated him. Altman was supposed to get the Lodge, its treasures, its basements, and now what was he going to inherit? Smoking wreckage? Smoking wreckage he wouldn't even be able to *access* once the connections to the surface world snapped.

The three of them, and the hound, reached the stairs,

which were beginning to stretch out, lengthening as the walls cracked on either side to reveal gashes of the void beyond. They raced up, the roar of the collapsing structures below them drowning out the sounds of their ragged, rushing breaths. The landings reappeared, but the gas lamps were dead, and the benches broken into splintered boards and bits of bent metal.

Altman was in good shape, but even he was breathing hard by the time they made it to the top – a shorter trip than the descent, but not by much. They piled into the hallway, and Altman looked back in time to see the staircase twist, like a wet rag someone was wringing out, and then snap. Only darkness remained at the end of the hall.

"Is it all gone, then?" Altman wailed, gazing at the void. "All those wonders, all those treasures, lost forever?"

"Oh, the deep basements still exist," the warden said. "Sanford just destroyed all the bridges, all the portals, all the passageways… you can't get there from here, not anymore. Not from anywhere, I'd wager. Their absence is an ache." She frowned down at her hands. "It's like I've had my fingers chopped off. I know they're gone, but I'd swear I could still feel them…" The walls trembled, plaster sifting down from the ceiling. "The house isn't stable. We should…" She trailed off, winced, and bent over, clutching at her chest. "Oh. Oh, it *burns*."

"Look," Ruby said, and grabbed Altman's shoulder. He looked back into the void, where Ruby pointed, and watched as the darkness filled with a deep red glow.

"What is that?" Altman whispered.

"Fire," the warden croaked. "Fire in the dark."

Was this a final trap Sanford had sprung, or a consequence of all that magic breaking down? Altman had heard enough stories about the charred remains of occultists found in their chalk-scrawled laboratories to believe either could be true.

Then, he felt the leading edge of the heat, like he stood too close to a bonfire and realized the red glow was getting brighter. "Run!" he shouted and sprinted down the hall. Ruby and the warden kept pace, but Van Shaw hissed, clearly in terrible pain.

They made it to the ground floor, where the chandeliers were swaying and dust sifted down from the ceilings. Was the whole building going to collapse, or would it burn to the ground first? Even when he lost, Sanford managed to strike a blow against Altman.

The warden led them through the shuddering house, and out onto the lawn, almost to the fence, where they all turned to watch the great house shudder and slump in the moonlight. The warden tottered forward onto her knees and groaned.

"Oh, good, you all made it out." Tillinghast was sitting in a wrought-iron chair just inside the gate. He'd acquired a cup of tea from somewhere and sipped it.

Altman and Ruby both sat on the lawn, gasping from their exertions, listening to glass panes crack and rafters groan. "It's going to fall into the earth!" Altman shouted.

"Into a pit," the warden whispered. "Into a pit of fire." She curled up on her side and shuddered, and Altman moaned as smoke began to billow out of the broken windows, and the walls sagged outward. Ruby began to cry, unless... was she laughing?

"It's a pity," Tillinghast said. "I didn't come to Arkham to destroy one old house. Still, there's plenty of real estate in Arkham, and we can always find another place to call home, can't we? The warden can see to the arrangements, I'm sure." He rose and put his cup down on the chair. "We have a little time yet before dawn. I'd like to change out of this befouled suit, and then I have some business to attend to. I'll see you all in the morning, hmm?"

"You can't leave!" Altman said. "The warden is… she's… I don't know, but she might be dying!"

He sniffed. "She'll suffer, but the Order of the Silver Twilight is more than a building. She won't die until the Order itself does. It certainly won't cease to exist under my watch, and you'll take good care of it when I pass it over to you, won't you, Altman?" With that, Tillinghast strolled down the path, out of the gate, and into the darkness beyond.

Altman sat down and touched the warden's shoulder as she shuddered and gasped beneath his hand. Watching the great house burn, his dreams collapsed before his very eyes. But Tillinghast was right. The Order was more than real estate. Sanford had left behind wealth and influence, and Altman would inherit those in time. He looked helplessly at Ruby. "I suppose… even with all this… we made the right choice, didn't we? We chose the right side. Sanford lost, and Tillinghast won, in the end."

"Is this… what winning… looks like?" Ruby gasped.

# CHAPTER TWENTY-TWO
## *Final Dispositions*

"I'm done," Ruby said after dawn finally came. Tillinghast had sent a taxi for her, and the two of them were on opposite sides of the counter in his shop, which was now located uptown, for some unfathomable reason. "I betrayed Sanford, watched his whole world fall, and even got the stupid red rock of R'lyeh for you. It's time for me to cash out and move on. I won't even ask you to replace my broken watch." She put the cursed thing down on the countertop. She'd tried to use it when Sanford confronted them in the room where he died, but it was too soon, and the crystal had cracked.

"Playing with time wasn't nearly as much fun as I thought it would be, anyway. Whatever your Great Work is, you can finish it without me."

"Mmm. You aren't curious to see what I'm trying to achieve?" He gazed at her through half-lidded eyes. The fact that all Sanford's relics, apart from the ruby, had been lost when the basements were torn loose from reality didn't seem to trouble him much. But then, Tillinghast was never easy to read.

"I don't know, and I don't care," she said. "Curiosity about that sort of thing has never done me any good. Now, will you pay me?"

"You're truly determined to leave my employ now?"

She crossed her arms. "I did what you hired me to do. I don't want to do anything else."

"Very well. But please, have a drink with me first."

"The sun is barely up," she said.

"You haven't slept, my dear, so in a sense, it's still the night before." He took two small black cups from beneath the counter, and a glass of something thick and scarlet, and poured them each a small measure. "Let us part friends, hmm?"

Was it poison? It hardly seemed necessary. He could have just stabbed her in the neck if he wanted her dead. And besides, the wine looked delicious, and she was suddenly so thirsty, and the cups were beautiful, weren't they? "Friends," she said, and reached for the cup he'd indicated. The moment before the rim of the cup touched her lips, she thought, *This looks like it's made of the same stuff as the Grail of Dreams*–

She tasted something warm and salty, and the darkness whirled all around her.

Ruby groaned, sitting up on a heap of stones beneath a sky the color of bruised plums. "No," she whimpered. "No, no, no, no." The wreckage of a city destroyed lay tumbled all around her, with distant fragments of high walls visible in the distance. She got to her feet and stumbled away, down the heap of rocks until she reached the bottom, where she stared at a great wooden chest the size of a steamer trunk, with the shape of a triangle around an eye burned into the wood. The chest was locked, but a golden key rested on top, neatly aligned below the base of the triangle.

Ruby knelt, and reached for the key, hands trembling. She unlocked the chest, and lifted the lid, and inside, she found heaps of gold coins, and emeralds, and diamonds – all the riches she'd ever dreamed of. There was also a small wooden box, square, and when she opened that, she found a black cup, a silver knife, and a sheet of paper covered in flowing script.

*My dear Miss Standish,*

*Enjoy your riches in your new home. Or, if you've reconsidered, and would prefer to remain in my employ until my Great Work is completed, simply deposit a few drops of blood in the cup, and drink, and return home. You'll receive the contents of the chest, and further rewards, when we're finished, and I daresay you'll enjoy them more here.*

*Yours most faithfully,*
*RT*

She sat in the ruins for a while, looking at the pulsing lines in the sky, and weeping, for everything she'd done, and everything she feared she *might* do in the future. Whatever

Tillinghast demanded, she could not deny, and he'd already demanded so much.

Then she cut the back of her hand, and dripped blood into the cup, and sipped, and whirled through the darkness to find herself sprawled on the floor of Tillinghast's shop.

"My loyal retainer," he said, smiling down at her.

"What was that place?" Ruby whispered. "I never want to see it again."

"Oh, you might. You may well see it in your dreams. But no matter. Once you've rested a bit, I need you to retrieve another little lost relic for me..."

Altman stood on the lawn beside Sarah Van Shaw, and together, they surveyed the remains of the Lodge. The rosy morning light made everything beautiful... except the sight before them. The stately old home had been reduced to a few charred timbers sticking up at odd angles, and the foundations were collapsed into the warren of tunnels below, the magic that held it all together broken. "We can rebuild, can't we?"

"I'm no builder," Van Shaw said.

The police, fire brigade, and medics had come and gone, and her hands and arms were wrapped heavily in bandages. There was a bandage across her left eye, too, and burn scars on that cheek. She should have been in the hospital, but she'd refused to go. The medics thought she'd been burned escaping from the fire, which had been blamed on a gas explosion, but in truth the burns had appeared spontaneously on her body when the Lodge fell.

The warden (warden of *what*, now?) kicked a paving

stone. "This is a plot of unstable, ghoul-infested land now. I wouldn't bother with it. Best we make our home elsewhere. Tillinghast was right. There's money, at least. We can find some other moldering pile to make our own." She shook her head. "At least I can leave this place now. The bindings that held me here burned up when the building did. If I pledge myself to protect another house, perhaps… perhaps I'll heal." She touched her covered eye and winced.

"What do we do now?" Altman asked.

She rolled her one good eye. "You'd best find yourself a hotel. I'll make my own arrangements."

"I mean… with the Order. Things are in such disarray."

"It's hardly your problem," she snapped. "Tillinghast is in charge for now, and he told me to secure a new headquarters. I'm sure he'll have tasks for you, suited to your strengths, whatever they might be. Someone must deal with the membership of the Lodge, reassure them. Word is going to get out that Sanford is gone, and the Lodge house burned, and the members will have strong reactions to *that*, let me tell you. Some of them are rich, and think they're important, and you'll have to smooth all those ruffled feathers and keep them in line. Even so, we're going to lose members, if we aren't careful."

"Dealing with people has never been my strength," Altman said. "At least, not unless I've got them held at knifepoint."

"Then why on heaven and earth did you want Sanford's job?" Van Shaw asked. "It's *all* dealing with people, when it's not dealing with monsters instead."

Altman stiffened. "I didn't want to take orders anymore,

is all. And the only way to avoid that is to be the one *giving* them."

Van Shaw grunted. "You aren't giving anyone orders yet, are you? Just serving Tillinghast instead of the magus, now."

Altman clenched his fists. Sanford wouldn't have tolerated that kind of backtalk from her, but then, he wasn't Sanford, and he'd negotiated a different sort of relationship with the warden. "Nor for long. Once Tillinghast is finished with this Great Work of his, I'll be – *we'll* be, the ones in charge here."

"May it bring us much joy," she said sourly, and walked off through the grass, half a dozen dogs suddenly appearing to follow at her heels. She still had *that* much power, then.

Altman looked at the burned remnants for a long moment. Then he headed for the street, wondering if he'd be able to hail a cab up here. The Bentley was a twisted heap of metal somewhere with a corpse pretending to be Sanford inside it–

Randall Tillinghast was leaning against a silver Rolls Royce, his arms crossed, when Altman turned the corner. "Hello, my crown prince," the old man said, smiling in his own secret amusement. "I have a new royal coach for you." He patted the hood.

"I'm not negotiating any new deals with you," Altman began, but Tillinghast waved that away.

"Nonsense. This is just a bonus. The terms of our agreement only required you to stand aside, but instead, you actively assisted in Sanford's downfall. Or you tried to, anyway. That deserves something extra."

"You didn't get your hands on his treasures, though, and

without the house and the basements, there's precious little left, it seems to me."

"The loss of the relics is a grievous one. I am also a bit perturbed to lose the Scholar of Yith. I'm sure she knew things that would have helped smooth the path of my work. As for the house, I have owned many of them, and seen many burned before. But tell me, Altman, are you trying to talk me out of rewarding you?" Tillinghast chuckled. "Take yes for an answer, my dear boy. You want to be the new Carl Sanford. You know he would take this as his due and then demand more."

Oh. "Then I demand—"

Tillinghast raised a finger. "Don't go that far." He stepped away from the car. "I assume you need a place to stay, since your bedroom is now a smoldering hole. You can always go to a hotel, I suppose, but you might be more comfortable at Gloria's house. There's room."

"Gloria is dead," Altman said. "Or, worse, she's lost down there, forever, wherever the basements are. If they haven't burned up, too."

"Is she? In that case, there's even more room. There's a key hidden under the flowerpot in her backyard, not that a man of your skills needs one." Tillinghast winked and strolled away.

The keys to the Rolls Royce were in the ignition, and after a moment of long indecision, Altman drove to Gloria's house. He had plenty of time to think on the drive, but his disordered mind would not cooperate. His thoughts were like a flock of pigeons scattering under the shadow of a hawk.

Would Tillinghast fulfill their deal? What would he ask

of Altman before all this was done? What was his Great
Work? Would there be anything left of the Silver Twilight
Lodge for Altman to take over when the time came, and
would Sarah Van Shaw let him enjoy it if there was?

He parked in Gloria's driveway. Her yellow convertible
was nowhere to be seen, and he wondered if it was parked
near the Lodge somewhere, or if Tillinghast had taken it
away. He found the house key under the flowerpot (that was
faster than picking the locks again) and let himself in. He
stood wearily inside, head slumped, unable even to decide
what to do next. He should drink a glass of water, maybe, and
then he'd collapse into bed. He'd endured many long nights
before in his checkered life, but none longer than this one.

Altman went into the kitchen and stopped, frowning,
when he saw an object on the kitchen table. When he went
closer, he saw it was a note addressed to him, written in
vivid purple ink.

*Dear Altman,*

*Do help yourself to my house. I won't need it anymore.
You can also help yourself to my position – Mr
Tillinghast doesn't need me anymore. He has you to
do his bidding now. I hope you enjoy the role as much
as I did.*

*A faithful servant,*
  *Gloria Dyer*

He scowled down at the letter. Had she written this before

she came to the Lodge? Or had she somehow survived the shoggoth, and the collapse, and escaped? He supposed it was possible. Just barely. He'd lost track of her in the chaos, so she might have made it out. Altman was too exhausted to speculate further, so he crumpled the letter and tossed it into a wastebasket, and then went upstairs to sleep on the silk sheets on Gloria's bed. He hoped there would be no dreams.

He suspected his hopes would be unfounded.

In the Miskatonic River, close to the Garrison Street Bridge that connects the north and south sides of Arkham, there is a small island, considered nameless to most. Those with occult wisdom know it is called Themystos' Island, though there are debates about who, or what, Themystos is, or was. What is known is that the island is a desolate place, covered in tall grasses, and home to ancient crumbling monoliths and a large altar stone. Whatever dark rites were performed there ceased long ago, and the ancient bloodstains have long since been washed away by time.

The morning after the Silver Twilight Lodge fell to Randall Tillinghast, and then fell into a smoking hole in the earth, Carl Sanford beached a canoe on the stony shore and limped through the tall grass and trudged toward the center of the island. He wore a dirty white cloak, the torn remnants of a once-fine suit, and fur boots, and his body was as battered and bloody as his clothes were tattered.

The ends of his shirt sleeves hung open, both cufflinks missing. The white die had served its purpose, granting him a boon of life-saving luck – he must have rolled a six, he supposed, because the falling roof stones had included two large slabs that fell just right to lean against one another. They created a triangular cavity beneath the rubble that sheltered him and protected him from being crushed. Sanford had excavated himself, expending much of his magical reserves in the process, only to find his enemies had managed to escape before the deep basements were torn free from the world above.

But that was of no consequence. They could be dealt with later. His enemies thought he was dead, or trapped forever, but they were wrong. The destruction of the keys had severed the connections between the Lodge house and the laboratories, workshops, and ritual chambers occupying that stolen space below, but those secret rooms were still intact, albeit damaged. The deep basements were now islands in the dark, and the passageways to the world above and to other worlds were blocked by stone, rubble, and void... but Sanford had his ways. Oh, yes.

The magus hadn't destroyed *all* the keys on his bracelet. He'd kept one, tucked into his vest pocket, just in case. That key opened a portal from the cut-off basements to a certain black cave near the river: a single, secret connection to the world above, known to Sanford alone. After digging himself out of the rubble, he traversed those damaged halls until he found the passageway he wanted. That afternoon, he limped out of the deep basements, and through a shimmering portal of velvet darkness, and on into the cave. He had a canoe hidden near the river, and he took that to the island, arms aching with every stroke of the oar across the wide and muddy Miskatonic.

Carl Sanford *always* had contingency plans. That's why he was the magus, and why Altman never would be. On balance, Sanford thought he hated Altman even more than Tillinghast. The shopkeeper was, at least, a foe who'd earned his respect. Altman was just an arrogant young murderer with pretensions beyond his station. And he thought he could simply take what Sanford had worked decades to build?

The former head of the Silver Twilight Lodge trudged to the modest rise at the center of the island. He stood there for a moment, looking at the red rays of the sun rising at the end of the river, turning the waters the color of flame. It was a new dawn. A new day. A new beginning. Sanford smiled. And all his enemies thought he was dead.

He made his way through the grass to the mossy standing stones, etched with near-invisible runes. This spot had been sacred to the long-dead cult of some long-lost god, but now it was only ruins. So, too, was Sanford's empire.

But Sanford would not disappear into the bottomless pit of history, no. Sanford would see all his glory restored.

There was an immense altar stone in the center of the island, a waist-high slab of ancient black rock, pitted and gouged, covered in lichen and mysteriously stained. Sanford set his hands against the stone, gritted his teeth, and set his feet. He pushed on the stone, and after a moment of reluctance, it began to slide.

The stone was cunningly counterweighted, and if you knew where to apply the proper pressure, it could be moved through a short arc on the stony ground. Sanford pushed until he heard a click, indicating that the altar was locked in its new position. The movement revealed a vertical shaft descending into the ground, with a ladder fixed to one side.

Sanford descended the ladder, wincing as his body protested at any movement. He'd put himself through a lot in the past several months – or, from the vantage point of those who'd remained on Earth, the past several hours.

When he reached the bottom, in the dark, he groped until he found the matches, right where he'd left them, and the lantern, too. He struck the match, lit the wick, and watched light bloom in the darkness. A solid lever of wood and metal jutted from the wall next to the ladder, and Sanford engaged it with a grunt of effort. A catch released above, and the stone slid back into place above him. Down in the bowels of the earth again. Fortunately, he was at home in such places.

The contents of the little stone-walled room at the bottom of the shaft gleamed in the light as he shone the lantern around him. It was hardly an accommodation suitable to his dignity, just a ten-by-ten space without much in the way of creature comforts. But his most precious relics were all here: the wall mirror, the scrolls, the cups, the knives, the statuettes, and more.

When his vault had been breached for the second time last year, Sanford knew his relics were no longer safe there, or anywhere in the basements. So he made a great show of increasing his security, while secretly transferring the relics through the portal in the basement, first to the Black Cave, and then to the nameless isle, where no one would think to look for them. He wasn't starting over from nothing. Almost, but not quite. He had his relics. He had a passage to his basements, and though the halls were shattered, there were still things of value in the wreckage… and maybe even one last ally, in the form of the Scholar of Yith, if she'd survived the upheaval.

Sanford had made it to the top before. He would make it again. He was even more motivated now than he had been in his youth, because now he knew how sweet it *was* to be on top.

This hidey-hole held more than just his relics. There was a cot down here, too, and the keys to a car stored in a garage in a nearby town, and cash, and – blessing of blessings – a fresh suit… though he should probably rinse off in the freezing river before he changed clothes.

All that could come later. For now, Sanford dropped his torn cloak, took off his filthy coat and vest and shirt, and kicked off his stinking boots. Then he stretched out on the cot, his muscles groaning. He would rest for a day or two, and then begin to plan. He would need to leave Arkham for a while. Loath as he was to abandon his city, it was too dangerous now with Tillinghast fully ascendant. Fortunately, Sanford had contacts overseas who might prove useful. Once he'd gathered his strength anew… he would commence his ascension.

Sanford closed his eyes. He expected dreams of snow, and fire, and revenge, and the devastation of his enemies.

He was not disappointed.

# ACKNOWLEDGMENTS

My thanks as always to the team at Aconyte, especially Charlotte Llewelyn-Wells and Gwendolyn Nix for their editorial acumen, and to the *Arkham Horror* developers for allowing me to play in their sandbox once again. My agents, Ginger Clark and Nicole Eisenbraun, do great work on the business side so I can concentrate on making stuff up.

On a personal note, I'm grateful to my spouse, Heather, and our teenager, River, for putting up with me muttering about tentacles and zoogs and the Beings of Ib for months, and for playing board games with me, even the very long and complicated ones. Thanks to my nearest and dearests: Sarah, Katrina, Emily, Amanda, and Aislinn, for their unflagging support, even when I'm being weird. Molly Tanzer is always there for me to bounce ideas off, and she's a great writer of Mythos fiction in her own right (check out "The Thing on the Cheerleading Squad").

Finally, I don't know Daniel Harms at all, but his book *The Cthulhu Mythos Encyclopedia* was always next to my desk as I wrote this book, and I consulted it often to refresh and clarify my memories (after forty-ish years of Mythos reading, it gets a little jumbled in there).

## ABOUT THE AUTHOR

TIM PRATT is a Hugo Award-winning SF and fantasy author, and finalist for the World Fantasy, Sturgeon, Stoker, Mythopoeic, and Nebula Awards, among others. He is the author of over twenty novels, and scores of short stories. Since 2001 he has worked for *Locus*, the magazine of the science fiction and fantasy field, where he currently serves as senior editor.

*timpratt.org // twitter.com/timpratt*

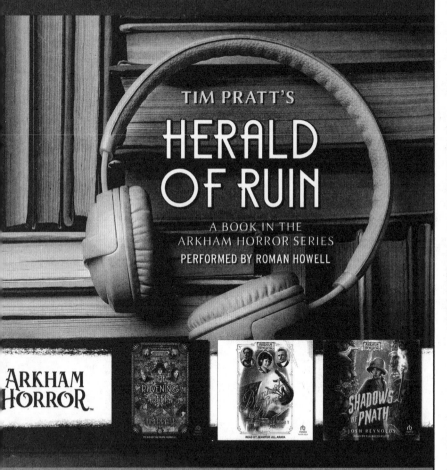

# THE DEFINITIVE GUIDE TO THE WORLD OF ARKHAM HORROR

*Venture deeper than ever before into the legend-haunted city of Arkham and its neighboring towns of Dunwich, Innsmouth and Kingsport. Explore 115 fabled locations with more than 500 illustrations in this gorgeous, full-color hardcover guidebook.*